JUSTUS

JUSTUS

ARTHUR L. LAPHAM

Publishing House
St. Louis   London

Concordia Publishing House, St. Louis, Missouri
Concordia Publishing House Ltd., London E. C. 1
Copyright © 1973 Concordia Publishing House
Library of Congress Catalog No. 73-79486
ISBN 0-570-03231-8

MANUFACTURED IN THE UNITED STATES OF AMERICA

This book
is dedicated with love
to my wife,
Alice,
and our children,
Mary Alice, Rosanna,
and Justus.

CHARACTERS

Justus — *Roman captain of Herod's guards*
Herod — *King of Judea, called the Tiger*
Nicolas — *of Damascus, Herod's counselor and chamberlain*

Jesus   Mary   Joseph

Guards Under Justus

Tarsus   Tactus   Mundus   Hezron   Cassius

Aizel — *A Jew, Herod's adviser on Jewish law and protocol*
Mariame — *Aizel's daughter who loves Justus*
Annas — *High priest of Jerusalem's Temple; Abbethdin (vice-president) of the Sanhedrin*
Joazar — *Nasi (president) of the Sanhedrin, the chief judge*
Magi — *Three seekers of the "New King" — Melchior, Balthasar, and Gaspar*
Salma — *Herod's chief astrologer*
Tarfon — *Head jailer and court bailiff for the Sanhedrin*

Judges of the Sanhedrin

Ismeal	Levitas	Josephus	James
Urias	Theophilus	Ben Levi	Ben Heron
Altazar	Abba	Zezebee	Jonathan
Eleazar	Doras	Caiaphas	Sceva

Nathan — *Chief scribe of the Sanhedrin*
Umbla — *Nicolas' slave*
Ebana — *Mariame's slave*
Sarah and John Zadok — *Witnesses against Justus*
Ben Bag Bag — *A physician*
Judith — *Landlady and friend to Justus*
Silas — *Justus' friend*
Followers of Jesus — *Nicodemus, Matthias, Edith*
The Apostles — *Peter, James, John, Thomas, Matthew*

JUSTUS

PART I

I

JUSTUS turned over and groaned, half hearing the hard fist-poundings on the pinewood door of his house. The sound of each great blow rumbled through the room, rebounding off the walls, and the big man, shaking sleep from his mind as he rose from his bed, stumbled through the semidarkness, cursing under his breath.

He muttered, "All right, I'm coming," then stubbed his great toe and shouted, fumbling peevishly at the latch, "All right, I said. I'm awake. Don't break the damned door in."

He jerked the door open and blinked in the moonlight at a young soldier with raised fist, who checked his swing and saluted.

Justus, ignoring the gesture, merely glared, holding his wrath in check against that moment when he might need to release it on the intruder.

The cold wind from the street leaped into the house, stirring the folds of his silk sleeping robe, and he could see the soldier's tremulous breath on the frosty air. The man still stood at attention, apparently steeled for a tongue lashing, and the metal of his armor clanked as his muscular body shook with fear and cold.

Justus spoke sternly, "Tarsus, what is the meaning of this? Why didn't you stop that pounding when I called out? Never mind; don't answer. Just come in and close the door before I freeze."

He turned, removed the slotted night-cover from the standing lamp, then held a thin reed out to the flame. He lit a large

13

brass brazier hung by three smoke-blackened chains from a ceiling beam, and as the flames from the two lamps met, the shadows ceased their dance on the white plastered walls.

He knew that he'd scared this courier almost out of his wits, but he thought, *"It'll do the arrogant bastard good,"* and turned again to speak gruffly.

"You'd better have a damned good and sufficient reason for coming here at this hour."

Tarsus swallowed hard. "Sire, the chamberlain himself sent me to bring you at once to King Herod's chamber."

"Old Nicolas? What the hell can he want with me this time of night?" Justus walked into the bedroom, feeling disgruntled. Herod's life was always in a state of strife, and when he couldn't sleep because of the pain from his advanced disease, he lay awake, thinking up new, often imaginary perils from possible sources of treason.

Justus got into his uniform, modeled after the uniforms of the Roman army, which he'd worn since he'd become an orderly at 8 years of age, and told himself for the hundredth time that while the position of captain of Herod's bodyguards carried certain rewards to be envied, uninterrupted slumber was seldom one of them.

While Justus dressed, Tarsus walked, cat-like, about the big living room, eagerly eyeing the pieces of furniture and works of art that Justus had collected over the past few prosperous years. Even this house Herod had provided for Justus after the quiet murder of Zak, a Jewish Zealot suspected of threatening the throne.

Tarsus knew from hearsay that Justus had acquired most of his art objects from Roman traders, but he could wager some of them had been plundered from the houses of certain victims of Justus' dagger. The statues were all of Greek and Roman gods, which the pious Jerusalem Jews would consider idols, and two were brazenly pornographic, intriguing studies of the pagan gods at play.

Tarsus gaped at a nude Venus next to a sly-lipped Mercury, and gently stroked the pink marble body, unaware his superior had come back into the room.

"All right, blow out that lamp and let's get moving," Justus told him. "You could easily break that Venus with your great calloused paw." Then, as he moved toward the door he asked, "Did the King seem to be angry?"

Tarsus grinned as he snuffed out the ceiling lamp's flame with thumb and forefinger. "Sire, have you ever seen the King when he wasn't mad about something?"

This attempt to establish undue familiarity with his captain was too obvious, and Justus instantly rumbled, "Am I to take that as attempted insubordination—or possible disloyalty toward your sovereign?"

"Oh, no, Sire. My captain knows I have only admiration and affection for Herod the Great. Our King is the Tiger of Judea . . . indeed, our beloved King . . ."

"Aw, shut up; that's enough. Do you have horses?" Justus buckled his flat sword to the wide leather belt of his uniform, then, seeing only one small gray horse tethered to his hitching post, he cried, "Why didn't you bring my mount, you thoughtless fool? Well, just for that, you can walk back to the palace . . . and don't stop on the way at some cheap whore's house."

He mounted the gray horse and dug his heels into its ribs, telling himself that something important indeed must be afoot at the palace if he was needed there at this ungodly hour. But of course that would not be surprising, for it was true that someone was constantly trying to raise a general revolt against the ailing Tiger. There were certain harmless sects of Jews in the city who thought the world was about to end, but there were also others decidedly more to be feared, who lived only for that fortunate day when Israel would be freed of Rome's domination, inflicted upon them by their puppet sovereign, Herod the Great.

Justus spurred the animal down a dark, narrow street, thinking nostalgically of Roma Eterna and ruefully asking himself why he had ever come to this troubled, alien country.

He'd been a personal courier for Caesar Augustus for two years before he'd first come to Jerusalem bearing a personal message that Herod should prepare his people for a tax increase within a year. Grinning now, he recalled the face-flinching rage which Herod had sought to hide on reading Caesar's letter, while Nicolas, the chamberlain, had tactfully calmed him.

Throughout his stay in Jerusalem, Justus had been treated with great courtesy by Herod, who, despite his reputation for cruelty, could apparently be generous enough with a person whom he liked—or to someone who might conceivably be of use to him at some future time. Justus was still not quite certain of his category.

Just one year after Justus' visit, Herod had come to Rome and in the course of business had asked Caesar Augustus to assign Justus to him as a temporary bodyguard. Caesar had sworn that Herod need have no fear of violence in Rome, but the Tiger knew that a large number of the city's vast population of Jews had fled Judea because of him and that there were Zealots among them who would welcome the chance to assassinate him. So in the end his insistent request had been granted.

Throughout the first days of Justus' assignment, once more showered with gifts, he had begun to think Herod's evil reputation must be exaggerated. But one night the Tiger had drunk too much and insisted on being taken to a woman, rather than having one brought in to him. Justus took the King to Vanessa —the most expensive whore in Rome.

Vanessa, though young in years, was a clever business woman who had kept herself unavailable to all save senators, royal clients, and wealthy merchants, thereby waxing lavishly rich herself. Her handsome villa near town boasted two massive bodyguards—former champion gladiators in the Roman circus—and Justus had paid them well from the Jewish monarch's purse. Then Herod had gone with Vanessa to her chamber, leaving Justus to play dice with the guards outside her door.

The woman had disrobed to stand nudely tantalizing before the King, but when Herod dropped his robes, she saw festering sores about his thighs and belly and backed away, protesting that she would not lie with him; then, as he'd reeled drunkenly toward her, she had cursed him, and Herod smashed his fist into her face, tearing an ugly gash in her lips with his heavily ringed forefinger. At Vanessa's anguished scream, the two guards rushed for the room, but as the first reached the door, Justus swiftly sank his dagger into the man's broad back. Then, as the other guard sprang forward, Justus drove the blade into the man's throat, and the dying guard vomited on the white bearskin rug before he fell face down to stain it with his blood.

The King savagely raped Vanessa on her bloodied silken sheets, while she lay silent. She was terrified that Justus, who stood transfixed with disgust, would take her life as well. Thus Justus had seen that night in Vanessa's villa the bestial side of Herod. He would not underestimate the fat, revolting swine again.

On the very next day, well before high noon, a messenger delivered a gilded box—a splendid diamond ring from Herod. The following day Herod had petitioned Caesar for permission to take the handsome guard back to Jerusalem, and Justus had not hesitated in his own decision. He welcomed the appointment of captain of Herod's guards, for he had an unshakable feeling that his future and his fortune lay no longer in Rome but in Judea.

In the past 7 years he had killed many times for the Tiger, each time being richly rewarded . . . and gradually, in unrealized, unceasing greed, he had begun to believe in himself as the destined protector of Herod's throne, meanwhile calculating that if the King lived long enough he would one day leave Judea a wealthy man.

He still believed that he could. The only trouble with this bloody job was that the Tiger always managed to panic late at night—never at any sensible hour of day.

Now he dug his heels once more into the horse's sides and raced the animal down the last rocky, uneven street that led toward the palace, wondering about the nature of this particular crisis. Herod was always sure somebody was plotting against him. He'd had his own two sons and his wife put to the sword in his mad suspicious efforts to protect his interests.

Justus privately thought Herod had been overzealous in those drastic actions, but it now might well be that the Jews were starting a new revolt. Certainly there were some Zealots who did not care much for their King—even though he had raised the Great Temple, which was known as one of the world's incomparable wonders. "*Yet, on the other hand,*" thought Justus, "*perhaps I have unwittingly angered Herod; or else some jealous advisor has whispered false accusations into the royal ear. If that is the case, I'll have to talk fast and smooth to save my skin.*"

He approached the palace with apprehension. Leaping from his mount, he raced up the marble steps, leaving the exhausted beast untended.

II

Aizel's old voice cracked as he raised it. "This is a matter of principle, Mariame."

Mariame reacted to her father's remark with woman's most maddening weapon—a pouting lower lip and steel-cold silence.

Aizel moved from his chair to stand by the couch where his

18

daughter lay on her back, pretending to study the frieze on the walls and ceiling.

"Please, Mariame, listen to me. I tell you there's no future in carrying on this foolish flirtation with Justus."

"No future for whom?" Mariame answered, low voiced. "Me, or you, Father?"

"You know what I mean," Aizel said. "I haven't many years left, but with the grace of God I intend to do everything in my power to see you suitably wed before I die."

Mariame's eyes moved from the ceiling past the old man to rest on a Persian rug that hung on the gray plaster wall of the palace apartment and the color of the richly woven wool reflected itself in her sullen eyes. She had no wish to look at her father—much less to continue this irksome conversation.

Aizel expended a deep, all too familiar, sigh. "You are only a child, still too young to comprehend these matters."

He saw Mariame slowly roll her eyes up in resignation at having to listen to what was coming next, but he went on, "You know full well that I think, at all times, only of your good. There are not ten men in Judea worthy of marrying you."

"You mean not ten who're rich enough, do you not?"

Aizel looked wounded. "Kindly do not speak to me in that tone of voice. I am only trying to do what I feel is best for you."

Mariame's almond eyes drifted to her pink toes. "Father, just ask yourself one question. Are you trying to help me—or benefit yourself?"

"Oh, Mariame. What a cruel, utterly heartless thing to suggest. You know I am living only for your happiness."

"Yes, but I've noted that money and worldly goods seem to figure predominantly in your paternal interest."

"Daughter, believe me; I know what it is to be cut off from wealth." Aizel paused as though to reflect, then went monotonously on. "You were too young to remember, but my father once had riches, position, and power. He was a most intelligent, able person, and very generous as well. There was nothing my older brother, Ben Ame, or I ever once desired that was not ours for the asking." The old man's eyes misted. "My father loved us both — even though Ben Ame and I were very unlike, and sons of different mothers. But I do realize now the problems that plagued him in his attempts to prevent my mother's dominating Ben Ame. Your grandmother, my dear, was a most domineering woman — the only person on earth who could make my father and Ben Ame do something they had no wish to do. Perhaps it was her influence that caused Ben Ame to grow up such a greedy, bitter man. My father tried his best with him, but as you have seen, he was not successful."

Mariame closed her eyes and placed a slender hand on her forehead — wondering how often she had heard Aizel tell about his father and Ben Ame. How many times had this self-pitying old gentleman told and retold with exaggerated martyrdom the story of his father's death and Ben Ame's unlawful capture of her grandsire's estate! She could recite the story by heart, and she'd come to hate the name of Ben Ame. She had long known that her uncle's treachery had deprived her father of his rightful heritage, and this had led the impoverished Aizel to the Tiger's court for employment.

She heard him moaning now, "What else could I do, Mariame? Where else could I possibly go? The King offered me this job as his adviser on Jewish law and protocol, and I had no choice but to take it."

Silently Mariame nodded, her fine eyes clouding as she strove to shut out this piteous plea for approval of a long-past action.

Aizel droned wearily on, "Of course I knew, when I accepted this post, that my own people would reject me — knew they would hate any Jew who aided the Tiger in any way at all. But I ask you again, what else could I do to earn a living? I was neither a tradesman nor a farmer; all I knew was my study of the Law. I had to bring you here, for I had promised your dear, sweet mother on her deathbed to raise you in the tradition of the nobility." Aizel paused to glance sidelong at his silent offspring. "Naturally, I'd have done it anyway, without that pledge to your mother, but my oath to her is one of the reasons I must insist that you cease seeing this barbarian from Rome. Why, he's no more than Herod's hired assassin."

Mariame still held her tongue, thinking how ambivalent it was for her father to expect her to marry a Jew, when the Jews had deserted him. He should have been a rabbi, or at least a judge of the Great Sanhedrin, yet he remained loyal to these heartless people who had rejected him. She was a Jew —a devout one—but she felt apart from her people, and she wondered, opening her eyes to look to her father, if her life in the palace had not caused her to disavow her heritage.

"Look at him," she thought. *"I know I should be like him . . . yet, somehow I'm not. I don't feel bound to marry only a Jew . . . I'm not prejudiced in the least against the Gentiles. I would marry Justus . . . I don't care what his religion, or nationality, is . . . it's the man himself. One thing I have learned, living in this palace, is that Herod himself isn't restricted by faith or national boundaries. He's a friend to the Romans . . . and even to certain Jews who're not afraid of him or who serve his purposes. . . ."*

She said aloud, cunningly, "Well, Herod isn't a Jew, and you'll have to admit it would please you highly if I should marry him."

Aizel hesitated, stunned that she seemed to have read his mind. Then he said, "Herod is King of all Judea. He's old and sick, and if you'll marry him you'll be Queen when he dies. He certainly can't live long, and you might well become another Cleopatra."

Mariame's heart fluttered; she felt a weakness in the pit of her stomach. So her father's suspected secret ambition was out at last! She knew that her young, fresh beauty had impressed the aging king, for sometimes she had felt his hot stare as she walked across the main court chamber. Court gossip was that Herod desired her for his mistress. Indeed, the lavish gifts the fat old fool had bestowed upon her left little doubt that he was playing a deliberate waiting game to get her in his bed—if possible, without marriage. She sat up, feeling panic.

"Father, if you really love me, please dismiss any thoughts from your mind of my ever marrying Herod. It's no secret he wants me for his concubine. I've seen the way he looks at me, and I've tried my best to discourage him without being downright offensive. I could never become either the Tiger's mistress or his wife. I would rather be dead."

"But Mariame, try for a moment to see . . ."

"No, Father. Don't interrupt me." Tears formed in Mariame's eyes as her voice rose, hysterical. "I don't want to sound ungrateful, because I know that you *think* you're acting in my best interest, but I could never, never go to Herod's bed. Surely you can't ask me to suffer the vileness of that old, fat, sick body next to mine? Why, I cringe when that beast even touches my hand, and I've heard the whores of Jerusalem refuse even to come to the palace for fear that Herod may be their bed partner. *No!* I tell you I'd rather lie on my deathbed than on the couch of that repulsive, disease-ridden monster."

The girl's voice ended on a fierce shriek, and Aizel wiped his bony wrist across his nose. He sniffed and coughed to pretend he had a cold, as his small eyes followed Mariame's delicate hand brushing great tears from her cheeks. Then he moved to the couch and began to fondle her lustrous hair. "No, now please. Don't cry, my daughter. Calm yourself, my dove. I promise you, now that I know how you feel, never to throw you to Herod."

Mariame stopped crying, kissed his sallow cheek, and wound her arms about his neck. "Oh, thank you. Thank you, Father.

Oh, I do love you so much. Please, let's promise each other never to let anything come between us."

"I promise, my darling, I promise."

Relief spread across Aizel's face, and he clasped the girl to his heart. She seemed to him once more the small trusting child who so often had run to his arms when she was frightened or hurt. Still, he drew back, wagging a warning forefinger. "But remember, I do however order you not to carry on this flirtation with Justus. He is a mercenary and, as I said, Herod's hired assassin. There are many more eligible, deserving, fine young men around this court."

Mariame nodded, smiling, as she wiped away her tears. She would listen now, without protest, and perhaps she might even follow Aizel's instructions, but Aizel unwisely continued, "For example, three foreign princes are visiting the palace tonight. Nicolas introduced them to me. One of them, Melchior, is an extremely handsome, gracious man. I'll have Nicolas introduce him to you tomorrow. You'll like him, I feel sure."

Like a leopard Mariame sprang off the couch. "Oh, will you never learn? You mean this Melchior is rich and royal. Father, you're simply hopeless, hopeless, hopeless." She ran from the room and slammed the door behind her, leaving the little man transfixed in sincere surprise.

"Women," he said beneath his breath. "Where is the man who can ever understand them? Why should a man be undesirable because he's handsome, royal, and rich?"

III

The long corridor reeked with a stench that no incense could mask; no matter how hard he tried, Herod could never disguise this evidence of the cancer that was eating his life away.

As Justus hurried toward the audience chamber where the Tiger made momentous decisions, the guard, who stood sword

23

in hand, saluted, telling him, "The King awaits you with impatience, Captain."

Justus hesitated, contemplating the fate that could befall him in the chamber, but there was no turning back, so he adjusted his sword, drew a deep breath, and, with his hard fist, dealt the massive cedar door a blow that rattled its hinges. He waited until he heard a muffled voice from within, then slowly entered the great familiar room that never failed to fascinate him. Persian rugs draped the walls, and the smooth tile floor reflected the flames of flickering lamps that threw off nearly invisible curls of smoke. But the room, unlike Justus' quarters, contained no statues or works of art, for Herod had taken care to remove any object that could be considered an idol by the strict Pharisees who visited the chamber. The King could avoid some conflict with the Jews by not flaunting idolatry in their faces; he knew when to be stern with the Jews and also when to bend. But one thing was certain: the Tiger was the King of the Jews, and those who failed to recognize that fact usually lived an abbreviated life after a public announcement of any belief to the contrary. Indeed, Justus' own sword had taught a fatal lesson to several loose-tongued Jews who had spoken out against the King.

Tonight the Tiger stood at a large oak table near a window boarded up to keep out the cold night air. He was dressed in a long, flowing blood-red robe, and even his gray beard and hair, though yellowed with age, gave little external evidence of that fatal disease consuming the short fat body which was now taut with rage.

Justus' entrance into the room was acknowledged only by glances from Herod and Nicolas, two old men who, in their late seventies, reminded him of a pair of decrepit game cocks sparring for an opening.

Nicolas of Damascus, Herod's counselor and chamberlain for over 30 years, was imposing in his floor-length robe, but

24

his slight stoop and short-clipped gray beard betrayed his slight stature and age.

He was a highly educated Greek, who had found his niche in Jerusalem. For years his schemes and plans had brought him the secret pleasure of living a vicarious life as King of Judea, yet he was perhaps the only human being the King trusted completely. He had met Herod in Rome at the time of the King's appointment, and Herod, at Caesar's request, asked him to become his historian. Nicolas had returned to Judea with the Tiger, and he was one of a few men who actually greatly admired the monarch. There were times, though, when even his life was in danger, for when the Tiger roared, none could predict how a whim might twist his mind.

Justus stood still now, aware of Herod's anger, wondering if it would be suddenly turned upon him instead of Nicolas, who was keeping the heavy table between his sovereign and himself. Justus felt a little sorry for this old friend, but he knew from past experience that in the end Nicolas' will would subtly prevail over Herod's—though the final decision would be made to seem Herod's idea.

"That old fool would have died anyway!" the Tiger was shouting. He slammed his open right hand on the table to emphasize his point, even as Nicolas pleaded, "But Sire, Rabbi Simeon was a highly distinguished member of the Sanhedrin. He was a son of the famed scribe Hillel. His word has never been questioned," the chamberlain waved a long forefinger, "and for years he has told of having a vision that he would live to look on the face of the Christ. He has often said he wanted to die, but that—according to his God's Word—he could not until that day."

Herod snorted. "Bah. His mind has been obviously damaged. What sane person could maintain his senses in the Temple. It's worse than a slaughter house, and I sometimes wish I'd never built it. The stench and smoke from the priests' offerings would drive any sane man out of his mind. Why the foul smell even reaches this palace when the wind is right."

Nicolas shrugged. "Yet Rabbi Simeon lived in the Temple since its construction—and he was one of its most honored teachers."

"Granted. But it was only a coincidence that he should die after viewing a child," Herod shouted.

His voice echoed through the room while Justus stood waiting, confused. What did his presence here have to do with this conversation? So far as he knew he'd never even met this Rabbi Simeon. He stood quite still, awaiting acknowledgment of his presence, wondering if there had been a mistake about his being summoned. But he dared not speak until he was spoken to, so he listened unmoving as Nicolas went on, "Sire, though you do not faithfully follow the Jews' religion, you must know that he was greatly venerated in the Temple. And remember, too, Simeon said upon seeing this child—'This day, Master, Thou givest this servant his discharge in peace; now Thy promise is fulfilled, for I have seen with mine own eyes the deliverance which Thou hast made ready in full view of all nations; a light that will be the revelation to the heathen and a glory to the people of Israel'—or words to that effect. Simeon was always very flowery in his speech."

"Yes. And I still say he was crazy."

"Nevertheless, Sire, he was saying in effect that this child will destroy your power and reign over Israel. And so, because of Simeon's death—immediately after seeing a child—we can't afford to discount its implications."

"So? Is that all you got me out of bed to hear?" Herod looked around for a chair. "I don't feel well, Nicolas. If you have no more to tell me . . ."

"Nay, Sire, there is more. Just after old Simeon had made his declaration and fled through the Temple to his death, a prophetess—Anna, by name—who like Simeon has lived and served in the Temple many years, also viewed the child. And she, too, proclaimed him to be the Messiah."

"Of course." Herod sank into a chair. "She undoubtedly was influenced by that old fool. But anyway—who was the child and what was he doing in the Temple?"

Nicolas leaned on the table. "Sire, as you know, under the law of Moses, a Jewish male child must be presented to Jehovah, then redeemed for an offering of five shekels. Also, the Mosaic ritual requires that a woman attend the Temple for purification not less than 40 days after giving birth if the child is a male— 80 if the child is a female."

"Then you think the mother had taken the child to the Temple for these rituals?"

"I think so, yes."

"Well, what of our spies in the Temple? Did they fail to learn the parents' identity?"

"Yes, I'm afraid so."

"Then they will pay with . . ."

"Sire, the spies say nothing unusual occurred till Simeon ran into the inner Temple where he fell dead—and by that time attention was focused on Simeon, not the parents. They were seen only by the prophetess Anna before they disappeared in the crowd. I'm sure our men did all they could."

Justus stirred, shifting his weight from leg to leg, thinking, "So the King wants me to investigate the Temple spies."

Herod pulled at his beard. "How do the Jews feel about this whole occurrence?"

Nicolas hesitated. "I will tell you, Sire, but there are other matters I should first speak of about this child."

"All right. What else has been done?" Herod shouted. "You seem to believe these stories!"

"Sire, it is of no consequence whether *I* believe them or not. The question is: will the Jews believe them and start an uprising? If those rabble-rousing Zealots who defy your just and legal reign find some religious sign in this child, they may rally the Jews into a general revolt. Therein lies the real danger, for certainly this child, in and of itself, cannot challenge your throne."

Suddenly Justus saw the impact of Nicolas' words mirrored in the Tiger's face, and seeing the King grimace with pain, he started to step forward, but decided to remain where he was because his presence had still not been fully acknowledged.

Nicolas let Herod mull over the situation, obviously sure that no amount of physical pain could match the mental torment the man must now be experiencing. He waited a full moment, then continued, "I have questioned High Priest Annas, and though I did not tell him my reasons, I am sure he knew my purpose." Nicolas glanced at a piece of parchment which he had taken from beneath his robe. "He says their prophet Micah, who lived 700 years ago in Judah, wrote, 'But thou, Bethlehem Ephratah, though thou be little among the thousands of Judah, yet out of thee shall He come forth unto Me that is to be Ruler in Israel.'" Nicolas looked up. "And Sire, there are many Jews who have interpreted this to mean that their Christ, or Messiah, would come from Bethlehem."

Herod winced. "Does Annas place any faith in this prophet?"

"Frankly, that is hard to determine. Annas is jealous of his position as high priest. So, while he may believe in the prophecy, he will be reluctant to name this child or any other as the Messiah."

Herod nodded. "Would he help us find this child . . . this false Messiah?"

"I think so, though not directly. Annas would be afraid of the consequences among some Sanhedrin members if he seemed too friendly toward us."

"Then all we know is, according to an old prophecy, the Christ will be born in Bethlehem—that is, if any of it is true." Herod looked up. "I assume you think the child in the Temple was born in Bethlehem. If so, all we'll have to do is ransack Bethlehem. Justus, come here."

Justus stepped forward, but Nicolas continued, "But Sire, suppose the child is no longer in Bethlehem? As you know the Romans held the census of Quirinius 40 days ago, at which time all Jews of the House of David were required to travel to Bethlehem to be registered. It is therefore possible the child was born in the town during the census, and the parents were on their way home when they stopped at the Great Temple. This is highly probable, because Anna stated that she didn't know the parents. So we must face the fact that the child may have been born months ago, and this was the mother's first chance to present him for the temple rites. Many parents travel for days to have their children blessed in the Great Temple rather than in their local synagogue — some even have traveled all the way from Rome for that one purpose. The Jews take great pride in the Temple — which you so wisely built for them."

Herod sighed. "All right, all *right* . . . what *do* you suggest?"

Nicolas raised his head. "I will tell you . . . I have waited to reveal an incredible piece of good fortune because of which I asked to have Justus summoned. Late this afternoon an unusual caravan arrived from the East led by three Magi."

"So? Get to the point; my stomach pains me," Herod said, rubbing his swollen belly.

"Well, these three appear to be of noble origin; yet, upon arriving at the edge of the city they questioned many people before taking time to rest themselves."

"What did they ask?"

"Sire, only one question: *'Where is he that is born the King of the Jews'?*"

Herod stared hard at his chamberlain; Justus could see that he had begun to feel there were reasons now for not laughing this matter off. He also knew that the Tiger would move with dispatch, since he was determined no other would ever be King

29

of the Jews so long as he lived. He had even planned, before his death, to will the throne to a man of his own selection. Herod was the power of Israel—and no one, not even Caesar Augustus, ever forgot that fact.

He was yelling now, "I want to talk to those men! I want to know why they're trying to spread these lies! Justus, go and find them!"

Justus saluted and turned, then halted as Nicolas spoke.

"That won't be necessary, Justus. The Magi are in the palace." The old man bowed to the King. "I took the liberty, Sire, of inviting the princes to rest here, and even now they are within the walls of the palace."

Herod smiled. "Good. Justus, you will do away with them all in their sleep—thus preventing any further rumor of there being another king."

Justus' right hand unconsciously moved to his sword, and he felt no pangs of conscience. He was the Tiger's personal executioner, so killing lay in the line of duty; murder was merely loyalty to the King.

But Nicolas shook his head. "Sire, I suggest we wait. We can use these Magi; and Justus can handle them with ease after we've finished with them. But first I would like to call in our astrologers."

Herod groaned. "Oh, no. What for? Let's get this over with, Nicolas."

"Sire, these Magi told me they have seen an unusual star which foretold a Messiah's birth."

"A star? Nonsense. This gets more and more ridiculous!"

"Perhaps. But remember, Sire, the Jews set great store by their prophets. They might make a strong case that a Christ has been born. As I said before, we're dealing with a highly explosive situation. If the Jews in general—I'm not speaking now of their hair-splitting Pharisees—are led to believe these reports, they might start a rebellion against you and Rome."

"Well, go on," Herod sighed, giving ground. "What else have you discovered?"

"Just this: there is a prophecy of Balaam: '*There shall come a Star out of Jacob and a Scepter shall rise out of Israel.*' It was upon this prophecy the Magi based their discovery of the new star. Also, many ancient prophecies foretell that the East will arise, and that men in a short time will see, coming out of Judea, those who will govern the universe. Even some Roman scribes believe all of this . . . although I doubt not they had you in mind, my King, when they wrote such matters."

Nicolas, adding the false flattery which Herod might or might not see through, smiled as the King said resignedly, "Well, let me hear my astrologers. Perhaps they can discount this foolish fable about a star."

"Justus, bring in Salma," Nicolas ordered. "He should have arrived by now."

Justus stepped into the corridor, and as his lungs savored the cooler air, he was amazed that the inner room's smell of disease had been more powerful than the stench he'd noticed here as he entered the palace.

Salma, the old astrologer, was leaning against the wall with his eyes closed, while his young assistant nervously paced the hall; Justus thought the old man was probably dozing, for Salma was a mysterious creature who passed every night with his stars.

As Justus stepped toward the old man to summon him to the audience, Salma gave a start, almost dropping the armful of maps and charts, so patiently plotted throughout his lonely life; then he scuttled quickly past Justus, ahead of his assistant.

Inside the chamber he moved to the table in front of Herod, unrolled his charts, and waited.

Nicolas spoke at once. "I'm told that 8 weeks ago a star of unusual magnitude was visible from Babylon, which from that

31

city, appeared to stand in the West, in Jerusalem's direction. Is that correct?"

The ancient seer paused to look over one chart, and another, and Herod's small eyes followed his movements. Then, after a maddening delay, Salma shook his head.

Herod smiled. "So. There was no star?"

"Not that I have observed, Sire. However, it is possible that from Persia or Babylon, an anatole—or early morning star— might have seemed to be in line of sight with Judea. The Eastern astrologers place special emphasis upon each star. For example, Pisces is the sign of the West, and in Jewish tradition, the sign of Israel. We Jews believe that Saturn is Israel's protector, and the Babylonian seers at the school of astrology in Sippas believe Saturn to be the special star of Syria and Palestine."

"We know all that. Now, get to the point," Nicolas ordered.

But Salma droned on. "I find no observation of an unusual nature, but it is possible, at the time of such an observation from an eastern area, our own area was under a heavy over-cast which could have prevented a similar observation from Jerusalem. If I had the exact date of their observation, perhaps I could examine my weather records."

"What say *you*?" Nicolas asked, looking to Salma's assistant.

The younger man bowed as he answered, nervous because this was his first audience with Herod the Great. "Sire, my master speaks for us both. We work in conjunction, and he is —as you know—the wisest astrologer in Israel."

"Well, I don't know the exact date of the star's appearance," Nicolas said, "but could there have been some comet that may have been mistaken for a star?"

Salma nodded. "Yes, to the inexperienced eye. However —from what you tell us—I doubt that a comet would have been mistaken for the star of which you speak. The star did not seem to move, nor did it have a tail." The old man looked at his charts again. "Furthermore, I find no recent records of a comet of sufficient magnitude to be mistaken for a star."

Herod looked triumphant. "Then we must conclude the Magi lied to you, Nicolas."

"No, Sire. There could be another explanation," said the aged astrologer as his long thin finger ran down a column of strange figures on his chart. "On the 30th day of Shebat [ca. mid-Feb.] past, Jupiter moved out of the constellation Aquarius toward Saturn, in the constellation of Pisces. The sun, at that time, was entering also in Pisces, and its strong light covered the constellation."

"So?" asked Herod.

"Then, on Nisan 27th [beginning of April] Jupiter and Saturn rose in Pisces heliacally, which means the first rising of a star at daybreak, with a difference of eight degrees longitude."

"Oh, stop rattling on, and get to the point," roared Herod. "Stop talking in riddles, Salma."

But the old man would not be hurried. He continued deliberately, "On Sivan 14th [ca. end May] there were clearly visible for two hours in the morning sky, Saturn and Jupiter in Pisces at twenty-one degrees with a difference of zero degrees longitude and zero point ninety-eight degrees latitude."

"Now, Salma, you *must* get to the point!" Nicolas warned.

Salma went on serenely, "Again, on Tishri 10th [ca. last week Sept.], a second conjunction of the planets took place, in the eighteenth degree of the constellation of Pisces."

Nicolas turned toward Herod. "Tishri 10th was the Jews' Day of Atonement. That was more than 8 weeks ago — which would allow the Magi normal travel time by camel from Babylon or beyond."

"But I thought the whole question concerned their sighting of a new star!" Herod cried.

"Sire, it is as I stated." The astronomer looked up from his charts. "This conjunction of Jupiter and Saturn could appear as a single star, and I believe that to be a reasonable explanation. There have been times when even *I* have mistaken a conjunction for a new star before I examined my charts. I do not believe there was a new star — the travellers may have seen, and misinterpreted, this conjunction."

"Ha! So these princes were not so smart after all?" Herod sat forward, drumming on the arm of his chair. "Nevertheless, these men could stir up the Jews, so Justus' sword shall provide them with a quiet end to their search."

"But, Sire, how should we ever then ascertain the child's identity? Do let us use these men to lead us to him. Surely they can extract more information from the Jews than we can. The Jews would have no cause at all to distrust *them*."

Suddenly Herod grabbed his fat stomach and belched obscenely, spraying a foul mist at Nicolas. In order not to offend the King, the counselor hastily turned and told the astrologers that they were excused. Then, while Herod took a great gulp of drugged wine, Nicolas dispatched Justus to the Magi's chamber to say that the King wished to see them.

Justus located the Magi, and addressing them in Greek, learned that they spoke his tongue with the ease of educated men. Like himself, the princes obviously knew several languages, and their dress was definitely typical of royal households. They had changed from travelling robes. Their persons were heavily scented, and their hair glistened fresh with oil as though they had fully expected an audience with Herod.

The princes seemed friendly enough, but Justus sensed that they were politely avoiding a personal conversation with him. Their leader, Balthasar, carried a small gold chest as he led the other two down the long, torch-lighted corridors to King Herod's chamber.

Entering the room, Justus saluted as the three visitors salaamed; then Balthasar, holding the small ornate box in his dark,- slim hands, moved forward, saying, "It is with great pride that we present this small token of esteem and respect, for you — whose many accomplishments are one of the world's true wonders, oh, Herod the Great. Our names are Balthasar, Gaspar, and Melchior. We come from east of Babylon, on a mission of love and peace."

Herod opened the box, doubtless expecting jewels or gold, and hastily hid his disappointment, crying, "Ah, yes. Here, Justus, light some of this fine incense so that I may honor these wise travellers as we converse." He turned to the Magi, smiling. "I have long loved the incense from your country. May its sweetness perfume our thoughts and tongues so that we may talk freely, in friendship and love."

Justus stepped forward, took the box from the King, moved to a gold incense burner and lit a cone of the gray stuff, feeling all the eyes in the room on his broad back. The curls of gray smoke wound their way from the container's slots, spreading a sweet pungent odor, and Justus thought happily that these Magi could not have chosen a more appropriate gift . . . anything, *anything* masking the terrible smell of sickness here would be welcome.

The silence was broken now by Herod as he inhaled the foreign incense for the very first time and lied, "Ah, it is a pleasure once again to breathe the air of beautiful Babylon through your gift. It brings back pleasant memories of years ago when I visited your land. Now, tell me, what is the purpose of your journey?"

Balthasar bowed. "Sire, we have come to pay homage to the new King of the Jews."

Justus flinched, fearing this answer would anger Herod, then straightened, alert to act at the Tiger's command. Instead, to his great surprise, the King remained quite calm. "Ah, yes," he said. "We have heard you have seen a new star that proclaims a king of the Jews." Herod's smile was sinister-sweet. "I am — as you see — old and sick of body. My physicians tell me I have not long to live. Perhaps, upon my death, this person whom you seek will ascend my throne."

Balthasar bowed again. "Ah, Sire, we do hope that your learned physicians are in error. Your long reign has been a most prosperous one for your subjects. No other country in the Roman Empire can boast the accomplishments made possible through your leadership."

"Thank you. But, is it not true that you believe a new king of the Jews has been born?" Herod still seemed unusually calm. "I believe you call him the Christ?"

"Sire, the prophecies have shown us the way. We seek the new King of the Jews — and the universe."

"In spite of the fact that you stand before me — the King of Judea?" Herod asked softly.

"Sire, we are merely repeating the written words of ancient ones far wiser than we," Balthasar answered.

Herod sat back, slit-eyed. "My chamberlain has told me much of your beliefs. I honor any man's belief in his god and the prophets. You can trust me. The Jews here have always been free in their religious worship — just as the Romans and others have. If, therefore, you have faith in these prophecies, I wish you well; I will extend you aid in your holy search."

"Thank you, Gracious One," Melchior half-whispered.

"Nicolas tells me that for days you have followed an unusual star which has led you here. I regret to say my astrologers have not seen such a star, but then, for several nights the skies over Jerusalem have been cloudy, so perhaps they have missed this unusual occurrence. Also, I have been told that there are ancient sayings none can disregard, which indicate that a ruler will arise out of Bethlehem."

Justus noted that Melchior now smiled faintly at Herod's words. The Magi had obviously expected no help from Herod, for even in the East they had doubtless heard of the Tiger's mad slaughter of anyone who appeared to threaten his throne.

Now, for some inexplicable reason, Herod was telling the princes where they might find the Christ, and even as Melchior smiled, the other two Magi looked at each other, plainly dubious about what they just heard.

Herod continued, "Yes, I have consulted the high priests of our Great Temple. They have confirmed the ancient prophecy, and I am not one to question such wise pronouncements, for I have been circumcised and am of the Jewish belief, even though, for certain reasons, I do not participate regularly in the faith."

The Wise Men nodded. They had heard of Herod's general attitude toward the Jews and their religion, and also how, believing in no god, this classic hypocrite alternated with the winds of politics between Roman and Jewish beliefs.

"Has the Great Herod seen the child?" Gaspar asked suddenly.

"No, I had not even heard of his birth until your arrival was heralded—and, as I have said, the star of which you speak was not visible to our astrologers. But I too am eager to see and worship the Messiah, and I only regret that this accursed illness prevents my going with you to find him."

"Of that we are truly sorry," Gaspar said in a soft voice.

"Yes, for if this child, as a man, is one day to sit on my throne, it is fitting that I should be one of the first to pay him homage. Will you, therefore, travel to Bethlehem and find this child and then inform me of his exact whereabouts?"

Gaspar bowed, but did not commit himself. "Sire, we pray that we do find the new King of Kings."

"Then go—and peace go with you. You will travel with safety under the protection of Justus and my other personal bodyguards."

Herod avoided the Magus' eyes as he looked at Justus, but Balthasar promptly answered, "Sire, we do not wish to offend you, but we would prefer to travel alone so that the rabble will do no harm to the Christ. We know that there are many who will doubt, and we have no wish to attract attention."

"Prince, do you question my intentions?"

Melchior stepped forward. "No, Sire. We only want to prevent any strife and misunderstanding. We are simply peaceful men on a mission, bringing gifts of gold, incense, and myrrh to the babe."

"Then go, and I shall eagerly await tidings of your success. We shall have a great feast of celebration upon your return."

Herod rose, indicating the audience was at an end. The Magi salaamed and quickly left the room, and Herod laughed aloud. "Those fools!"

Nicolas moved to his couch. "They do not trust us, Sire."

"No . . . nor do I trust them. Those three are even more slippery than the Great Sanhedrin's judges," the Tiger answered, rubbing his belly. "Justus, have one of your best men follow them. I'm certain they'll try to slip out of the palace tonight; you mark my words. In fact, send Mundus to shadow them all the 5 miles to Bethlehem. It is a small village, and he should have no trouble finding the child. Then take three of your best men, go and wipe out any vestige of this so-called Messiah . . . and the stupid Magi as well."

Justus took his leave and hurried down the long corridor toward the guard's barracks, cursing Herod for having selected Mundus to follow the Magi. It wasn't that the man couldn't do the job, he thought, as the hard leather of his sandals echoed on the stone floor, but simply that Mundus could not really be trusted. The buck-toothed Roman would slay his own grandmother for a price, and Justus would have sent the bastard back to Rome, save for the fact that Herod, having heard how bloodthirsty this soldier was, had personally petitioned Caesar for his services. This villain had a reputation not only for being an artist with the knife, but for having a sadistic, perverted nature that took actual pleasure in killing.

Like Justus, Mundus had grown up in the Roman Army, had traveled extensively with the Legions, and despite his illegitimate birth and rough childhood had learned court manners and customs so that he was at ease in any company. Justus knew that the man secretly despised nobility, but that did not disturb him so much as the revolting fact that Mundus was a homosexual who revelled in corrupting young boys. Furthermore, if anyone threatened Justus' complete acceptance by Herod, it was this monster, for Herod had made him a lieutenant over the protests of both Justus and Nicholas. Justus knew that this was Herod's way of keeping a constant rivalry alive between them. Justus feared that Mundus might poison the Tiger's mind against him, since Herod lived in constant fear of betrayal by any man close to him.

As Justus entered the barracks, five men were playing dice on the cold stone floor, with a half-filled jug of wine near their feet, and Tactus was cursing his luck as Hezron pulled a stack of copper shekels toward himself.

"All right, break it up now," Justus snapped, "and get to bed . . . all of you. There may be work to do later tonight. Where is Mundus?"

He glared at the men who looked up from the dice.

"In there." Tactus pointed to a closed door at one end of the long room; and Justus walked past several soldiers sleeping under woolen covers, oblivious to the noisy game of dice.

He pounded on the door, then opened it just in time to see a naked Jewish boy, no more than 10 years old, scurry beneath the cover next to Mundus, who raised himself on one elbow, slyly grinning.

"Get up," Justus roared. "The King has orders!" He then turned in disgust from what he knew had been going on, to watch the soldiers preparing for bed, hearing Tactus still grumbling at Hezron as the latter placed his winnings in his helmet.

39

In a few moments Mundus came out, buckling a short, flatbladed sword to his waist—his sadistic grin exposing four protruding front teeth.

"This had better be important," he said as he placed his helmet over his close-shaved head.

"Come out here," Justus growled, indicating the empty hall. In the corridor he told Mundus about the mission, instructing him to use a black horse and to wear Jewish robes to avoid detection while he was following the Magi.

"Report back to me as soon as possible," he said, then, as Mundus turned to leave, "and get that depraved little Jew-boy out of your quarters at once, you evil dog."

Mundus spoke grimly. "That remark may cost you more than you've bargained for, one of these days."

Justus spat on the barracks floor. "I doubt it. I also doubt that Herod would countenance the things you do with the sons of his concubines. Take care that I'm never forced to tell him all that I know."

IV

Justus sent word to the other guards to allow the Magi to leave the palace in peace and to notify Mundus as soon as they had departed. He then reported his actions to the chamberlain, who had returned to his own chambers after summoning the court physician to ease the Tiger's pain.

Leaving Nicolas' apartment, Justus heard the sound of soft, rushing footsteps. He turned to find Mariame half hidden in a doorway, and she rushed into his arms whispering fiercely, "Oh, Justus, I had to see you tonight."

"Mariame!" Justus held her off. "What are you doing here at this hour?"

"I told my maid to watch for you. I simply had to see you."

"Is something wrong?" Justus asked, as the dim torch-light illumined her beautiful face.

"Justus, do you love me?"

Justus scowled. "Don't answer me with an irrelevant question, please. Just tell me why you are here."

"I told you—I had to see you. Now, answer me, at once. *Do you love me, Justus?*"

"Must you know that right at this moment?" Justus asked.

The pitch torches threw a golden glow on her olive skin. He could see that the girl had been crying, and suddenly, not knowing why, he countered, "First, tell me: do *you* love *me?*"

"Oh, yes. Yes," Mariame whispered shakily. "Yes, I do." For the first time in her life she was honestly telling a man that she loved him, and the impact of her confession made her tremble inside. She looked deep into Justus' eyes seeking a similar admission, and saw that he was struggling with his own emotions. He said, after a moment, "You must know how I feel about you, Mariame."

"I don't," she cried. "How am I ever to know how you really feel unless you tell me? Please, *please* . . . tell me that you love me, now. I need to know . . . I must . . ."

Justus held her close. "Oh, don't," he said. "I can't imagine why you're acting like this, but if you'll only stop these tears, I'll tell you a hundred times, I love you." He pressed her head to his heart, then raised it in his big hand, and placed a soft kiss on her lips.

"Now tell me at once; what has brought all this on?"

Mariame gulped. "It's Father. He wants to marry me off . . . to Herod . . . or to some nobleman—no matter who, as long as he's rich and powerful. My father thinks of me as a chattel—I know that now. Oh, Justus, take me away . . . marry me—and take me far from this palace."

Justus stiffened. "So, that's how it is," he said and held Mariame closer, trying to think. For the first time in his life he had told a woman he loved her. This was new — and how could he be sure he wasn't reacting to her own display of emotion? He needed time to study this situation, and he did not want to commit himself at once. Then, too, what would Herod say, or do, if he took this girl in whom the Tiger had recently shown great interest?

He slowly withdrew from Mariame's arms, speaking quietly, "Mariame, how can I say this? You are the only woman I've ever told I loved and truly meant it. But there is the King to consider — and your father."

Mariame's eyes met his. "My Father and Herod have nothing to do with us. If you love me, take me away — somewhere, anywhere — tonight."

"That's foolish talk," Justus told her sharply. "We can't just run away. Besides, the King has ordered me on a special assignment tonight. Listen. I give you my word — we will talk tomorrow. Now come. I must take you back to your father's apartment. Suppose he waked up and missed you? Calm yourself now — and promise you'll try to sleep. Nobody's going to force you into matrimony tonight, you know."

Mariame laughed for the first time. "No, I guess not," she said. "I'm sorry I got so hysterical." They walked slowly hand in hand, toward Aizel's chambers, but she stopped twice to kiss Justus and extract more promises than he could make. Nevertheless, he made them, and their whispered words of love were gradually hushed by long kisses as they stood against the wall beside the door to Mariame's quarters.

Then suddenly Aizel flung open the door, gasping, "Oh God, Mariame! How dare you do this to me? Come inside at once. And as for you, you Roman assassin . . . go, before I report your behavior to the King."

Justus sprang back as Mariame ran weeping into the apartment, and Aizel slammed the door in his face.

He stood for a second, glaring; then turned on his heel, torn between hatred for old Aizel and mortal fear of Herod.

V

Mundus took a long drink of water from the clay pot in Justus' palace apartment and wiped his mouth with the front of his mantle.

"They left just after I stationed myself at the south entrance . . . on those damned camels, headed toward Bethlehem."

Justus nodded. "And did you see, by chance, an unusual star?"

Mundus scratched his head. "Yes, now you mention it, there was a very bright star on the low horizon just about an hour before daybreak. The sky suddenly cleared, and there it was."

"Did the Magi follow it?"

Mundus looked contemptuous. "Justus, sometimes I wonder about you! How could they follow a star? The star was on the horizon—way on the other side of Bethlehem. The Magi simply set out on the road to Bethlehem and stayed on it."

"Where did they go when they reached the village?"

"I don't know . . . I lost them."

Justus glared. "You *what?* How could you possibly lose three men on camels? What happened?"

"Well . . . about 2 miles out of Bethlehem, my horse either stumbled on some damn rock or stepped in a big hole—I don't know which. Anyway, the horse fell, dumping me; then he ran off, and it took me nearly an hour to catch the black bastard in all that darkness. So, when I finally rode into Bethlehem, I couldn't find the damned Magi. But anyway, I don't think they stayed in the town—at least nobody would tell me, if they knew."

43

Justus gritted his teeth. "Herod will kill us both. I guess you know that. Who did you ask about the Magi?"

"The only people I saw; some shepherds. They said three men on camels had passed them earlier, but when I told them Herod had ordered me to find the Magi, they wouldn't say anything more—just kept repeating what they'd said at first."

Justus considered. "Then we shall have to lie to Herod to save our necks. Go at once; get Tactus and Hezron and four fresh horses . . . . I think we'll be going to Bethlehem shortly. Now, make tracks. You've caused me inexcusable trouble tonight."

Mundus took to his heels, and Justus hurried to Nicolas' chamber where he told the chamberlain's slave, "Wake your master, quickly."

The old man was angry after Justus' explanation—first, at being awakened so early, second—and more important to the captain, because Mundus had lost the trail of the Magi.

"The King will have Mundus' scalp over this," he said, shaking his skinny finger, "but that can't be helped, unfortunately. The only possible thing is to tell Herod the truth. Come quickly, now."

Herod belched with pain, his breath befouling the air of his bedroom. "Why must I forever be plagued with incompetent fools? And after all I've done for that damned Roman," he moaned, shaking his head. "Now, I must think how to punish him, I suppose."

Nicolas spoke up quickly. "Mundus can wait, Sire. We must take immediate action . . . any delay could mean complete disaster. The Magi may have left Bethlehem, but they have not returned to the palace, as they promised."

Herod shouted shrilly. "I knew they were liars. I told you. Why did I tell them to go to Bethlehem? This is your fault, Nicolas! If we don't find this child, it will be your fault!" The King grabbed his stomach, grimacing.

"Please try to calm yourself, Sire. You know how excitement affects you. There is a way . . ."

"What way? Damn you, I wanted to kill those princes."

"Sire, attend me: the Magi evidently did find the child in Bethlehem, or they'd have stayed to continue their search — although, of course, they could have been in hiding when Mundus searched the town. That is possible — so I suggest that we search every house in the town and arrest all the parents who have an infant."

"Don't be a fool! Don't you know the parents of this child would lie about his being the Messiah? No. We must slay every male child in the village. Justus, take three men with you — and don't leave a male child alive in Bethlehem."

Nicolas said hastily, "Nay, Sire. Why not only those children under 2 years? As you know, the Jews suckle their babes to that age, so, by slaying all those under 2 years we will eliminate any chance of error, and the task will be far less difficult."

"Very well. Justus, kill only those 2 years old or younger," Herod commanded. "There can't be more than 25, anyway, in such a small village. Now, be off. And remember, I'll attend to you as well as Mundus, if you fail to do this job right."

Justus bowed and left the chamber. He summoned Mundus, Hezron, and Tactus, and within the hour the four were half-way to Bethlehem.

Mundus was smiling as they rode at a fast gallop, and Justus was sure he could read the sadist's mind. If he did a good job, perhaps the King would not punish him severely for his failure in following the Magi — and of course he would not mind about killing children. "The bastard would like and enjoy his bloody work," mused Justus.

The captain eyed Hezron and Tactus as their horses raced down the chalk-white road, thinking that he couldn't have picked two better men for this mission. They had no fears and no consciences that might lead them to hesitate. Indeed, he and these three, all highly skilled in killing, would undoubtedly end this matter to Herod's liking. "Still," Justus thought, "small children . . . I have killed men on the battlefield and committed many murders under orders . . . but innocent children . . ."

Oh, well, what difference did it make? Perhaps he would get a promotion out of this day's work. Perhaps a successful completion of this project might even ease the way for his marriage to Mariame. Her father's opposition would not count alongside Herod's approval.

He shouted above the roar of the horses' hoofs, "Remember, *every* child. Spare none under the age of 2. If you fail it may mean the deaths of us all."

At the edge of the town, as the men reined in their horses, he ordered, "Tactus, come with me. Hezron, go with Mundus. We'll take the south half of the town; you two, the north. We'll all meet at the inn when the work is done." Then, as Mundus and Hezron raced off toward the north side of the village, Justus pulled his horse's reins and, standing in his stirrups, motioned to Tactus. "You take the southwest half; I'll take the southeast. If you run into trouble sound an alarm for me. And remember, you are protecting your King, so be thorough. Now, away with you!"

The morning sun was just beginning to warm the air as Justus rode to the center of Bethlehem and tied his horse to an iron ring outside the small synagogue. He had no sooner finished than he saw a young woman entering the synagogue, and shouted, "Halt, in the name of Herod."

The woman turned, her dark eyes wide with fear. "Sir, I was only going to give thanks to Jehovah for the birth of my son." She nodded down at the child in her arms, wrapped in a white linen cloth.

"Woman, I must slay your son," Justus told her, matter-of-factly. He drew his dagger, grasped the baby's arm and ran the long thin blade into its heart. The infant gave a gasping cry as the blade sank to its hilt, and the woman fell to the ground clutching the baby to her breast.

The small body spilled its lifeblood, turning the swaddling cloths to crimson as Justus wiped his blade on the edge of his mantle and walked away, his eyes avoiding the sight. As long as he did not look back, he thought he could not feel the full impact of his actions.

As he reached the synagogue steps, the mother screamed after him, "May the Lord cause you to suffer for this deed!"

He found the synagogue empty, then started up the narrow street, searching every house. This was simply another job he had to do for Herod. He could not afford to feel remorse or guilt.

As he broke into every house in his section of the city, he came to the realization that these people had become so subservient to Rome and to Herod's harsh rule that they meekly submitted to his violence. It seemed their spirit was gone, and instead of joining together to fight him they seemed to understand that resistance would be futile and fatal. Though their weakness aided him, he cursed the Jews for being so spineless as to allow a single man to break into their homes and kill their children—even if Herod had decreed it.

By late afternoon he began to tire of the senseless killings. He still felt no remorse—only fatigue. Only two young fathers had attempted to stay him. One, fat and jolly-faced and still in his teens, had rushed at him with a short kitchen knife. As Justus drove his sword deep into the young man's ample belly he saw that the man's love of his son was sufficient for the sacrifice of his own life. But it had been a foolish act, for the child immediately joined his brave father in death.

The other father with a glint of spirit had cracked a clay pot over Justus' helmet, and Justus, in a moment of compassion, spared the father by merely knocking him unconscious with the flat of his blade. As he calmly walked from the house, Jus-

47

tus was pleased that he had spared the father so he might sire another child to replace the son he had just lost to soothe Herod's sick mind . . . .

Now, approaching the inn, he knew the massacre must be complete, for Mundus, Tactus, and Hezron had already tied their mounts outside the small, two-story stone building.

Entering, he saw the three guards at a small table drinking wine, gobbling up cheese and bread, and he noticed that their tunics and mantles were spattered with dried blood.

Justus dropped to the hard wood bench and took a swig from the wine bottle. "Well, how did it go?"

Mundus turned upon him the buck-toothed smile of a self-assured Roman. Justus hid his irritation with the man for acting superior because he was born in the city of Rome.

"Ha! I had no trouble at all," Mundus boasted. "I did away with fifteen or twenty children—and about a dozen parents."

Justus said nothing. He knew that Mundus was exaggerating, but it was plain that he'd killed a great many Jews, for his tunic was red, the edge of his cloak was stiff with dried blood, and even the hair on his right forearm was darkly matted.

"We too were successful," Hezron said. "Not a child in our section escaped."

"Yes, but did anyone of you slay the King of the Jews?"

Mundus poured another cup of wine for himself. "No. We found no such child. We were just discussing that when you arrived."

"Nor I," Justus said, "not even anyone who could possibly have been a disguised member of any royal troupe."

Tactus looked up. "Then there was no such child?"

"Yes, there was such a child. He was here at one time, and of course we may have killed him, unknowing. The thing is, are we sure we've slain all the children under 2? You know what will happen if Herod would determine that we've failed?"

Mundus ducked his head behind his cup. "Oh, yes. I'm absolutely positive about my section."

"I also," Tactus said, and Hezron hastened to say, "I'm sure there are none left alive in mine."

Mundus looked at Justus. "By the way, we found no trace of the Magi. Did you?"

Justus shook his head, unable to speak through a mouth full of white goat cheese.

Hezron looked at him, pleading, "Captain, can't we rest before we go back to Jerusalem? I'm tired from all that work and lack of sleep."

Justus grunted. "You shouldn't shoot dice all night. I've told you, time and again. Still, perhaps it would be best to wait till nightfall and slip out of town." He gulped some wine, secretly glad that one of them and not he had suggested this; then he turned, raising his voice: "Innkeeper! Bring us more wine and cheese and some meat."

The innkeeper came to the table, wiping his greasy hands on the dirty apron that covered his fat belly. "I'm sorry, sir, but this is all the food I have. I sold the rest to three men riding camels, who set out this morning for Babylon."

Justus shouted, "What's that you say? Where were these men from?"

The innkeeper looked frightened. "They didn't say where they were from. They only said they needed food to last them until they reached Babylon."

"Did you hear their names?"

"Well . . . yes, sir, I did hear one call the other Melchior."

Justus sat forward. "What else did they say?"

"Nothing. Except that they'd fulfilled their mission, and were free to return home now that they'd seen the light of the world—whatever that meant." The innkeeper was obviously shaken now, for he had placed these blood-covered soldiers as four of Herod's bodyguards.

Justus persisted. "Did they stay here last night?"

"No, sir. They came about sunup, seeking food and water."

"Do you know where they'd been?"

"No, sir. But they came up the side of the hill from where the animals are kept . . . ."

"Show me where that is," Justus ordered, springing up.

The innkeeper moved to a window and pointed down a steep hill back of the inn. "Down there, sir. They came from that direction. My stables are down that way."

"Are there homes down there?"

"Only one near the cave we use for a stable. But during the census when the city was overcrowded, there was a small family staying in the cave because I had no room for them in the inn."

Justus' heart beat hard as he grasped the man by the hair.

"Quick now. Who were these people?"

"I . . . don't know, sir, truly. Just a young couple from Nazareth who'd come for the census. I suppose the man was of the House of David—though I didn't ask."

"Did they have a child?"

"Not when they came, no, sir. But the wife gave birth to a son the night they arrived. That's why I gave them the stable. It was too cold for the woman to deliver her child in the open."

"Where are they now?" Justus roared, giving the man's hair a twist.

The innkeeper screamed. "Oh, sir, truly I don't know."

"You do—and if you fail to tell me, you'll never live to see the morning's sun!" Justus cried, twisting harder.

"They . . . they have gone to Egypt," gasped the innkeeper. "They left this morning, just after the men on the camels did. And they paid me with gold for the use of my house, although I didn't ask any payment, for I am a generous man. Oh, sir, I had no idea they were important people. If I had known I'd have thrown out someone and given them my best."

"Let's see the gold," Justus commanded, and the innkeeper

nervously fumbled at his inner robe, withdrawing a small leather bag with a drawstring. He felt in the bag, extracted a strange gold coin, and held it out.

"Here, sir."

Justus looked at the coin, put it in his mouth and bit it. He said, "Yes, this is pure gold. Now, which road did these people take, man?"

"I think they went by the desert route, for they had much water on their animal." The innkeeper looked at the strange gold coin, plainly lamenting its loss, and Justus, reaching under his tunic, produced a handful of silver.

"Here. Now fill a water skin." He turned, shouting, "I think we have found what we were looking for!" and the men sprang up from the table. "Now we must catch them, if we have to ride all night."

He looked down at the coin again. There was no question that this was a gift of the Magi, and a coin specially minted, for on each side of it in raised lettering, a simple Greek word gleamed in the lamplight: ΧΡΙϹΤΟϹ – CHRIST!

VI

Their long ride through the rough country was painful, and Justus continuously felt the cold night air biting his nose and ears. They had stopped twice to rest, for the horses, despite a chilling desert wind, glistened white with a foamy lather in the clear moonlight. At each rest stop Hezron and Tactus had complained of the pace Justus had set, but Mundus had merely drunk from the wineskin he'd gotten from the innkeeper, grinning and telling his captain, "We're wasting time. We can never possibly find that child out here."

Finally, Hezron's mount had gone lame from a sharp rock, and Justus had ordered the tired soldier to rest his mount and return, as best he could, to Jerusalem. He knew that Hezron was secretly thankful for the accident, and anyway, any fighting that might occur could be handled easily without him.

Hezron sat down to stretch his tired legs and to watch the three riders dissolve in the cold shafts of the moon. The beat of the horses hoofs shook the ground till the wind quieted their thunder, and then the soldier dozed, lying close to his supine mount.

As they rode on, Justus' body grew numb, while his mind sought a possible excuse to make to Herod, if they should now fail to find the child, and surely some explanations could be offered if they should fail in this desolate desert area. What if the innkeeper had lied about the family's taking the desert road? But, no, the man had told the truth . . . he'd have had no reason to lie, since he had no suspicion as to the child's importance. Well, it was useless to speculate; if they failed now, the Tiger would be beside himself with fury, and that would be that.

Perhaps he could lie to Herod. It would be a simple matter to get Mundus and Tactus to go along with a lie, for they, too, would be in the same danger and would be held equally responsible. No. Herod need never learn that they had let the child escape, for, after all, the parents were taking the baby to Egypt, and no one except the innkeeper knew their identity, and he could be disposed of. The Magi, who had returned to Babylon, would have no reason to contact Herod again. Oh well, he would cross these bridges when he came to them. Meanwhile, he felt sure they were on the right track; he had seen fresh dung, then the tracks of an ass that had been led down a dirt road, when they'd last stopped to rest the horses, and Tactus had said at the time, it was lucky this wasn't a paved Roman road or they'd never have seen the animal's tracks.

Justus' mind continued to weigh the outcome of this tiring journey, conjecturing that they must be swiftly closing in upon their prey. They should catch up with the fleeing family near dawn, which wasn't far off, and he was glad the night had been clear so that they could follow the rough road that was little more than a path. If this had been a black night, they'd have had to wait until dawn to track down their quarry . . .

Now, the first dim outlines of high hills in the distance began to focus in the widened pupils of Justus' eyes, and he told himself that the long night vigil had given them a cat-like quality.

Later, as the sun's first rays began to light the sky, his confidence continued to grow, then suddenly he shouted, "Look! What's that on the rise ahead?"

Justus strained his eyes and detected a hint of color. Yes, there was an ass, and someone in a red mantle, riding him.

He gave his horse the spur, and though the tired beast was slow to respond, he could see they were closing in fast, for now he could make out a man in a dark brown cloak leading the donkey. Justus smiled. This was their goal, without a doubt, he thought, just as Mundus, yelling, "Let me do the honors for the King!" spurred his horse ahead.

Now as the sun neared the horizon, Justus could see that the person riding the beast was a woman, holding a baby swathed in white.

He shouted at Mundus, 20 yards ahead, "No, wait. I'm in command here. I must slay this usurper to Herod's throne!"

But Mundus rode on at full speed, ignoring the order, and Justus spurred his horse until he feared the beast might fall beneath him.

In another moment the headlong approach of the soldiers caused the young couple to stop, and the man leading the ass moved to the woman's side. Meanwhile the small animal, welcoming the halt, stood quiet before the onrushing fury of the three armed riders. The woman, her head covered in a white cotton veil that fell to her shoulders, cradled the child in her arms — its face hid from the cold behind a white swaddling cloth. If there had been a sympathetic eye to see, the couple with

53

their precious cargo would have looked pitifully small against the desert's vastness as the fierce riders bore down at full gallop.

Mundus reined his mount to a halt a few feet in front of the couple, and the horse's hoofs threw a cloud of dust that drifted groundward. The Roman leapt into action, drawing his sword.

"No, stop! This is my job, I tell you," Justus shouted. He vaulted off his mount, just as Tactus, bringing up the rear, dismounted and moved to the opposite side of the couple, back of the ass and near to the saddle bags.

Justus drew his sword, and suddenly fearing his authority, Mundus lowered his own sabre and stepped back.

The young woman looked at Justus who now stood, sword in hand, heart-thudding, sure that this was the Christ Child. He would make the kill, and Herod would reward him, not only with a promotion but with great wealth.

The sun continued its upward course, its rays gently tinting the surrounding hilltops. Justus glanced at the bearded man who stood quietly, the rope leading to the donkey's harness taut in his left hand. The woman sat sidesaddle and her husband's right hand fumbled toward hers as the two of them stared transfixed at the men from Jerusalem.

Then Justus took another forward step, and as the man pressed back, his movement caused the ass to shift its legs so that the woman swayed to keep her balance. Justus could now see her face clearly, and he noted that her dark eyes were wide and shaped like almonds. The headdress only partially covered the black hair that tumbled off her shoulders, and he noted an almost imperceptible quiver of her full lower lip.

"Let me see your child," he ordered, "uncover the babe."

The woman obeyed, turning back a corner of the protective cloth; her husband, looking helpless, gazed first at her, then at the baby boy, as she turned him toward Justus.

"Ah, so it is a male," Justus thought. "Well, this confirms it all . . ."

He glanced at the husband, realizing there'd be no serious trouble with him since he was unarmed, but he also sensed that he would have to kill this man in order to get to the child. Somehow he had the look of a father who would die protecting his son.

Justus raised his sword—all at once a ray of sun broke over the distant horizon, bathing the woman in brilliance, and her face glowed with color. Her black eyes streamed silver tears that rolled down her high cheekbones and fell on the face of the uncovered child. Her pale lips opened and closed as she wept, not speaking; her whole person glowed with an ethereal beauty that Justus, the Roman, had never seen before, as she pressed her child to her visibly pounding heart.

She stared into Justus' eyes, questioning in a language stronger than any words; then the sunlight touched the boy child's face and he awoke. He stirred and let out a short cry, quickly lost in the desert's vastness and the soft hum of the wind, and Justus stepped closer, arm still raised, ready to speed his blade on its path of destruction. His right arm halted, chin-level, awaiting an order from his brain, and he glanced again at the woman on the ass, thinking, "What's wrong with me?" He hesitated, once again sighted his target, but his mind would not speed an impulse to the nerves of his sword arm. He felt suddenly sick at his stomach as he tried again, and his arm again refused to move. Something in the woman's face would not let him wield the sword, and he trembled, amazed at himself, yet unable to move beneath the strange paralysis that held his brain and body in thrall.

"Kill him," Mundus shouted. "Don't let a baby's cry stay you. Kill him! Kill them all!"

Justus whirled to see the Roman, sword in hand, rushing toward the couple, screaming, "Kill them! If you've gone soft, I'll do it!"

With a quick, sure swing Justus brought his sword's flat side against Mundus' wrist and heard the bone snap as Mundus' sword struck the ground.

Mundus fell to his knees, and Justus shouted, "Damn it, I told you I am in charge here! Next time maybe you'll learn to obey your superior." He glared at the soldier crumpled up at his feet, obviously fearing a sword-thrust to the neck. Mundus' eyes shone glassy. He hobbled on his knees—away from Justus, holding his wrist with his good hand. Justus turned again to the travelers, thinking, "Now, I'll finish this job." But again he hesitated as he looked into the face of the mother. She had not shielded her eyes from the sun. Justus glanced at the husband, then at the child, and back again at the mother. He simply *could not* even raise his sword arm, and he could not understand *why*.

Tactus was still on the other side of the ass, his dagger held in his right hand, poised to pounce on the travelers from the rear, and Justus heard himself shouting, "Tactus! No! If you harm them, I'll kill you! Attend to the horses, and then to Mundus."

For some reason he took a step back from the couple. He lowered his blade completely, but his mind was totally blank. He moved almost as in a trance; his gaze fixed on the woman. He could hear the wind and the horses' movements, but all else was silent. After what seemed an hour, he took another backward step, pointed, and cried, "Egypt is that way. Be gone! I don't know why I spare you—but go, and do not return to this land so long as Herod is King."

The woman smiled at Justus, while her husband cautiously took his place at the head of the small beast. As the ass took its first step, the mother's eyes were still wet, and she spoke for the first time. "Thank you, sir. My son will thank you some day, too, I know."

The sun glowed brighter as the couple moved on. The

mother sat very straight on the tossing back of the little animal; the man walked slowly, his face turned toward the sky.

While Tactus was splinting Mundus' arm, Justus sat on a rock, utterly silent, watching the travelers till they passed from sight over a distant hill. His mind was still blank, but his body was shaking now, and his face was incredibly streaked with tears.

VII

Tactus was doing a good job, setting the broken bones of Mundus' wrist, but there was a contempt in Mundus' eyes that the man could not conceal. Justus sensed that he should have killed him. This was not the first time that Mundus had come out at the losing end of a disagreement with him, but it was the first time he'd been wounded. Justus weighed the advisability of killing both him and Tactus; however, in spite of Mundus' wounds, he doubted that he could win in a fight with both men. Tactus was easily the best swordsman he'd ever seen. He could whip any three of Justus' other men, and, knowing Tactus as he did, he was sure he would side with Mundus. Also, even with one hand, Mundus would be a formidable adversary, so the two soldiers must be handled separately—later.

Justus continued to sit on the stone, half-dazed, waiting for Tactus to finish wrapping Mundus' arm. He was still confused as to why *he*—of all people—should have spared those travelers. No matter how he analyzed his actions, he could not justify them. It wasn't the child—only yesterday he'd killed children without remorse or hesitation—nor was the young mother with her strangely compassionate look the reason. The day before he'd killed other children as their mothers looked on, helpless. He hadn't hesitated a second because of the young mother before the synagogue; he'd seen in her face the same mother's love that he'd seen in the face of the woman on the donkey.

57

So . . . what was it? *What* had caused him to fail the King?

"*Well, actually,*" he told himself, "*I had no proof this was the Christ Child. All I knew was, the innkeeper said a child was on the desert road to Egypt. The one we were really after could have taken a different route. The innkeeper could have lied to throw us off. These could have been just ordinary travelers, for truly they didn't look like royalty. The man could have been a farmer or maybe a carpenter, and a Messiah would have to be of royal birth, not of these people . . .*"

He paused in his reverie to point to a leather sack he'd just noticed tied to the saddle of Tactus' horse, "Tactus, what's that?"

"Nothing. Just some loot I took from the couple."

"Let me see it."

Tactus pretended not to have heard. Finishing the splint, he attempted to divert Justus' attention by giving a sharp jerk to Mundus' sling, and Mundus let out a yell of pain, shouting, "Damn you, dog of a dog! Clumsy fool! I'll kill you!" He slapped Tactus with his good left hand. Tactus tumbled backward from his crouched position into the dust. Tactus stared with an animal hatred at his lieutenant. His reflexes responded automatically, and as he scrambled up, he drew his sword with lightning speed. Mundus, unarmed except for his dagger, struggled to rise from his sitting position, and Justus sprang forward from the stone, drawing his sword as he rose. With a quick stroke he brought the blade's flat side down on Tactus' bronze helmet, and the two metals met with a dull clank as Tactus' helmet bent under the blow. The soldier fell forward but quickly rose, shaking his massive head to clear his thoughts.

Mundus looked at Justus, amazed, and took a backward step. It was plain that he now expected his captain to turn the blade on him, and his eyes darted to the left and right, surveying the situation, seeking an escape. He held the dagger in his left hand, ready to fight, if necessary. Tactus, still shaking his head, tried to circle Justus, who moved to keep them both in front of him, so they could not attack from opposite sides.

"Tactus, put down that sword. Don't be a fool. You know I can kill you both, so don't press me. Herod will boil you in oil, if anything happens to me. Mundus, drop it! Why fight when you know you'll lose? Drop the blades—both of you. That's an order!"

Mundus, still unsure of his safety regardless of the outcome of a fight between Justus and Tactus, was the first to react and lowered the dagger to his belt.

"Now you, Tactus," Justus ordered again, and to his relief Tactus responded to his authority without argument as years of discipline took over from the anger.

Justus then lowered his sword and told Tactus to get the horses that were nibbling the sparse vegetation. Turning to Mundus, he said, "You're lucky to be alive. You've tested my patience twice today. I should have let Tactus kill you."

A childish smile crossed Mundus' face and Justus thought, "Damn, why didn't I kill him? What's wrong with me? It has to be done, . . . this bastard will be trouble one way or another until he's dead."

As the Roman struggled on to the back of his tired mount, Justus said, "Mundus, you ride ahead of me. Tactus, you follow in the rear, and if either of you gives me any trouble, you'll regret it when we return to Jerusalem."

He kicked his heels into the horse, and neither he nor Mundus spoke as they rode on toward Jerusalem. Their silence reflected the wasteland's stillness, and the only sounds came from the horses and the creaking of leather saddles.

Far to the rear Tactus followed like a jackal stalking a wounded animal—afraid to approach and unsure of the reception he might receive.

They rode on till the sun reached its peak and began to descend, still slanting its searing rays on the lonely riders. The men, lost in thought, continued in silence.

Mundus, sometimes grimacing with pain from his wounded arm, rode slightly ahead of Justus, and Justus kept a steady, monotonous pace, thinking now of Mariame. What could he possibly do about her? Without the King's approval he could never have her for his wife . . . he stared ahead, suddenly awed, thinking, *"Imagine! I want to get married! Me, of all people . . . it probably wouldn't work. I'm not going to change, and she'd have to learn my way of life."* How in the world had he got into this fix? Only Herod could force Aizel to give him the girl in marriage, and besides, Herod desired Mariame for himself.

But Mariame could wait, he thought; he had a more pressing problem with Mundus and Tactus. Of the two, Mundus, because of his intelligence and inborn hatred, was the more dangerous. He cursed as he watched Mundus swaying in the saddle in front of him obviously in deep pain. "It serves the bastard right," he said to himself. "If I attack Mundus, Tactus will rush to his defense. No, I must convince Tactus to kill him . . . then I can deal with Tactus later."

Justus glanced over his shoulder at Tactus, who, half asleep in the saddle, was lagging farther and farther behind. "He is all brawn and no brain," he whispered to himself. "I can control him; though he'd fight with Mundus against me, it should be easy to rekindle his hatred for Mundus. Tactus knows he'll profit more through my favor . . . I have the Tiger's ear."

He raised his head and called, "Let's rest the horses," his voice sounding strange after the long silence.

"I'm so tired, I'm afraid I'd never be able to get back on my horse if I dismounted," Mundus said, supporting his injured arm with his left hand.

Justus slid from his tired mount, moved to the rear of Mundus' horse, and untied a waterskin. He drank of the hot, tasteless water, passed the skin to Mundus, and looking back, saw that Tactus had also stopped to sit in the meager shade of a large bush.

After Mundus had drunk, spilling water over his face and neck, Justus took the waterskin and poured water into his helmet for his mount. He did not water Mundus' horse, and Mundus did not seem to notice. He filled his helmet again and poured water over his sweat-soaked hair; then, swinging back onto his mount, he said, "I'm going back to see Tactus and then going on ahead." Justus turned around and rode toward Tactus who still sat slumped in the shade. He did not see Mundus, eyes closed with pain and fatigue, fall forward on his horse.

Approaching Tactus, Justus held his arm high, signalling friendship, and Tactus rose to meet him. The horse stopped as Justus gently pulled on the reins, and Justus said, "Tactus, this is an order. Kill Mundus! His horse is tired and without water, and the man's half dead already. If you don't kill him now, he will kill you in Jerusalem—and if you fail, I warn you; don't ride into Jerusalem." He watched Tactus' face, seeing his order seep into the slow-witted giant, and added. "Do you understand me?"

"Yes, sir, I understand," Tactus answered hesitatingly. "But won't the King punish me for killing Mundus?"

"Hell no, you oaf. I'm not going to tell him, and furthermore, I'll see you're rewarded. Also Tactus, remember: we killed the child in the desert."

Tactus blinked. "Huh?"

"I said, that child we came upon back there is dead. We killed him, didn't we?"

Tactus smiled slyly. "Oh, yes, sir. I see what you mean. And you say you'll reward me?"

"Yes, you can rely on that, but no one must know the child isn't dead. Our lives could depend on that secret, understand?"

"Uh, yes, sir . . . captain, could I please have a drink of water?"

"Sure. Take the whole skin." Justus threw the half-full water bag to the sweating soldier and wheeled his horse toward Bethlehem.

He circled the town and set out for Jerusalem, visible in the distance. The sun was slipping behind the high hills, and it would soon be dark. His body cried out for food and rest; his lips were chapped, and his legs were completely numb. He had been in the saddle, without food, twenty-four hours.

He patted the horse's neck in appreciation of the beast's endurance and thanked his stars that Herod had supplied his guards with fine Arabian mounts.

As he glanced up at the high hill he could see lights from the towers of Antonia, and he told himself he could never even try to explain his actions to Herod, for he'd tried unsuccessfully, all day, to rationalize them to himself; so if Herod ever did learn of his failure, he'd lose his head. But Tactus would surely murder Mundus; then only the two of them would know, and he, Justus, could see to it that Tactus died an early death. Meanwhile, he'd report total success to Herod.

But now a sudden thought struck him. He had been stupid to leave Mundus in Tactus' hands. He should have seen to that death himself. He should have stayed with Tactus to see the job properly completed. While he had been certain Tactus would obey his instructions, still the soldier was weak-minded, and Mundus might have persuaded him . . . but no, Tactus was intelligent enough to recognize that Justus had the ability to punish as well as reward. No . . . Tactus would surely dispose of Mundus . . . .

On the other hand, he'd have the whole Roman Army after him if Tactus didn't kill Mundus. If they should together report his disobedience to Herod, he would have to flee the country. Maybe he could go to Egypt, find the child, and bring it back to Herod. But there was still the chance that Herod would believe him rather than Tactus and Mundus. Tactus was a simple bastard, but surely he would dispose of Mundus . . . he hated the buck-toothed sadist.

Now, as he passed through the Dung Gate into Jerusalem he suddenly turned toward home instead of the palace, deciding to bathe and eat before reporting to Herod. Also, as a precaution, he'd best get his things in order, in case he had to flee from the Tiger in a hurry.

The night had begun to chill as he entered the cold house, lit the lamps, and went to get his saddle bags to fill, thinking not even the anger of an angry Tiger could cause him to hurry more, for he had now to eat and drink in order to keep going. He found a skin of wine, some cheese, bread, and smoked mutton, and ate and drank as he sorted certain valuable portable treasures.

After filling the saddle bags, he went to the small courtyard back of the house and threw himself, clothed, into the rainwater cistern. The cold water snapped his nerves to a spurious tingle, and his mind cleared considerably. There, despite the bitter cold, he took off his wet garments, threw them in a ragged pattern over the stone floor, and washed himself.

Finished, he ran naked into the house, dried off with a great rough cotton towel, and dressed in a new tunic and a mantle with the tassels of the Jews. He was about to leave when a voice cried above loud blows on the front door, "Justus, open up!"

He stopped in his tracks, frozen with fear, as the voice cried again, "We know you're in there! You're under arrest for murder. This is the Great Sanhedrin's police, and we have the house surrounded. Open up before we break down your door!"

He threw the saddle bags under the bed, then, considering the situation, slowly opened the door for the intruders, feeling certain they could not arrest him, the Tiger's captain.

VIII

The cold cell was lit by a single massive oil lamp. Justus threw a wavering shadow as he tugged at the chains that held him fast to the thick limestone wall. This straining had become a compulsive habit, even though he knew full well, after a week of trying, that his struggle was futile.

"You're a fool if you think Herod will raise a finger to help you," Nicolas said, eyeing the haggard, unshaven captain.

"But I acted upon his orders," Justus yelled, and the cords of his neck stood out as he strained forward. "The King *ordered* me to slay those children."

"Of course. But he'll never admit to ordering a massacre. I know you acted under orders. The high priest, Annas, suspects you acted on orders straight from Herod. But the Jews are seeking vengeance for these killings, and seeing they can't have Herod, they'll take you." Nicolas paused to let his words sink in, then continued slowly, "It's the only solution for Herod, Annas, and the Sanhedrin."

Justus glowered. "I thought the Great Sanhedrin believed in the Law. Are they going to punish a soldier for following orders?"

"No one will stop your trial; it would be political suicide. I don't know whether or not they'll follow the Law; that will be up to the Sanhedrin's individual members. But I do know, no one will be fool enough to try to stop your trial. You've been arrested by the Sanhedrin, Justus. You are under their power unless either Herod or Rome states that you are not subject to their jurisdiction. But Herod will not intercede—and Rome will never know. The King will not tell Caesar; and even if he knew, I doubt that the Emperor would do anything to help you —though you were his own blood kin."

Justus knew that Nicolas was speaking the truth. He was

unimportant to Rome, and Caesar would not raise a finger to help him. No. Caesar would sit back, pronouncing platitudes on law and order; in the end he'd be the first to demand execution; and the Tiger would play a waiting game, always keeping in mind the protection of Herod.

"Nicolas," Justus finally said, "what are my chances?"

Nicolas shrugged. "Who knows? I have asked Aizel for advice on the Sanhedrin's law. He's not optimistic, but then, I feel his judgment is colored by a certain dislike for you."

"Have you seen Mariame?"

This was the question Justus had wanted to ask since Nicolas entered. For the past week in the silence of his cell, he had thought of her constantly, and in the quiet he had talked aloud to himself telling her time and again of his love, hearing only his own voice repeating her words so indelibly imprinted in his mind and heart, "Justus, I love you. Take me away."

"Mariame is fine," Nicolas said. "You know, of course, she is like a daughter to me. Ah, why did she fall in love with you, I wonder?"

Justus looked defiant. "What's wrong with me?"

Nicolas sighed. "Don't you really know? Justus, I have been fond of you, and have often gone out of my way to help you. I like you because I've seen in you certain traits of my own. But don't you know what a conscience is? I've never seen a spark of remorse in you—never once since I've known you."

Justus stared at his feet as the old man continued, "Mariame is young, Justus. She is a sweet, innocent girl who's been sheltered all her life. Do you think she deserves to share a life like yours?"

"But Nicolas, I love her. I could change."

"Son, there are three things you need to understand. First, you'll never be anything but a soldier, albeit an excellent one. Second, you could never give Mariame the kind of life she's accustomed to, and that situation would soon turn love into hate. Third, you are in prison, awaiting trial for murder."

Justus looked up. "Nevertheless, Nicolas, will you tell her I'm thinking about her—and that I love her?"

The chamberlain nodded. "Yes. In spite of my better judgment, I'll deliver that message."

"Why? Because I may die soon?" Justus shifted his body against the chain. "Is the Sanhedrin also going to arrest my men who were with me in Bethlehem? It would seem they'd be as guilty as I."

"Mundus and Tactus have disappeared. They never returned from your mission to Bethlehem. Herod knows from Hezron that they were alive when you left Bethlehem and has alerted the Roman garrisons at Caesaraea and Tyre to arrest them if they try to sail for Rome."

Then Tactus killed Mundus and is trying to escape, Justus exulted. And if he didn't kill Mundus the two have fled anyway, so they'd be no further trouble. Herod would never learn of his failure to kill the Christ Child now.

"Why are you smiling?"

"Oh nothing, just thinking. Are they going to arrest Hezron?"

"You must understand that the Law—as the Sanhedrin sees it—is a complicated, sophisticated pronouncement of God's law," Nicolas said, waving one skinny arm in the air. "But, fortunately, Hezron is, like Herod, an Idumean.* Herod and Rome have limited the jurisdiction of the Sanhedrin to the Jewish race only."

Justus' smile broadened. "Why, don't you see? The Sanhedrin can't try me. I am a Greek in the Roman Army, on assignment to Herod by Caesar himself. They can't do it. You just said as much."

_____
* Idumea—also Edom, a small country southeast of Palestine.

66

"My poor young friend," Nicolas said in a fatherly tone, "do you forget your mother was Jewish? The Sanhedrin has not, believe me. No. Annas has thought of that. He says they have civil and criminal jurisdiction over you."

"Who told him my mother was Jewish?" Justus cried. "I've told only a few people. Did you tell Annas?"

Nicolas shrugged. "Herod knew."

"Oh, yes." Justus slumped again. "But why should the King do this to me?"

"Aizel also knew."

"You mean he'd go so far, just to keep me away from Mariame?"

"Well, honestly, I don't know who told Annas. But it was not I. I like you too much, Justus."

"But I'm not circumcised. My father was Greek. I'm no Jew!"

"Nevertheless, the King won't come to your defense. You are a soldier accustomed to danger, and you knew the risk you took on accepting the captaincy of Herod's guards. Accept the facts. You'll rest better if you do."

"Ha! Who could rest in this hole, knowing he had to stand trial before a bunch of pious hypocrites? Now tell me this: is there a chance Herod may ask Annas to help me?"

"No. He will pretend he knew nothing of your mission to Bethlehem. He will say he gave you no such orders."

"And the punishment?" Justus questioned, holding his breath.

Nicolas spoke gently. "You know the Sanhedrin's punishment for murder. You have seen many beheadings."

PART II

IX

THE FRESH CLOTHES felt good on his clean skin, but the fresh shave with warm water had refreshed him most. The two weeks that had passed since his cold bath in his courtyard had seemed like a lifetime, because he had always been most fastidious.

Now he asked Tarfon, the chief jailer and the Sanhedrin's court bailiff, "Why have you let me bathe and given me my clothes?"

"Today you stand trial before the Great Sanhedrin," Tarfon told him. "Our great judges wish you to look your best, so that your appearance needn't affect their judgment. They wisely know that the beggar, dirty and filthy, engenders prejudice in all except the most righteous men. Thus our judges, wisely following the Mishnah, wish nothing, even unconsciously, to sway their evaluation of evidence for or against you."

Justus nodded approval, remembering how he himself had looked with contempt on beggars down at the city's gates. It would be hard indeed to feel that such were his equal, even under the Law.

He said, "You don't think they're going to give me a fair trial, do you?"

Tarfon answered piously, "I have no doubt the learned judges will give you what God's law prescribes.

"Then I'm being tried by God, not the Sanhedrin?"

"Our laws came down to Israel through Moses and other ancient judges who received the Law from God."

Tarfon went on, mouthing words he'd overheard in a previous case before the great court. Justus paid little attention as he adjusted his clothes. Evidently the Jews had searched his quarters, for this was his best white linen robe, and there was his favorite girdle of red silk, as well as his money pouch. He finished dressing and decided that he looked good enough to appear before the greatest of kings. He had worn similar clothes when he'd accompanied Herod to see Caesar in Rome . . . the only difference was that he now had the mantle with Jewish tassels that he sometimes wore in the hope of passing unnoticed through Jerusalem. Why, he wondered, had they selected this mantle instead of his uniform? Perhaps they'd wanted him to look not too well dressed—or maybe to look like a Jew.

Surveying himself in the small metal mirror brought by the guard, he saw that he didn't look too bad after a fortnight's imprisonment. In spite of his light red hair, he looked pretty much like a young Jew—perhaps the son of a rich merchant.

Tarfon moved impatiently. "We'd better hurry. The morning sacrifice is surely over now, so the Sanhedrin will shortly convene."

Justus glanced around the cell, sizing up the odds of escape now that his leg irons had been removed, while Tarfon, sensing this animal instinct, stepped back and called to his companions in the hall outside.

He said coolly, "If I were you, I'd forget any plans for escape that may be dancing in that handsome head. With the Sanhedrin you have a chance to live—with us, none whatsoever. My men would be charmed to choke the life out of you. You have the reputation of being a soldier with nerves of iron—well, this trial will be your battlefield. But if you make the slightest move to escape, you'll never reach that battlefield."

Justus looked at the hard-faced men who'd obviously been selected because of their size and temperament and let out a chest full of air. Resigned to the fact that escape was not presently possible, he knew that his best course of action would be to play for time and await the guard's relaxation. He said aloud, "All right. What am I to do? I suppose the Sanhedrin has certain court procedures that I must know—and I wouldn't want to disrupt the orderly dispatch of business."

"Actually, your trial has begun. The Great Sanhedrin's judges met at the Temple at daybreak and made a sacrifice to God, asking Him for wisdom and permission to convene. This is always done in the trial of a criminal case where the punishment may be death."

"How do they know it may be death? I haven't been indicted. Your guards and the Sanhedrin police say I'm charged with murder, but I know not of whom, nor where. Surely this isn't fair. How can I present a defense to a crime I know nothing of?"

Tarfon, knowing that he could not answer this question to his own satisfaction much less Justus', snorted, "Come on, you'll find out soon enough."

He led his prisoner through a maze of corridors, up several flights of stairs, and Justus, never having been in this part of the Temple, saw that it was much like Antonia, though he sensed a different air about the building.

The tread of their footsteps echoed down the hall, punctuated by an occasional grunt from one of the three huge guards; then the small procession stopped at a heavy wooden door, and Tarfon entered the room beyond it, leaving Justus with the huge guards who moved even closer to him, their eyes bright with anticipation. But Justus thought, "Oh, no. I'm not fool enough to try to escape with you blood-thirsty jackals waiting to pounce."

As he continued to eye these huge men—perhaps the largest Jews he'd ever seen—his mind ran over the possible facts confronting him at the trial.

First, though he'd be tried for killing the children of

Bethlehem, the Sanhedrin would likely try him for only one or two murders and allow the rest to be used as prejudice against him, for Nicolas had intimated as much already. Anyway, Nicolas had said that Herod would have no part in the affair, for he considered himself above the Sanhedrin.

Another thing, there was the matter of his men who participated in the Bethlehem children slaughter. Did the Jews know they sought to kill their long-awaited Messiah? With Tactus and Mundus still missing, did the Sanhedrin and Herod know he had allowed the Christ Child to escape? There was no indication that anyone other than himself knew the possible truth.

His mind weighed the idea of using his weakness as a point in his defense. Should he tell the Sanhedrin he'd spared the Christ Child's life? Perhaps it could sway them from giving the verdict of death by beheading. But again, no. The trial would have only one result no matter what he said: the judges would seek to kill him in vengeance, regardless of his story. They'd listen to no one except the crying mothers, fathers, and kin of the dead children. They would murder him — a soldier who had only carried out the orders of his King.

Suddenly the massive door squeaked open, and Tarfon motioned him forward, then the door closed, and he felt small as the room's immensity dwarfed him. The ceiling, 40 feet high, was supported by huge straight beams obviously hewn out of Lebanon cedar. The room, empty now except for Justus and the guards, had two doors, the one through which he'd entered, and a towering double door at the room's opposite end that almost reached the ceiling. Its great brass hinges reflected the torch lights on their highly polished surfaces.

The Sanhedrin's great hall, 120 feet long and 60 feet wide, had no windows but was lighted by lamps evenly spaced along its walls. To Justus' left rose three tiers in a semicircle, each about 5 feet wide, and he quickly counted the thick cotton-filled pillows evenly spaced on each tier: twenty-three to a row.

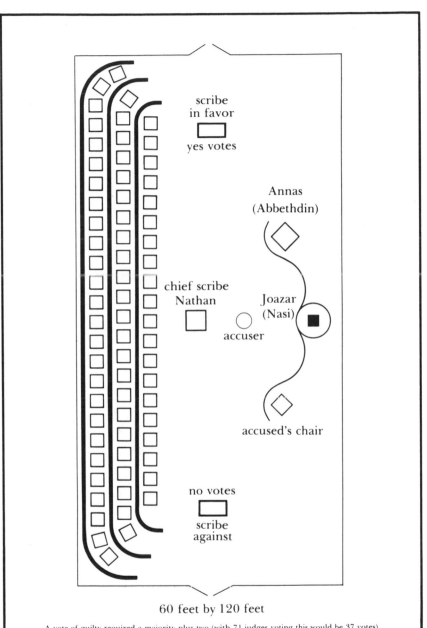

scribe
in favor

yes votes

Annas
(Abbethdin)

chief scribe
Nathan

Joazar
(Nasi)

accuser

accused's chair

no votes

scribe
against

60 feet by 120 feet

A vote of guilty required a majority plus two (with 71 judges voting this would be 37 votes).

At floor level in front of these tiers, constructed of huge granite blocks from the mountains of Midian, stood three tables and stools. Justus knew the court scribes sat at the tables recording evidence, arguments, and the votes of the judges; the chief scribe sat at the center table — the assistants at each end.

In the center of the theater-like room stood a great heavy oak chair richly carved with flowers, inlaid with gold and silver in designs representing the 12 tribes of Israel, and this was obviously the chair occupied by the Nasi, the Sanhedrin's president, for it faced the tiers where the judges would sit.

To the right of the Nasi's throne was a smaller, less ornate one, the chair of Annas, the Abbethdin or vice-president of the Sanhedrin, whose duty it was to preside in the Nasi's absence. In all other matters Annas voted in the regular order of his seniority as a judge, and he had no additional duties or powers during any session of the court when the Nasi was present.

Tarfon motioned Justus to follow him to a simple chair before and left of the Nasi's throne, placed at an angle so that it faced both the Nasi and the judges.

"You will sit here during the trial. From here you can see all that takes place, and the judges who'll sit there, can see you at all times," Tarfon told him, pointing to the rows of pillows.

"And the accusers?" Justus asked, looking all around the empty room.

"They will stand there, facing you and the judges. They will look into your face as they testify, and you into theirs. So do not divert your eyes while they speak. It is thought by many to be an indication of guilt."

"Thank you for the advice," Justus said. Then, puzzled by the sincerity in the guard's voice, he asked, "But surely you don't mean to help me toward an acquittal?"

Tarfon shook his head. "No, I don't want to help you. I personally hope you will be beheaded. But I am the court bailiff; I want you to have every right allowed by the Law: no more, no less."

Before Justus could answer he heard a chanting from outside the huge entrance doors, and he knew the Sanhedrin must be approaching.

Tarfon again motioned for him to sit in the defendant's chair and withdrew to the rear of the Nasi's throne. The massive doors opened, and Justus could see the judges moving into the hall.

At their head came Joazar, the Nasi. His head was covered with a bright blue silk turban pinned with thin gold spikes at strategic places. His flowing soft woolen robe was also dyed blue, and on his chest hung the ornate insignia of his office: a heavy gold breastplate inlaid with pearls and rubies that formed a design representing the twelve tribes of Israel. The gold and silver embroidery on his robe almost seemed to give life to the flowers and trees that covered it front and back.

Justus gazed with wonder upon the rich splendor of this solemn procession moving toward him. The Jews might hate statues and works of art, but they spared no expense on their religious robes.

Joazar, the Nasi, now held his hand aloft and stood facing Justus, who was still seated. The chanting of the judges stopped in unison, their two columns coming to an almost military halt; then they moved from the columns to their places on the tiers. It was evident the younger judges sat in the front row and that these dignitaries increased in age to the top row.

There were sixty-nine, ranging in age from 40 to near 90, and, counting the Nasi and Abbethdin, a total of seventy-one judges, alike in appearance only because each had a full beard. No two were dressed exactly the same, yet each wore a turban and had a gold chain around his neck, supporting various styles and types of delicately carved gold and silver breastplates. The splendor of the various colors in their robes and turbans charged the room with excitement, although a death-like silence prevailed as the judges seated themselves cross-legged on the cushions.

The tomb-like silence fell like a pall over Justus' spirit as he surveyed the seventy-one faces, vainly seeking a friend. He recognized no one except Joazar and Annas, who sat erect in their chairs, with stern looks on their faces. Justus felt cold sweat in the palms of his hands as he looked into all the un-smiling faces surrounding him and towering above him. Joazar clapped his hands to call the Sanhedrin to order.

Justus had seen Joazar at the palace on several occasions. He recalled the story behind Joazar's rise to eminence through Simon Boethus, his father.

Simon Boethus had a beautiful daughter. Herod's infatuation for her was fierce, but he could not lure her to his bed. Herod was even willing to marry her, but Simon Boethus did not hold a position of sufficient dignity to warrant such a step. In desperation Herod had removed Jesus, son of Phabet, from the position of high priest and installed Simon Boethus in his place. This elevated the family to a place of honor and made the marriage possible. Despite his unholy call to the priesthood, Simon Boethus had done a creditable job. When Joazar's sister died shortly after her marriage to Herod, the family remained in favor with the Tiger. Joazar had moved up through the ranks of the Sanhedrin, to become Nasi, succeeding Matthias, who, believing a false rumor that Herod had died, had whipped up a group of frenzied young Zealots and directed them to tear down a massive Roman eagle Herod had placed above the Temple gates to honor Caesar. When the King learned of this uprising, he'd sent Justus with his troops to capture the culprits; then he had executed the offenders, including Matthias, and promptly elevated Joazar to his present position.

"Stand up!" Joazar suddenly ordered, looking at Justus with piercing eyes. "What is your name?"

Justus snapped to attention. "My name is Justus."

"Then, Justus, I inform you that you have been arrested to answer certain charges which will be lodged against you by witnesses from the town of Bethlehem. You are under no indictment or charge at this time."

Justus thought, "Then why have I been held chained in that cold cell? Why was I arrested if I'm under no indictment? I am charged and still not charged."

Joazar continued, "Have you ever witnessed the proceedings of the Great Sanhedrin?"

"No, sir, I have not, for I am not a Jew. I am not a citizen of this country. I am a Roman."

"Sire," cried a voice from the top tier of the judges.

"Yes?" Joazar looked away from Justus. "Do you wish to speak, Rabbi Ismeal?"

"Sire, the person Justus claims he is not a Jew nor a citizen of Judea. I raise the question: is he then subject to this senate's jurisdiction? If he is, in fact, not a citizen of Judea, but a citizen of Rome, then I think we have no jurisdiction to sit in his judgment. The jurisdiction for any crime of his would be with the Romans."

Justus looked up, surprised that his statement had set off this defense by a dried-up old rabbi who sat on the top row.

"No!" Another rabbi rose in the third row to face Rabbi Ismeal. "If this man, as a soldier in Herod's guards, committed a violation of our law in Judea, we have jurisdiction. The question is one of geographical jurisdiction. We have jurisdiction over *all* criminal acts in Judea."

"My brother, Rabbi Urias, is in error in his thinking," Ismeal said. "Can we sit in judgment upon the crimes of Caesar? Can we, temporarily under the rule of the Romans, bring to trial any citizen of Rome who might violate our laws? Can we prosecute a Roman citizen who does a particular act that violates our code, but which may not be a violation of Roman laws? No. I say we cannot. Therefore, if the man Justus is not a Judean citizen, it follows we have no more legal right to sit in judgment upon him than we would have to put Caesar himself on trial."

"If the wise Ismeal will confine himself to one question at a time, I think this matter can be resolved," Urias said.

"Then answer me, if you can."

"We will have no bickering back and forth between the two of you." Joazar clapped his hands to command attention. "Rabbi Urias, you may answer his remarks if you wish."

"Sire, the question before us is one of geographical jurisdiction," Rabbi Urias repeated. "The case before us involves the murders of children in Bethlehem. Over Bethlehem in Judea we have jurisdiction. It is true, I'll admit, under the laws of Rome, that we must upon a verdict of guilty seek the Romans' approval or confirmation of our verdict before punishment can be administered. Thus, by reason of the clear implication that we must get the Romans' approval before such punishment is carried out, we are given jurisdiction over crimes committed in this country, regardless of the citizenship of the accused. If our verdict is for acquittal, then the case is closed; only if we vote to inflict punishment must we obtain Rome's consent. Thus it follows as night follows day: we have jurisdiction."

But before Urias could sit down Ismeal was back on his feet. "No. You have not answered the question before us. Regardless of any approval we must obtain from Herod or from the Romans, our jurisdiction extends only to violation of Judean laws by Jews."

Ismeal's skinny hands flailed the air as he continued. "This man, under no charges until a witness lodges a formal complaint against him through legal testimony, has, in my opinion, the right to question the Sanhedrin's jurisdiction to hear any complaint against him. Of course he will be charged with murder, but if he is not a Jew, we have no recourse except to step aside and let him be tried by Herod or by the Romans—for they have the legal right to judge their own, while we do not."

"Ha! Do you think Herod would try him?" Urias' face turned red as he pointed a crooked finger at Ismeal.

"I think the question is not for us to decide."

"Then, you would have this murderer go free?"

"Just a minute, Rabbi Urias," Joazar commanded. "We appreciate your passion in this matter, but do control yourself. I instruct the members to disregard the last remarks of Rabbi Urias. Sir, I instruct you to be more cautious in your statements."

Ismeal let Joazar's warning settle upon the silent rabbis, then he said, "Sire, I would challenge my brother Urias' ability to sit fairly in judgment of this case, in view of his last statement."

Justus was surprised at this defense from an old Jew whom he didn't know, and he wondered if this rabbi might be a friend of Nicolas.

"Are you taking up the defense of this man?" Joazar asked, indicating Justus.

"No. I am taking up the defense of this wise and august senate." Ismeal flourished his hand. "I repeat, until it is established that the defendant is a Jew, this tribunal has no jurisdiction, regardless of the site of the alleged crime. For us to try a defendant without the legal right to do so would be a crime more serious than the one alleged against this man." Pausing to take a deep breath he continued, "But in addition to our lack of jurisdiction, I challenge Urias' ability to fairly judge this case. He is obviously acting under passion and has prejudged the defendant's guilt."

"Are you asking that we vote to decide Urias' qualifications as a judge in this case?" Joazar asked.

"Sire, I ask first that we vote to determine Urias' qualifications; second, that a vote be had upon our right of jurisdiction in this particular case."

Joazar nodded. "It is granted, to prejudge a case is a disqualification; that rule is well known to the members of this senate. I will, therefore, call for a vote to determine if we should rule Urias disqualified from further service in this case." Joazar looked around at the Sanhedrin's general members. "However, I know that each of you will vote, not with malice toward another member, but with the Law foremost in your minds and hearts. If I hear no motion for further argument, I call on the scribe Nathan to call the roll to cast your vote. A vote of aye will disqualify; a vote of no will not."

As Justus surveyed the seated Sanhedrin, Nathan, who sat in the center near Joazar, called the roll, and each judge, as his name was called, rose to say aye or no. In accord with the tradition of the Sanhedrin, the younger members voted first, so that their judgment might not be affected by the vote of the older, and perhaps wiser, members. Each aye vote was recorded by the scribe to Justus' right, the no votes by the scribe to his left. The scribe Nathan recorded both votes as he called each member's name. It was also the duty of the scribe on the right to transcribe anything said in favor of the defendant, while the one on the left kept a record of statements against him.

As the roll call continued, Justus tried to keep track of the count, but as it rose higher, for and against the disqualification, he lost count. It was evident, though, from the start of voting that it was a close question. As the top rows of older men began to vote, Justus stirred in his chair, still puzzled that, in spite of their hatred for him, these stern-faced men were casting votes on a matter of law and principle.

His thoughts were interrupted by Nathan's calling Joazar's name, then he turned and looked into Joazar's face as the latter spoke firmly, "I vote 'no.' "

Justus glanced at the two scribes bent over their tablets, adding the tally of the votes. Then, in the stillness, the scribes arose almost simultaneously, as if on command, and marched to Nathan's desk where they huddled, showing their tablets to each other and whispering together.

Nathan nodded and the scribes returned to their tables. "Sire," Nathan said, bowing to Joazar, "the vote is complete and verified."

"How many votes are 'aye'?" the Nasi asked the scribe to the right.

"Sire, there are thirty votes 'aye.'"

"There were thirty votes to disqualify Urias," Joazar repeated. Then, looking to his left he asked, "Scribe, how many votes are 'no'?"

The scribe bowed to Joazar, and stated in a low, weak voice, "Sire, there were forty-one votes 'no.'"

Again Joazar repeated the scribe's tabulation. "There are forty-one 'no' votes. Therefore, it is the vote of this senate that Urias is not disqulified from sitting in judgment on this case by reason of any prior opinion regarding the defendant's guilt."

Justus looked at Ismeal, hoping to see some reaction, but the old one's face, almost completely hid by his gray beard, remained expressionless. Only his dark eyes gave evidence that Ismeal was thinking about his next move.

"Is there any question upon the vote?" Joazar asked, eyeing the passionless faces of the Sanhedrin; then, after a long pause, he said, "There being no motion for further argument or a recount of the vote, we shall move to the next business."

"Sire, I again respectfully submit, we have no jurisdiction to hear this case," Ismeal said.

Urias rose from his pillow; his large nose protruding from his black beard glowed red, giving evidence of the rage that boiled within him as he pointed at Ismeal with one long bony finger. "You continually raise this point of our having no jurisdiction to hear this case. Do you do so to avoid any guilt that may fall upon Herod when the facts of the murders are brought to light? I say that if anyone is disqualified to hear and judge this case it is you, Rabbi Ismeal!"

Joazar, obviously fearing that the personal argument of Urias would spread through the Sanhedrin, arose and clapped his hands before the other members could speak. "As Nasi of this senate I again caution you all that our deliberations should be without passion either toward the defendant or each other. The present argument stems from a statement made by the defendant Justus that he is neither a Jew nor a citizen of this country. There is no evidence before this body other than his short statement. Rabbi Ismeal desires that we now vote to determine if Justus is subject to our jurisdiction. Perhaps he has more evidence than we have. There is no question in my mind concerning our jurisdiction over the offense of murder. I do, however, have reservations concerning the Sanhedrin's right to try a man who is Gentile and not a citizen of Judea. I personally ask if there is any objection to having ancillary or preliminary testimony concerning the defendant's statement. What say you, Ismeal?"

"Sire, I have no objection."

"No!" Urias shouted. "The defendant is not yet formally charged with a crime. When there is sufficient testimony to accuse him, he can raise the question of jurisdiction as he develops his defense."

"You mean after he has been prejudiced by witnesses, don't you?" Ismeal said.

"I have told you two for the last time to stop snapping at each other," Joazar shouted as other Sanhedrin heads swayed back and forth, following the argument between the two rabbis on the room's opposite sides. "Then to settle this matter, I propose a vote be taken to determine whether we should have a preliminary hearing to allow the defendant to introduce such evidence as he may desire concerning his nationality and race. A vote of aye will allow him such privilege; a vote of no will not."

"Sire . . ."

"Don't interrupt me," Joazar snapped. "After such testimony by the man Justus, the question of jurisdiction raised by Rabbi Ismeal can be taken to a vote, if he still insists. The scribe Nathan will call the roll."

As the count began Justus' mind, dwelling on what he would say if he had the opportunity to testify, flashed back to his childhood, sorting out points that might help him. Then, as the vote neared its end, it became evident that he'd at least have an ancillary hearing, but sweat formed in the palms of his hands as he realized he'd shortly be fighting for his life with mind and tongue instead of his hard, battle-trained muscles. His thoughts were interrupted by the scribe on his right announcing that the vote was fifty-one for the ancillary hearing.

Justus noted that there were twenty "no" votes and that even Joazar had voted "aye," so perhaps his chances to escape punishment were increasing. But he knew the biggest test still lay before him.

"The vote being fifty-one for an ancillary hearing, it is adjudged the defendant shall have the right to present such evidence as he may desire to sustain his plea," Joazar said. "What say you, Justus?"

Hesitating, Justus rose to face Joazar. "Sir, I am not familiar with the procedures and rules of this court. Am I to be given time to call witnesses? How am I to continue?"

"This proceeding is most unusual, and is not written in our Law. The members, however, have voted that you may make such defense as is possible to substantiate your claim that you are not a Jew or a citizen of Judea. I suggest, therefore, that you testify on such matters as may relate only to your plea of this court's lack of jurisdiction over you and nothing else."

"Am I to be sworn?"

"No, the Torah and our laws do not require oath, particularly in the case of the defendant testifying, for we believe that where a man's life is at stake the oath means little to him. We have a maxim, 'In most men religion is silent when interest speaks.' Such a temptation will almost invariably result in his lying under oath—adding that breach of God's law to the crime for which he stands trial."

"Are you to ask me questions?"

"Not now. Make your statement first. If the rabbis then wish to question you, they may do so; however, I now rule they may presently question you only on matters of your race and citizenship."

"And as to calling other witnesses?"

"That will depend on the state of the record at the end of your testimony. Should the senate feel additional testimony would be useful to afford you a fair hearing, then you will be allowed to call such witnesses."

Justus was puzzled by the Sanhedrin's almost bending over backward to give him a fair trial, when he knew that all these men undoubtedly longed to punish him. Perhaps they wanted to feel clear of conscience when they ordered him beheaded or stoned to death. He hesitated, not knowing where to begin his defense, almost hearing the silence as the men looked at him with unfriendly eyes. The deadly silence somewhat confused him and made him dizzy.

"My name is Justus," he said. "The name is Greek. I am 28 years of age. My father was a soldier in the Roman Army—as was his father. My father was born in Athens; I in Alexandria, Egypt.

"When I was 8 years old my father was killed in action, and General Valerius Elaccus, my father's commanding officer in the Sixth Roman Legion, asked that I be allowed to join his staff as mess boy. Actually, I almost became his adopted son, serving under him till he was killed in battle in Gaul. In his deathbed will and testament, the general asked that Emperor Caesar Augustus accept me as a member of his personal army staff, and Caesar did this out of respect for him.

"I was 18 years old when I went to Rome to serve Caesar. I became a member of his personal bodyguards and his personal courier. It was in this capacity that I first traveled to Judea with messages from the Emperor to King Herod." Justus paused, noting the judges' rapt attention.

"Three years later King Herod, while in Rome, asked that I be temporarily assigned to him as a bodyguard. Caesar gave his permission — and I have served King Herod since.

"Sirs, I am a Roman citizen — a military man on assignment to Judea. I am a Gentile. I therefore plead that this honorable senate cannot legally prosecute me for any crime because I am under the jurisdiction of Rome . . . and Caesar." Justus sat down, feeling that though he'd been brief, it was better to say too little than too much, inasmuch as his words might be twisted by one of these old men.

"Is that all you have to say?" Joazar asked; then, at Justus' nod, he asked the council, "Does anyone have a question he wants to put to this man?"

"Sire, I want to ask several questions," an old man who sat near Urias stated.

"Yes, Rabbi Altazar. You may proceed."

A cold sweat spread over Justus' whole body, fearing that Mariame's father had laid a trap with more than one judge of the court, he waited, breath-caught, as the old man rose to face him.

"I note that in your genealogy you either forgot, or carefully avoided, mention of your mother. May I inquire as to her nationality and race?"

Although the old rabbi's voice was soft, Justus knew that Altazar had cut to the heart of his plea.

He said, "Sir, she was born in Tyre."

"What was your mother's maiden name?"

"Ruth, daughter of Abraham Barsabbas."

"Was she Jewish?"

"Yes. My father met her during his military duty in that city and took her to Alexandria where they were married."

"Then the truth is that you are half Jew," the old man said with contempt.

"I do not consider myself half Jew and half Greek. I consider myself Roman. Does one drop of blood in my veins make me Jew when the other is all Greek? Who knows which of the seeds my father planted in my mother's womb developed me? How can I tell if her seeds added anything to my makeup? I am a man, so his seeds were obviously stronger. I do not know that any of her seeds gave me characteristics. But when would I become Greek, not Jew? Or when would I become Jew, not Greek?" Justus paused, feeling his argumentative answer was adequate, then continued, sensing another question from Altazar, "I have never claimed to be a Jew."

"You do not claim to be a Jew; yet, is it not true that you use your mother's maiden name on occasion?"

"Yes sir." Only someone in the palace could know this, so it had to be Aizel who had fed the information to these judges, Justus thought, going on, "I have used the name twice since I came to serve with Herod. It was his idea, and as a soldier, I obeyed his order. He asked that I pretend to be Jewish to help complete my disguise in tracking down a criminal. I would have preferred to use my Greek name of Justus, for who would believe I was Jewish with this hair?" Justus rubbed his hand across his short-clipped red head.

"But the truth is, you are half Jew and you use your mother's name? In other words, you claim to be Jewish when it hastens

88

your personal goals and deny it when it does not? Answer me. Is that not true?"

"I have already explained that," Justus said. "I do not follow the Jewish religion. I am Gentile. I do not carry the mark of a Jew. I am not circumcised! And because I am not cir-cumcised, I am not a Jew in the eyes of the priests at the temple. Thus, if I am not a Jew at the Temple, I cannot be a Jew here."

He felt a swell of pride, seeing his point had struck home with Altazar, and now he added, "Shall I disrobe and exhibit myself so that all may personally examine my defense?" There was insolence in his voice as he rose and began to remove his mantle. "It is perhaps not the largest defense in Judea, but I am sure that you'll find it adequate."

But the rabbis, obviously shocked at his behavior, stirred and murmured, and Altazar, wildly swinging his hands, mut-tered in his beard, at a loss with this man who had effectively turned the argument's tide against him.

Joazar clapped his hands, attempting to restore the general composure. "It will not be necessary that you disrobe. To re-quire such might prejudice you in the eyes of some of the judges."

Urias jumped to his feet. "Oh, yes! It would destroy the dignity of the senate."

"Dignity be damned! Let him do it!" one of the younger judges cried before Joazar could formally recognize him. "If we do not give this man every chance to prove his case the dignity of this senate should be lost, for we shall have already destroyed our honor and integrity, and have lost the blessing of God. The defendant's action will not embarrass the righ-teous—only those who attempt to force false standards of conduct in this court. We cannot turn our heads from any evidence this defendant may offer in his own behalf—no matter the source."

Joazar, apparently taken aback at this outcry, hesitated as

the members of the Sanhedrin began to look about, seeking reaction on the faces of other members.

The dignitary cleared his throat. "We will have no more speaking without permission. On reflection, I am in agreement with Rabbi Jonathan that it is our duty to give the defendant every benefit of our wise and righteous jurisprudence."

"Sire, may I speak a moment before you rule?" Urias asked.

"Yes."

"Let us assume that Justus is not circumcised. I hold that such a fact, in and of itself, does not make him Gentile. The duty to circumcise is a moral obligation placed on the parent. It is a dedication of the male child to God, but even though both parents may be Jewish, their failure to dedicate a child to God through circumcision does not remove the child's heritage through genealogy. Mere negligence . . . carelessness . . . lack of obedience to God on the part of a man's parents cannot destroy God's own spoken assurance that the Jews are His chosen people. The child is God's because of race, not circumcision. To hold otherwise would be a declaration by this senate that man can transcend and change the word and will of God. Justus, being a Jew through his mother, is a part of God's chosen people. And that is something over which God—and God alone has dominion. Thus, that dominion, having been established in the womb, cannot be changed by the defendant Justus, or by this Sanhedrin. He is a Jew first; perhaps a Roman citizen second."

"Sire," another judge said immediately, "I feel Urias' point is well taken, but I'd like to question the defendant on another point."

"You may do so, Rabbi Ben Levi, if you address your question to this matter alone."

"I noticed that you have not spoken of your religion," Ben Levi said, his short fat body expanding and contracting with each word. "Do you worship God?"

90

Justus shifted, mopping his brow. His mind quickly raced ahead, asking if this mountain of fat could be trying to shift the charge against him to blasphemy in addition to other charges, or was he throwing this into the argument to help him?

"If you mean, do I worship your God, Yahweh, the answer is no. Nor do I worship any gods of the Romans or Greeks. Not because I don't believe in your god or any of theirs, for to believe requires an evaluation of the pros and cons of a given religion. I have never given any religion — yours or theirs — an evaluation upon which to form either belief or disbelief. I have been a soldier — not a man of religion," Justus answered, honestly stating his position despite the possible danger of one of these pious Jews charging blasphemy.

Ben Levi huffed and puffed. "Nevertheless, our police found statues of Roman and Greek gods in your house. If you do not worship their gods, why do you possess these idols?"

"They were gifts . . . some I plundered. I treasure them for their esthetic beauty. If you have seen them, you know they are of Diana, Juno, Minerva, and a few others. I do not worship them as goddesses, though I do admit I admire the statues — or rather the skill of the sculptor who has captured the beauty of women in stone and gold. If you are trying to intimate that I am guilty of idolatry, I am not. To be so, I would first have to believe in and worship a god or goddess through images of him or her. Obviously, I could not commit an act of idolatry, not believing in any god. And I doubt if it is a crime *not* to believe in a god — even in this court."

"Does anyone else have a question?" Joazar asked as Ben Levi struggled downward to his seat. "If not, I shall now call on Justus to sum up his position and exhibit himself — after which I will call for a vote by this senate to determine if we have jurisdiction to try the defendant."

Justus rose, and after clearing his throat, launched into a

91

restatement of his testimony as well as portions of the prior argument by Ismeal that the Sanhedrin had no right to prosecute him. He stood facing the silent men, noticing that many of them did not seem to be paying attention, and that some kept their eyes diverted from him. Attempting to attract their attention, he raised his voice at what he thought were important points, and the more he bore down the more worried he grew. Sweat ran down his face and he began to repeat himself, unaware of the length of time he'd spoken, but he was aware that the longer he spoke the more inattentive the judges became. Then finally, pausing for breath, attempting to gather additional thoughts, he realized that he had spoken too long, and not knowing how to end his argument properly, he shrugged his massive shoulders, saying, "That's all I have to say."

The judges gave an audible sigh of relief as he sat down, wracked by self-criticism and nervous with anticipation as Joazar clapped his hands.

Then he suddenly remembered that he had forgotten to exhibit himself, and his face burned a deep red as he rose again. "Sir, I forgot to show that I was not circumcised," he said, and raised his clothes to show his body to the judges. As he stood silent in the awkward position, he realized how ridiculous he must look, but he had at least the satisfaction of knowing that he had no need to feel ashamed of his organ. He raised his head, seeing contempt or was it envy in the faces of certain judges, then quickly adjusted his clothes and fell back into his chair, convinced he'd led himself into a trap as he saw a smile cross Annas' face.

Joazar said, "Ahem," cleared his throat once more, and spoke in an overloud voice, "Before we vote, I must again remind you that though this is an unusual hearing, it has nevertheless been voted. Certain new and interesting arguments have been advanced in this court for the first time. You will now cast your ballot, and I know each of you will vote with the spirit of God within you—casting out any thoughts that are impure. A vote of 'no' will say the Sanhedrin does not have jurisdiction to prosecute the defendant. If you vote 'aye,' you will be saying this senate *does* have jurisdiction over the defendant. In other words, a 'no' vote will free Justus; and 'aye' votes will continue the trial. Because of the nature of these proceedings, before the trial can continue, a majority plus two votes will be required: the same as is normally required to convict any defendant of a crime." Then, after pausing to survey the amphitheater for questions, the justice said, "The scribe on the right of the hall will record the 'no' votes, the scribe on the left, the 'aye' votes. Nathan, call the roll."

"Rabbi Jonathan."

"I vote 'no.' "

"Rabbi Ben Heron."

"I vote 'no.' "

Justus' hopes rose. The first two votes were in his favor.

"Rabbi James."

"I vote 'no.' "

Justus smiled. Could it be he'd talked these pious Jews into voting to free him, despite their obvious hatred? His thoughts were interrupted as another rabbi voted "no." Four votes in a row in his favor; he wished he had a pen and papyrus with which to keep score.

Then, "I vote 'aye,' " Rabbi Josephus said, shattering his hopes of building a larger lead.

He kept count as each rabbi cast his vote, and the count rose to ten "nos" against five "ayes." The proceedings droned on, and the vote advanced to twenty in his favor against sixteen against him. His earlier hopes of building a large majority among the younger judges began to dwindle, but with each "no" vote, he looked up hoping again to receive a string of "nos." The balloting slowed as the older judges voted. No one seemed to want to rush his vote. Many rabbis voted with emotion, evidencing their conviction of their ballot's correctness. The air was charged with excitement as the judges watched how their fellow members were voting, and it grew increasingly plain that the vote would be close.

"I vote 'aye,'" Annas replied to Nathan; then Justus realized with a shock that the vote was even. Sixty-four judges had cast their votes, with thirty-two "nos" and thirty-two "ayes." Under the law of the Sanhedrin it took a majority of two votes for condemnation; therefore, with all seventy-one members voting, it would require a minimum of thirty-seven votes to convict. Justus began to sweat more profusely.

They needed five more "aye" votes to make the thirty-seven. If he could only get thirty-five votes, the ordeal would be over. He *had* to garner three votes from the remaining seven judges.

The next vote was "aye," and the vote stood at thirty-three against him, thirty-two in his favor. With six votes remaining, he had a fifty-fifty chance. The air of tension began to spread as the members sensed the importance of the last few votes.

"Rabbi Urias," Nathan called, and Justus' hopes descended. He was sure this prejudiced rabbi would vote against him, leaving him only three chances out of the remaining five.

"I vote 'no,'" Urias said in a loud, unnatural voice.

Justus started, unable to believe his ears. How could this old man who'd fought him so hard suddenly change and vote in his favor? *Why?* Was he trying to prove that he was a pious man who could set his prejudice aside to vote on a principle of law? Or did he feel that Justus could not ultimately win, and wanted to clear his conscience of guilt for his unfair previous attacks?

Justus had little time to consider Urias' reasons, for his mind was calculating the tally that now stood at thirty-three to thirty-three, with five votes remaining. He needed only two more votes in his favor. His eyes searched the top row of the amphitheater, seeking the old men who had yet to vote. The only possible friend he could see was Ismeal. Joazar would vote last, probably against him, so, somewhere in the other three, he had to obtain a "no" to go with Ismeal's certain vote to acquit him. Because these were the oldest and wisest judges of the Sanhedrin, he felt sure he could garner at least one other vote to go with Ismeal's. Perhaps Urias' reversal would have a favorable effect upon at least one remaining judge.

The next vote was against him, so he still needed those two precious votes out of four remaining. Sweat again soaked his tunic as the odds shifted to fifty percent, and for the first time, the judges reacted audibly to the vote. But their low sigh did not give evidence, one way or the other, of how they felt, though the simple majority had now voted against him.

"Rabbi Ben Levi," Nathan called, and Justus watched the fat rabbi struggle up, puffing under the strain of raising his stomach.

Ben Levi paused to get his breath, and a sucking sound came from his ruby red lips, breaking the great hall's stillness. Plainly aware of the dramatic impact of his forthcoming vote, he let the Sanhedrin prepare itself as he surveyed the room like an experienced actor, but his pompous attitude was shattered by Joazar's insisting, "Rabbi, how do you vote?"

A deep crimson dyed the portion of Ben Levi's face that was not hid by his massive beard. "I . . . vote 'aye,'" he said, recovering his composure with difficulty.

"Three votes to go," Justus thought. "*Thirty-three to thirty-five.*" If he'd had a god to pray to, he would now be praying for two of those three remaining votes. He shifted in his seat, straining with anticipation. No battle he'd ever fought had created the anticipation and tension that now caused him to quiver.

"Rabbi Eleazar," Nathan called, looking up from his tablet. The Sanhedrin members turned their bodies to be able to

95

see the skinny old judge, whose long hooked nose escaped from a white, untrained beard. His toothless state caused his chin to appear to touch the nose, allowing the scraggly beard almost to hide his mouth. With difficulty Eleazar announced in a frail voice through the beard, "I vote 'no.'"

A gasp spread through the hall as the judges realized only two voters remained: Ismeal and Joazar. One more "no" vote and Justus would be free. If both votes were "aye," he would have to stand trial. The judges, knowing their decision would have far-reaching effects on the Sanhedrin's jurisdiction, fixed their eyes on Ismeal, who would vote next. His vote could free Justus, for the ballot now stood thirty-four to thirty-five.

Nathan's chest swelled with the pride of his own importance as he called, "Rabbi Ismeal."

Hope crept into Justus' mind in spite of the tension that caused his knee to quiver. He wiped his brow with his forearm only to find that his mantle was soaked wet with sweat. His breath came hard, and his mouth and throat felt parched. "This vote will free me," he thought.

Ismeal, also aware of the critical status of the vote, rose and stood as straight as his aged body would permit, plainly proud of his role. Never in the 40 years of his membership in the Sanhedrin had his vote been so critical, for in his hands lay the power to free this soldier of Herod's.

"I will vote . . ." he stopped to let the judges prepare themselves for his answer, "I will vote 'aye.'"

Justus unconsciously crashed his fist into his open palm — and the sound caused a sharp report to bounce off the walls of the great hall, drowning the audible sighs and exclamations of the judges who now snapped their heads around from Ismeal to look at the prisoner, twisting and turning in his chair, shaking his fiery head in disbelief.

"How could he have voted against me?" he thought. "It was Ismeal's idea to have this hearing . . . he, who had argued for me the most.

96

These damned Jews! I knew you couldn't trust them. They say one thing and do another. Look at Urias . . . he did exactly the same thing."

His last chance stood with Joazar, who, as Nasi, had the last vote. The vote stood at thirty-four to thirty-six. Joazar could free him. "Please let him vote for me," Justus whispered to someone under his breath, knowing that while some of these men were not voting on a principle of law, they probably wouldn't feel kindly toward him regarding his killing of the children. He looked at Joazar with eyes that plead for acquittal, and he who had never weakened in battle nor in carrying out Herod's worst orders felt numb from the top of his head to his toes.

Joazar rose from his chair, looked over Nathan's shoulder to check the tally of the votes, and without speaking returned to his throne. The judges began to whisper as they debated among themselves as to how Joazar would vote, but the hum of conversation was broken as he clapped his hands for attention. His face was grave, and it was plain the decision weighed heavily upon him.

He began to speak. "Before I vote, I want to say that in all the years I have been a member of this wise and august body I have never seen a case in which the vote turned on the vote of the Nasi. Perhaps it is the will of God that my vote should carry the profound implications that have been argued here today. Each of you has cast your vote according to your knowledge and belief of the Law. Each has been guided by a highly respected sense of justice. No one can question your motives. I know each of you has voted according to his conscience. I further realize your convictions are based on a devout consideration as to God's will. I want to state that I, like you, must vote my own convictions upon this matter. I intend to side with no one. Some of you may be disappointed by the way that I will cast my vote. But do not be. My vote is equal to yours. Because I vote last, my vote may seem more important, but it is no more important than Rabbi Jonathan's who voted first. Nathan, I am ready to vote my conviction." He flourished his mantle and returned to his throne.

"Nasi Joazar," Nathan called, again with pride in his voice.

Joazar again rose in response to Nathan's call, then in a calm voice he answered, "I will vote 'aye.'"

Justus slumped in his chair as the judges suddenly began to talk among themselves, creating complete disorder, relieved the balloting was over. Some of them smiled, while others looked dejected and disappointed. It was evident that many judges were taking the vote as a personal defeat.

After Nathan had reported that the vote had been verified, Joazar again brought the assembly to order by a sharp clap of his hands, and called for the scribes' tally of the votes.

He rose again and spoke quietly, "There are thirty-seven votes that the Sanhedrin has jurisdiction over the prisoner. The vote being a majority plus two votes, it is accordingly adjudged and decreed that this senate has the right and jurisdiction to prosecute this man upon whatever charges are made against him by competent witnesses."

Justus hardly heard the Nasi's fatal pronouncement. He was sure that his chance of survival had died with Joazar's vote, and, along with it, his future with Mariame. He looked at Joazar with contempt, silently vowing, if he ever had the chance, to kill this old man who had so piously directed the Sanhedrin.

Joazar clapped his hands once more, "Under the Law we cannot hold court after sundown. Because of the late hour I do not feel we could possibly conclude any case against the prisoner today; therefore I now call a recess in the proceedings against this man. I know that the prisoner will receive a fairer trial if the evidence against him is produced without interruption. Also, because of our rule of not stopping a trial to eat, perhaps many of you must be hungry, not to say eager for rest. Therefore, so that this too may not influence your deliberation,

I feel a recess is called for. Thus, unless I hear argument or comments to the contrary, I herewith recess this senate until tomorrow morning. Because no accusation has been laid at the feet of this man, I further order that we meet at the Temple at daybreak to ask Jehovah's permission to conduct tomorrow's session." He looked around the hall, and seeing no one rising to speak, continued, "We will assemble at the Great Temple at dawn to offer a sacrifice for wisdom in our deliberations and to ask permission of God again to sit in judgment upon Justus. This senate is adjourned in recess. The bailiff will remove the prisoner to his cell."

Justus glanced to his right and saw Tarfon approaching him. Sensing that there was nothing else to do, he rose and met the guard, and the two walked through the open door they had entered early that morning. In the hall two huge guards fell in behind, while Tarfon moved in front of him. As they walked down the stairs, he considered the possibility of escape, weighing his chances.

Suddenly he reached a decision. It must be now or never. As they turned a corner of the steep winding stairs, he whirled upon the larger guard, above and behind him, slamming his fist into the groin. The guard doubled over, screaming in pain, as Justus' other fist made a pulp of the giant's nose. The guard slumped to the stairs unconscious as the second guard lunged, but Justus slashed his Adam's apple with the back of one hand and the guard, gasping for air, fell forward to tumble down the damp stair. Then with the animal instinct of a well-trained warrior, Justus turned on Tarfon who, one step in front of him, had taken two steps more before realizing what his prisoner had done. Tarfon, cautiously approaching, stepped over his gasping companion as he drew a short, heavy sword that hung from his waist.

"You stupid dog of a dog!" Tarfon hissed. "You'll die for this."

But Justus stood his ground, legs tensed, ready to spring. He yelled "Yeaa Ho!" flying through the air and swung his mantle so that it covered the head of his adversary, who stood two steps below him.

Tarfon slashed out in blindness with his sword as Justus' heavy body drove into him. The two men rolled down the stairs, and the sword fell from Tarfon's hand with a dull clank on the stone. Justus pounded his fist into Tarfon's face as they rolled over and over; then as they came to the next turn in the stairs, Justus slipped his knee between the man's legs. He snapped it up into the groin with all his strength, and with a howl of pain, Tarfon released his grip and fell backward unconscious.

Justus scrambled for the man's abandoned sword, his hopes for survival increasing; then, out of a corner of his eye he caught a glimpse of a lighted torch swinging toward his head. He tried to dodge, but the heavy pitch torch laden with fire bounced off his head onto his right shoulder. He felt no pain as darkness blanked out the bloody-faced guard swinging the torch, but he knew in a split second before unconsciousness came, that his impromptu attempt at escape had failed.

X

The head of Justus felt every throb of his heart. Slowly he raised his hand to the large knot on the right side and felt dried blood matted in his short-clipped hair. Then he withdrew the hand and opened his eyes to see if it was bloody.

"So you're awake at last," Nicolas said. "It's a miracle that you're not dead. You are a fool, Justus. You should have known you couldn't escape."

Justus groaned as he strove to raise himself from the floor. "Well, I tried. I'd rather die fighting than have those pious judges sentence me to death by stoning or beheading. What are you doing here, old man? Have you come to help me?"

"If you mean, am I going to help you escape, the answer's no."

"Then, what do you want?"

"The King sent me. He's disturbed about your trial. He is still afraid you're going to drag him into this unwholesome affair."

"He should be. He's the guilty one."

"He doesn't think so."

"Then he may as well change his mind because, when they accuse me of murder, I'm damned sure going to tell the Sanhedrin I was acting under his orders."

"He will deny it. He's already telling everyone who'll listen that you and your men acted on your own when you went to Bethlehem. And you know how very convincing Herod can be when he applies the proper pressure." Nicolas twisted his hands as though wringing the neck of a chicken. "He can make a good case against you."

"How? We had nothing to gain in killing children!"

"Tactus and the vase of myrrh . . ."

"What are you talking about, old man? I know nothing of Tactus and a vase of myrrh."

Nicolas shook his head. "Just as you know naught of the Christ Child?"

Justus was stunned. Had Tactus betrayed his failure to kill the child in the desert? Had he been captured? Had Mundus been captured? How much did Nicolas—and Herod—know of his fight with Mundus? His mind tossed about the possibilities, and he decided to wait before talking about the child. Looking Nicolas directly in the eyes, Justus repeated, "I tell you I know nothing of any myrrh, and that's the truth."

"Listen, my young friend. You can quit playing childish games with me. Both Herod and I know you followed the Christ into the desert, then let him escape, because you either became enamored of the mother or turned softhearted. Tactus was captured and told us, if that's what you want to know. And I want the truth from you. So don't leave out any details. Now Justus, what happened?"

Justus raised himself from the floor and sat with his head against the cold stone wall. "Since you know some of the story, I'll tell you the truth. I should have known you'd learn it sooner or later anyway."

Then in slow, deliberate tones he began to talk, leaving out nothing, reaching toward a climax. "And so that fat innkeeper showed me the gold coin, and then I knew the Magi had found the child they sought."

"What gold coin?" Nicolas asked, his face alive with interest.

"Wait," Justus said. "I have it. It was in my money sack when I was arrested." He withdrew the glistening gold coin he'd looked at and fondled many times since his arrest, cursing about his only failure in duty as a soldier. He handed the coin to Nicolas, saying, "See. It says CHRIST. I knew when I saw it . . ."

"Then the men from the East did find the child!" Nicolas whispered. "This was a gift of the Magi."

"Yes, so we followed them." Justus went on to tell of the long ride through the cold night and of their overtaking the travellers.

He said at last, "I don't know why I didn't kill the child. I've thought about it ever since, and tried to rationalize my actions; but I honestly don't know what caused me to hesitate. All I know is, I couldn't kill that baby. It wasn't the mother — though she was beautiful. I didn't fear the father; I had killed children the day before. Nicolas, I can't explain. Perhaps I'll never know . . . ." Nicolas sat silent as Justus shook his head and added, "But the truth is this: I have no way of knowing this was the child the Magi sought. All we know is that we followed a

102

narrow road from Bethlehem and found this couple with a young child. It could have been anyone from Bethlehem, fleeing with a baby. I really can't say it was the couple that gave the gold coin to the innkeeper. . . . No one knows, for we didn't ask."

"Tactus has proved otherwise."

"How?"

"With the myrrh. He sold a vase of myrrh, which he said he'd taken from the couple, to a young Jew called Joseph of Arimathea. The vase had inscribed upon it the word CHRIST, just as the coin. In fact, the vase was more valuable than its contents. One of our spies heard of the matter and reported it to me. I made inquiries, which confirmed that Tactus had sold the vase to this Joseph."

"So that's what was in the sack," Justus said. "Did Tactus tell you I had a fight with Mundus and broke his arm?"

"Yes."

"Well, while Tactus was splinting Mundus' arm, I noticed a strange leather bag tied to Tactus' saddle. But when I asked about it, he and Mundus suddenly got into a fight. I had to stop them — in fact, I knocked Tactus half-unconscious — and I never thought of the bag again till a moment ago. Don't you see? The myrrh must have been in that bag. Tactus must have taken it from the parents' animal during my fight with Mundus."

"If the myrrh was in the bag, there must have been more gold coins like this one," Nicolas said, fingering the gold disc. "There had to be more, because the parents wouldn't have given their last gold coin to that innkeeper for the use of a miserable room near a stable."

"Did Tactus say he killed Mundus?"

"No. But he did say you'd encouraged him to murder Mundus. No. If he'd killed Mundus, he'd have admitted it. His torture was too great for anything except the truth — and, too, this gold coin may well explain Mundus' flight. I couldn't understand why he'd flee till now, but there must have been a small fortune in that sack. He probably took it from Tactus. Also, he probably thought you'd kill him, or have it done, if he returned to Jerusalem."

"What finally happened to Tactus?"

"He's dead. Herod ordered his tongue cut out, and he died in the process."

Justus shuddered, recalling a time, when he was 12 years old, that he'd witnessed the cutting out of a Spanish bandit's tongue for a lie about the location of his hideout. He could still recall the bandit's unearthly scream.

"But why?" Justus whispered.

"Because the King must silence any rumor regarding the Christ Child. He arranged for the vase of myrrh to be stolen from Joseph, but the Jew had left the city. Nevertheless, in the end the King will have that vase. Thus, only you and Mundus know there was really a Christ, and Mundus has fled, but he'll suffer a speedy death if he's captured, for Herod has notified Rome that he has deserted."

A smile crossed Justus' face, but Nicolas added, "You needn't smile, for even if you do escape from the Sanhedrin, you must still face Herod."

Justus gulped a mouthful of air, thinking, "How did I ever get myself into this?"

It was almost hopeless. If Aizel hadn't told some judge that his mother was Jewish, he'd probably be free right now — at least from the Sanhedrin. Even Mariame didn't know his mother was a Jew; not five people in all Judea knew it, yet one of them had to be her father. His luck had run out.

"How is Mariame?" he asked quietly.

"She is well, but she spends all her time in her apartment, except for running to me for news of the trial. She has turned into a full-grown woman before my eyes. She asked that I tell you she loves you," Nicolas spoke in a half-whisper, eyes diverted.

"Nicolas . . . tell her I love her. No . . . don't. There's no future in it for her. Her father's won. But you can tell *him* that if by some miracle I'm freed, I shall not forget his malevolence toward me."

"I'm no messenger boy," Nicolas said. "Nor can I guarantee I'll do anything. But listen to me: you must keep silent about the Christ. I promise you nothing, but I want you to remain silent about the purpose of the children's slaying. I know, in spite of anything I can say, you're going to raise the defense that you acted on Herod's orders. We could have brought in Tactus to say you acted upon your own in the killings, but he can't speak now. I suppose we could use Hezron, but we don't want to. He's such a fool those judges might trip him up. Nevertheless, we will if necessary. Anyway, he's in a prison cell in case we need him. So it won't do you any good to speak of the Messiah, and it may hurt you."

Justus smiled. "And Herod too, eh?"

"Yes. But I will do everything in my power to help you, if you'll forget the purpose of the Bethlehem mission and the Christ."

"I'm not going to leave Herod out of it," Justus said doggedly.

"I'm sure you won't. I'm not sure I would either if I were in your shoes—but I do think you should seriously consider what I'm saying. Because, I repeat, if by some miracle you are acquitted by the Sanhedrin tomorrow, you'll still have to face Herod."

Justus sat silent as the old man's words sank in. Perhaps Nicolas was right in saying he had little to gain by stating the purpose of the killings.

"I don't know," he said. "I'll think about it."

Nicolas nodded and slowly raised himself from the small

stool, his bones creaking a little as he stretched himself. He looked at the coin in his hand. "Can I have this?"

"No," Justus said. "If I die, I want that with me. It's the cause of my trouble, and I want to make a pendant of it to wear around my neck. That is my millstone."

He reached out his hand for the coin, but Nicolas said, "Let me fix it for you." He took a thin gold chain from around his scrawny neck and detached the miniature gold breastplate of his office. Taking the coin, he punched a small hole through the soft pure gold with his dagger, and slipped the coin onto the chain. "Now," he said, dropping it around Justus' neck, "if you die, you'll die wearing the Magi's gift to the Christ. If you live, perhaps you can personally thank the Christ. But again, I advise you to leave Herod out of this trial. If you don't, he'll slit your throat where that chain sits, if the Sanhedrin gives him an opportunity."

"I told you I'd think about it," Justus said. "Now, please leave me alone. My head hurts where that damned giant hit me."

"You're lucky that Tarfon didn't kill you. But maybe he follows orders better than Herod's men." Nicolas knocked at the cell door and called the guard to let him out, then as he started out the door, he turned to say softly, "Keep quiet. And whatever you do, don't let the judges see that coin on you."

XI

The great courtroom looked grimly familiar to Justus as Tarfon and four guards ushered him to his chair. Whatever kindness Tarfon may have felt for him the previous day no longer existed.

Tarfon was angry because of his prisoner's attempt at escape, and he made no effort to hide it. The bruises around his

106

eyes and his stiff, slow-moving body gave evidence that Justus' fist and knee had done damage he could not forgive.

As Justus seated himself to await the judges' procession, Tarfon whispered, "If I'd cut your throat yesterday, it would have saved a lot of time—but I shall take even greater pleasure in carrying out your sentence when you're found guilty."

Justus pretended to ignore these remarks, but Tarfon leaned close and spoke louder. "Didn't you hear me? I'm going to take pleasure in seeing you squirm when I cut off that pretty head, you . . . dirty . . . murdering bastard!"

Suddenly Justus grabbed the man's short beard and gave it a hard jerk. "Listen, if you keep chattering like a widow, I'll give the Sanhedrin a real case to prosecute . . . killing their bailiff in open court." He gave Tarfon a push with all his strength, and the man fell to the floor.

Hate blazed in the bailiff's eyes as he scrambled up, but before he could draw his dagger he heard the judges' chanting, so he swore and returned to his station to await the dignitaries who now began to pour through the great doors.

When the Sanhedrin had all been seated and their general shuffling had stopped, Joazar rose, clapping his hands.

"I call the Sanhedrin to attention. You are Justus?"

"I am," Justus replied, still seated.

"Bring in the first witness," Joazar called.

Tarfon went out through the huge doors, and the judges sat silent, their eyes fixed on the opening; then the doors opened again, and Tarfon led in a beautiful young woman. She was dressed in a black robe, and the white shawl around her head only partially covered her lustrous hair.

Justus stared at the girl as she approached him, trying hard to remember. Had she been the one in front of the synagogue? No, this was the wife of the man who'd broken the clay pot over his head. He remembered striking the young Jew on the head

107

with the flat of his blade, knocking him unconscious; perhaps he might have even killed him.

When the woman came to a halt at the spot Tarfon had indicated, Joazar clapped his hands. "Has this witness been examined in private?"

In the second row a heavy-jowled judge rose from his pillow. "Yes, Sire. A committee composed of Rabbi Theophilus, Rabbi Abba, and myself has examined the witness."

"Thank you, Rabbi Doras. Does the witness understand the preliminary warning?"

"Yes, Sire. She has answered all questions fully."

"In every criminal case before the Sanhedrin a witness, prior to giving testimony, must be examined in private . . ." Joazar said.

Justus interrupted. "You mean, I don't get to hear the testimony?"

Joazar looked irritated. "If you will let me continue, I will explain. I assure you that you will hear of your actions in open court . . . . Now, Rabbi Doras, we will continue. What says the witness to the following question: 'Is it not probable that your belief in the prisoner's guilt is based on hearsay evidence?'"

"The witness answered, 'no.'"

"The next: 'Have you, or have you not, been influenced in your opinion of the prisoner's guilt by remarks of persons who you feel are reliable and trustworthy'?"

"The witness answered, 'I have not been influenced.'"

"And the next question: 'Are you aware that the Sanhedrin and the accused will submit you to a thorough, searching examination?'"

"Sire, the witness answered, 'I understand, and I am ready to testify.'"

"Then, the last question required: 'Are you acquainted with the penalty attached to the crime of perjury?'"

"Sire, the witness answered, 'I know the penalty for perjury is the same as that for which the prisoner stands accused,'" Doras said. "That, Sire, completes the preliminary questions asked by the committee. We feel the witness is qualified to give testimony and understands the serious nature of these proceedings."

"Then, upon your findings I shall administer the warning to the witness. She will now face the throne and pay heed to this solemn, God-given warning."

Joazar looked at the young woman who trembled with nervousness. Then he cleared his throat to begin the warning which he'd administered word for word since he'd become Nasi, and which, so far as he knew, was the same given by Moses as first president of the Sanhedrin. "Forget not, O witness, it is one thing to give evidence in a trial as to money, and another in a trial for life. In a money suit, if the witness bearing shall do wrong, money may repair that wrong. But in this trial for life, if thou sinnest, the blood of the accused, and the blood of his seed to the end of time, shall be imputed unto thee. Therefore was Adam created one man and alone, to teach thee that if any witness shall destroy one soul out of Israel, he is held by the Scripture to be as if he had destroyed the world. For a man from one signet-ring may strike off many impressions, and all of them shall be exactly alike. But He, the King of the King of Kings; He, the Holy and the Blessed; has struck off from His type of the first man the forms of all men that shall live; yet, so that no one human being is wholly alike to any other. Wherefore let us think and believe that the whole world is created for a man such as he whose life hangs on thy words. But these ideas must not deter you from testifying from what you actually know. Scripture declares: 'The witness who hath seen or known, and doth not tell, shall bear his iniquity.' Nor must ye scruple about becoming the instrument of the alleged criminal's death. Remember the Scriptural maxim: 'In the destruction of the wicked there is joy.'"

Justus flinched at the last words of Joazar's warning, but the young woman stood seemingly in a trance as she had done all through the warning that took the place of an oath. At its close, she merely said, "I understand."

Joazar, upon hearing her acknowledgment of the warning, now clapped his hands again. "Then we will proceed to the Hakiroth. The witness will answer the following questions asked of all witnesses appearing against an accused. What is your name?"

"My name is Sarah Zadok, wife of John Zadok, of the village of Bethlehem," the woman said in a clear, proud voice.

"Did the occurrence of which you complain take place during a year of jubilee?"

"No, sir."

"Did it occur during an ordinary year?"

"Yes, sir. During the year 4658."

"In what month did the occurrence take place?"

"In the month of Tebeth . . . or late December, according to the Roman calendar."

"On what day did the complained of act occur?"

"On the first day of the week—the fourth day of Tebeth."

"At what hour did the offense take place?"

"During the noon hour."

"At what place did this act occur?"

"In my husband's house on the Well Road in the village of Bethlehem."

"Do you identify this person?" Joazar said, pointing to Justus.

"Yes, sir. That is the . . . man." The woman burst into tears as she looked at Justus. "It was he who killed my Jonathan—my innocent, helpless child. That is the demon who killed my son."

Joazar, seemingly unaffected by the woman's tears, looked at Justus with cold eyes. He said, "The Hakiroth has been satisfactorily completed. We will now proceed to the Bedikoth which will embrace all questions concerning the alleged crime. Is there one judge who prefers to handle the questioning of the witness?"

A young rabbi who stood at his station on the first row spoke up quickly. "Sire, with your permission, I would like to question the witness upon direct examination."

"Very well, Rabbi Sceva. You may proceed."

Sceva, younger than most of the rabbis, wore a brilliant red robe over a white tunic. On his chest hung a pendant of gold encrusted with rubies and pearls; his beard was sprinkled with red, and his eyes were deep blue. He stood ready to begin his questioning, evidently nervous, rubbing his hands together.

Justus looked at Sceva, wondering why this man had immediately volunteered to question the star witness for the prosecution. He caught Sceva's eyes for a split second, and the rabbi, like a small boy caught stealing an orange, quickly turned his head.

"You are Sarah Zadok, wife of John Zadok?" Sceva asked, too softly.

"Sir?" The woman raised her head.

Sceva reddened, raised his voice, and repeated, "I said, you are Sarah Zadok, wife of John Zadok? Is that right?"

"Yes, sir."

"What is . . . or was, your son's name?"

"Jonathan Zadok," the woman answered, her eyes clouding again.

Sceva spoke gently. "Now I know all this is painful for you, Sarah, but please raise your voice so that the last judges in the top corner of the hall can hear. How old was your son?"

"He was just over a year. His birthday was the tenth of Casleu." *

"Please speak up so the judges can hear. I doubt that they all heard you." Sceva raised his own voice higher.

_____
* Casleu, or Chislew, ca. November 15 – December 14

111

"I said, he was almost a year old . . . no, just over a year old. He was born on the tenth day of Casleu."

"Thank you. That's better. Now, where was he killed?"

"As I told the other judge — in my husband's home on the Well Road in Bethlehem."

"Very well. Now, tell us in your own words, what happened."

"As I said, it was about noon, and I'd been preparing my husband's meal. He is a merchant, and I was expecting him home from the market. Anyway, I was cooking in our kitchen when the front door of the house burst open with a terrible crash that almost broke its hinges."

Joazar interrupted, "Please get to the point."

"Then . . . I saw him." Sarah pointed to Justus.

"What, if anything, was he doing?" Sceva asked.

"He was coming at me with a drawn sword."

"Did he say anything?"

"No, not then."

"Well, what did he do?"

"My son was playing with a toy in the kitchen . . ."

Sceva interrupted, "Your son Jonathan?"

"Certainly. I had only one child."

"Go on."

"My son was playing with his toys while I was cooking. That murderer . . ."

A voice interrupted. "Sire, we will object to the witness calling the accused a murderer."

Justus turned his eyes from the woman, up to the top row of judges where Ismeal stood alone. Would this man again take up his defense, and then desert him when it came time to vote? Still, he must be thankful. Ismeal might, at least, change some of the judges' minds.

Ismeal continued, "Sire, the prisoner has yet to be accused of murder — and even if he had been properly indicted, it would be only an opinion of the witness. The answer is improper: the

112

sole reason for this trial is to determine whether or not Justus *is* a murderer. The opinion of a witness invades the province of the court."

Joazar rose. "Rabbi Ismeal is correct. Sarah, I know that your statement was unintentional, due to nervousness and grief. However, in the future please do not state a conclusion or opinion. I further instruct the judges to disregard the witness's opinion testimony." Joazar sat down, nodding to Sceva. "You may proceed with your direct examination."

"Go on, Sarah."

The woman started to cry again. "I forget where I was."

Sceva frowned, evidently wondering why he had volunteered to conduct this examination. "Your child was playing in the kitchen when the defendant came into your home."

"Oh, yes . . . he came in with his sword drawn. He had blood running down his arm, and his cloak was spotted with blood. He started toward me . . . and I picked my child up in my arms. I couldn't run because he stood at the only door."

"Did he say anything?"

"Yes. He said he was going to kill my Jonathan."

"Did he say why?"

"Yes."

Disgusted with having to pull everything out of the woman, Sceva now almost shouted, "Well, what did he say?"

"He said he had to kill my child because King Herod the Great had ordered him to."

"Is that all he said?"

"Yes . . . except that he was sorry he had to do it."

"Then what happened?" Sceva asked, eager to cover up the last statement.

"Actually, it happened so fast that I don't know. I know that he lunged at me and Jonathan, that I screamed, and Jonathan started to cry. Then . . . Jonathan screamed, and his crying stopped. My child was dead . . . ." The woman sobbed and

113

crumpled to the floor, and Justus looked at her, his own eyes wet with tears.

For the first time, not knowing why, he felt a stab of conscience, poignant and deep. For the first time, knowing compassion, he realized that he had been cruel and heartless all his life.

XII

Joazar watched grimly as Tarfon helped Sarah Zadok to her feet and gave her a drink of water. Though hardened by many years service in the Sanhedrin, the old Nasi could not hide his feeling of compassion for this young woman. He looked at Justus, obviously wondering if the tears that now streamed from his eyes were sincere or merely an act to gain the judges' sympathy. He looked puzzled, for he knew Justus' reputation as Herod's most cold-blooded bodyguard—the King's personal executioner, ever ready to act without remorse when Herod commanded. Surely a man of such nature could not feel love or sympathy for anyone but himself, so perhaps these tears were shed in fear.

Justus, head bowed to his chest, blinked to clear his watery vision—at a loss to understand his own emotions. Never in his career of professional killer had he wept for any victim of his sword. Never before had he felt a knot in his throat, a gnawing pain in his stomach. He wanted to cry aloud to rid himself of this new torment, but he knew that the judges would interpret such an action as a bid for sympathy. He stared at the floor, helpless to stop his tears.

The woman passed the silver water goblet back to Tarfon, who now cautiously released her shoulders.

"Do you think you can go on?" Joazar asked.

"Yes, sir."

"Then, Rabbi Sceva, you may continue with your interrogation."

Joazar turned to the young judge, who had been standing alone during the episode, and he knew that Sceva, inexperienced, had been unable to decide whether to remain standing or sit. He had also, apparently, forgotten the exact testimony already given, but he was not going to show that he'd forgotten. He said, "I . . . have no more questions to ask this witness, Sire," and sat down as though drawn to his pillow by a magnet.

"Very well." Joazar hid his smile as he turned to Justus. "The defendant, Justus, or any one of the rabbis may now cross-examine the witness in the defendant's behalf."

Justus blinked and passed an arm across his eyes as he stood up quickly. "Sire, I have but one question to ask the witness. Lady, didn't you say I told you that I was acting on King Herod's orders?"

Sarah whirled to face him. "Yes, you said that. But I don't believe the King would want to kill my baby. You are a heartless murderer. My baby never hurt anyone . . . why didn't you kill me instead? Oh, I hope you suffer a thousand deaths for what you've done . . . ."

Justus realized as Sarah continued to spit fiery words at him that his question had brought forth a stream of invectives that she seemingly could not stop. "It's all true," he thought. "What she's saying is true." It was a senseless killing, brought about by the insane fears of a sick old man, desperate to protect his throne. As Sarah screamed a volley of hate-filled questions and denunciations, Justus knew that if he tried to answer her questions, he would only be adding oil to the fires obviously smoldering in the hearts of the whole Sanhedrin. As Joazar ordered Sarah to silence, he sat down afraid that the quicksands of further cross-examination might swallow him. One thing, though: it was Sarah, not he, who had brought in Herod's name.

"Do you have any other questions?" Joazar asked.

Justus shook his head.

"Does any judge have questions he wants to put to this witness?"

"I have."

Justus glanced up again, recognizing Ismeal's voice. "Damn," he thought, "is this old man trying to dig my grave? Doesn't he know it's impossible to attack this witness?"

"Yes, Rabbi Ismeal. Do you want to cross-examine in the defendant's behalf?"

"No, Sire — only in behalf of the Sanhedrin, to see that justice is done."

"Very well, you may proceed."

"Sarah, I know this is painful for you, and we have no wish to add to your grief. I have only a few questions to ask," Ismeal said. "First, in reviewing your excellent testimony, I want to ask: did you speak to the defendant when he entered your home?"

"Yes."

"What did you say?"

"When he came into the house . . . after he'd broken the door in . . . I asked him what he wanted."

"Did he have his sword drawn then?"

The woman paused. "No. He was drawing it at the time."

"Did he hesitate?"

"No."

"Then did he answer your question?"

"No. He just kept coming at me and Jonathan."

"He did not answer your question?"

"Well, yes, later. Just before he . . . killed my son."

"Sire," one of the judges said without rising, "we cannot clearly hear the witness."

Justus thought the judge must be lying because the hall was

quiet as a tomb; he probably wanted Sarah to cry louder in order to create more prejudice.

"I'm sorry," Sarah raised her voice. "I said: he did, just before he killed my son."

"Tell us what he said," Ismeal insisted.

"He said he was acting under King Herod's orders."

"Did you say anthing else to him?"

"No . . . I was so confused and afraid . . . I don't remember anything else."

"Did you tell him what he was about to do was a crime?"

"No, sir. He *knew* it was against the law to kill. Everyone knows *that* . . ."

Ismeal persisted calmly. "Did you tell him that if he killed your son he could be beheaded?"

"No. But everyone knows murder is against the Law. I was too busy trying to protect my son. Oh, why didn't he kill me instead of my helpless child?"

"Perhaps because his orders were to kill only the child," Ismeal answered dryly.

He sat down, and Justus, searching the old man's face, saw no sign of any emotion.

"Does anyone else have questions to ask this witness?" Joazar surveyed the chamber — his cold eyes finally coming to rest on Justus, who shook his head.

"Very well. The testimony of the witness Sarah Zadok will be taken as standing testimony, subject to its being properly corroborated by other testimony. It is a well-known rule that under normal circumstances a woman is not competent to give evidence in a criminal trial. However, when she is the victim or is directly involved in an alleged crime, she may testify, provided her testimony is corroborated by other witnesses. Because Sarah Zadok's infant son is the victim, I rule that her testimony falls within that exception to the general rule. The bailiff will bring in the next witness."

Justus looked at Sarah as Tarfon escorted her from the hall, wondering what would happen to her in the future. Would she have another child, or would she be so bitter that she would remain barren?

Tarfon reentered the hall, and at his side, with almost military gait, walked the dead child's father. The men's footsteps echoed off the stone floor, and Justus saw on the face of John Zadok the same look of fearless determination that he had seen when the man had attacked him. But as young Zadok drew closer, he saw something else in the eyes. John Zadok was feeling guilt and grief — guilt that he had not stopped Justus and grief at the loss of his most precious possession.

For an instant Justus forgot his own plight, trying to place himself in the man's shoes. "What would I feel?" he thought, "I doubt that I could restrain myself, even in court, from killing the man who slew my son, if I had a son . . . perhaps Mariame could have married me, and we'd have had a son, but now there's no hope, for I'll surely die tomorrow."

"Rabbi Doras," Joazar called out, "has your committee examined this witness?"

"Yes, Sire."

"Was he examined separate and apart from the other witnesses?"

"Yes, Sire, and he fully understands the preliminary warning. He has answered all questions fully," Doras answered quickly.

But Joazar began the same qualifying questions as before, "What says the witness to the following question: 'Is it not possible that your belief of the prisoner's guilt is based upon hearsay evidence?' "

"The witness answered 'No,' " Doras told him.

As the formal questions rolled without falter or variance from Joazar's tongue, Justus marveled that the Sanhedrin's rules, based on sound logic, were designed with one thing in mind: to protect the accused. He thought, "Yes, they have the procedure and rules to give a man a fair trial, but what good are rules of procedure if these judges vote, ignoring them?" There was scarce chance the judges would be satisfied with the excuse that he'd acted on Herod's orders, even though it had been brought up by their witnesses.

As Joazar administered the formal warning to John Zadok, Justus braced himself for the last sentence of the admonition, which more than any other thing would give the Sanhedrin grounds for voting the death sentence.

Joazar's voice rose with emphasis, nearing the climax. "Nor must ye scruple about becoming the instrument of the alleged criminal's death. Remember the Scriptural maxim: 'In the destruction of the wicked there is joy.'"

"I understand the words of the warning," John Zadok said in a steady voice.

"What is your name?" Joazar asked, again embarking upon the formal questions of the Hakiroth as to his name, the fact that the occurrence took place not during a year of jubilee but in an ordinary year on the fourth day of Tebeth at the noon hour in the kitchen of his home on the Well Road in Bethlehem.

"Do you identify this person?" Joazar asked, pointing at Justus.

"Yes, sir." John stared at Justus with hate-filled eyes, and for several seconds the two men looked at each other until something in Justus weakened, and he turned his eyes away.

"That completes the Hakiroth. Rabbi Sceva, you may proceed with the Bedikoth," the old Nasi announced.

"Sire, with the Nasi's permission, I would waive my questions in favor of Rabbi Zezebee who is more experienced," Sceva said, betraying the fear that he might again do a poor job in examination.

The Nasi nodded approval. "You may proceed, Rabbi Zezebee."

Justus glanced up to the center in the second tier of judges, recalling that Zezebee had spoken against him on the question of the Sanhedrin's jurisdiction. This little bald-headed judge had a voice like a lion, evidently developed to make up for what he lacked in physical stature. "Sir, what is your name?" he asked, too loudly, even for the vast courtroom.

"John Zadok."

"For the purpose of the scribe's recording of the testimony, have you received, and did you understand, the 'warning of Moses'?"

"Yes, sir."

"Now, John, there is testimony before the Sanhedrin that one Jonathan Zadok is dead. Was Jonathan Zadok your son?"

"Yes, sir, he was," John answered, looking directly at the blue turban that sat slightly crooked on the judge's onion-slick head.

"Will you tell us how your son died?"

"Yes, sir. He was stabbed by the defendant."

"Did you witness the occurrence?"

"Yes," John answered, choking. "I saw that fiend stab my son."

"I know this is painful; however, this testimony is needed. Please describe what you saw and heard."

Clearing his throat, Zadok began, "I was coming home for my noon meal. I'd been at the village market looking at wool, and as I neared my house, I heard my wife scream. I was just down the street, so I ran to my house and saw the front door had been broken in. I ran into the kitchen and saw the defendant withdrawing a short sword from my son's body."

"Did you actually see the defendant stab your son?"

"No, sir . . . but I saw the blade coming out," he repeated in a lower voice.

"What happened then? Did you hear the accused say anything?"

"Yes."

"What did he say?"

"He said, 'damn you' when I attacked him."

"You attacked the accused?"

"Yes. I tried to kill him with a clay pot—the only thing handy . . . I was not armed . . . I wanted to kill him for what he'd done, and I was afraid he might kill Sarah."

"Did you actually hit him?"

"Yes, but the pot broke on his helmet. It didn't even hurt him. When I hit him, he swung 'round, cursing me, and struck me on the head with his sword. I was stunned and fell to the floor."

"Are you sure he said nothing else?"

"That was all I heard. All I know is that . . . he killed my son. I saw it happen. I will see it forever, in nightmares."

"Thank you, John. I think that will be all," Zezebee stated firmly, indicating by his manner that having sufficient evidence to convict, he need not burden the court with further testimony.

Joazar, familiar with Zezebee's manner from previous trials, smiled a little; then as the low hum of the judges' whispering settled, he rose and faced Justus. "Does the accused have any questions to put to this witness?"

Justus shook his head, whispering an almost inaudible, "No."

"Rabbi Ismeal," Joazar called, "I suppose you have questions to ask this witness?"

"Sire, I most certainly do," the old man struggled up on his shaky, spindly legs.

"Then proceed. I suppose you are again interrogating for the benefit of the Sanhedrin—not the defendant?" Joazar spoke with sarcasm.

Red-faced, Ismeal snapped back, "If what I develop through cross-examination helps this senate to decide this case properly, then I shall have achieved my purpose. If it sheds light on the truth, then the accused is assured of a more honest, fairer trial. If my questions expose false statements and weak points, the Sanhedrin will benefit. It will mean we have judged the case on true facts and testimony—not prejudice, and that we will apply the proper law to the true facts. In short, any and all relevant and truthful testimony will benefit both the Sanhedrin and the defendant." The old man paused for breath. "Yes, even if the testimony I develop proves beyond doubt that the defendant is guilty, he will know—and God will know—we have performed our duty honestly, as God has directed us through Moses and the Talmud."

The Nasi sighed. "Thank you for your wise interpretation of your duties, as well as ours. Now please, let's continue."

Ismeal looked at John Zadok and hesitated as if wondering whether to attack the witness or to be gentle, then he began his cross-examination. "John, are you certain the defendant did not say he was acting on Herod's orders?"

"I didn't hear him say it."

"But, he could have said it?"

"I suppose so. If he did, I didn't hear him."

"Your wife has testified the accused told her he was acting on Herod's orders in killing your child. Do you think she is mistaken?"

"No. She told me the same thing after I came to, so I believe he did tell her that he was acting on King Herod's orders . . . but I didn't hear it. Everything was so confused at the time."

"Then, in that confusion the defendant might even have told you he was acting for Herod?"

"I don't think so . . ."

"But you're not sure—you only *think*—thus, he could have said it, and you didn't hear him."

John Zadok rubbed his brow. "Yes, I suppose so."

"Now, John, was it you who reported this incident?"

"Yes, sir. After I'd attended to my wife and son, I rode

straight to the Great Temple here in Jerusalem and reported the murder to the Nasi of the Great Sanhedrin, as well as to Rabbi Annas, the High Priest."

"Did you, at that time, identify the accused?"

"Yes, sir. I knew who he was, for I'd seen him before, in Jerusalem. He'd been pointed out to me by citizens of this city who knew and feared him. I identified him by name when I complained to the Nasi."

"Did you attempt to report the matter to King Herod?"

"No, sir."

"You didn't attempt to because you knew that Justus was acting on Herod's orders?"

Zadok lifted his head but remained silent.

"Answer me! You knew it would do no good to complain to Herod because you knew Justus was acting on his orders, didn't you?"

"I was afraid to seek an audience with the King . . ."

"You were afraid because, knowing Justus had acted on Herod's orders, you'd be stepping into a tiger's mouth. Isn't that correct?"

"Yes, sir," John whispered.

"Speak up! The judges didn't hear you!"

"I said . . . yes, sir." Zadok looked up.

"Very well." Ismeal reverted to a gentle and quiet tone. "Now let me ask you this: did you warn the accused that if he killed your son, Jonathan Zadok, he could be tried for murder? And that the punishment for murder is death by beheading?"

"No, because when I entered the kitchen the act was completed—his blade had already taken my child's life. It was already done. I had no chance to stop it, but even if there'd been time, I would not have wasted a warning on that animal."

"And you didn't hear your wife warn him?"

"No, I didn't," Zadok spoke angrily. "Nor did I hear the other parents warn him before he killed their children."

Joazar stood up. "Before our wise brother Ismeal can move that the witness' last statement be disregarded, I caution the Sanhedrin to wipe that statement from their minds. I further caution the witness to answer the questions, and not volunteer information."

Ismeal nodded grudging approval, obviously resenting, Justus guessed, Joazar's muffing his chance for a stirring climactic finish to this cross-examination. Without saying another word, Ismeal eased himself on to his pillow.

Joazar had not been watching Ismeal, and when he looked up, surprised to see the old judge had ceased his examination, he said, "I assume Rabbi Ismeal has concluded?"

"Only for the moment!" the old man shouted, and a smile broke over his crafty face.

"Does anyone else have questions to put to this witness?" Joazar asked.

The great hall was silent as the judges surveyed their fellow members, and Justus again felt small in the vast room as the judges' eyes rested upon him. He thought of Nicolas' warning about implicating Herod and told himself, "The king will have to seek his revenge against Ismeal, not me."

Joazar said, "There being no further questions, the bailiff will remove the witness." Then, as Tarfon escorted Zadok through the heavy door, he cleared his throat to continue, "Because of certain testimony of the previous witness, I shall make a short statement concerning the report of the alleged crime to me. First, it is true John Zadok did report the matter to me and to Rabbi Annas, near sundown on the fourth day of Tebeth, which has been testified to as the day of the child's death. We were at the Great Temple, and John Zadok told me that the defendant, Justus, a captain, he said, in Herod's personal bodyguards, had murdered his son about noon in Bethlehem. Rather than notify Herod, I ordered Tarfon to take several of the Sanhedrin's police and arrest Justus. Zadok also told me his wife had said Justus had told her that he was acting on King Herod's orders in killing their son. Because of the implications, I ordered the defendant's arrest before informing King Herod. Since that time I have talked to Nicolas of Damascus, the King's minister. He says that King Herod, denying he sent Justus to kill the child, refused to appear before this senate to testify and waives his right to intercede as Justus' commander."

Justus stared at Joazar, amazed. Though not trained in the Law he knew that Joazar was now placing hearsay statements before the Sanhedrin, obviously going to extremes to convict him.

Joazar went on quickly, "Before I hear an objection that what I've just said is hearsay, I want to say that my conversations with both Zadok and Nicolas of Damascus are repeated here, not to establish the truth of those conversations, but merely to affirm that those conversations took place."

"Sire," Rabbi Eleazar spoke in a frail voice as he rose, "we appreciate your concern for applying the correct rule of law to the evidence in this case. However, as I view your statements, none of the events and conversations about which you just gave testimony occurred in the defendant's presence. You are correct. It is all hearsay, and such statements should not be considered by this senate for any reason. We do not question your veracity, but we feel that your testimony, for, that's exactly what it is, should be disregarded. In spite of your office as Nasi, you should have been given all of the preliminary warnings of the Sanhedrin, as well as the Hakiroth, before you testified. That is the only procedure whereby such incriminating testimony and evidence can be brought before this body."

Justus noticed that Joazar had reddened as the old rabbi gave out his awkward, toothless pronunciation. It was obvious that Eleazar had touched a tender nerve, and now, though Joazar still had his hand raised, the old man continued, "I move

125

that the Nasi instruct the senate to disregard his statements—
in toto, without reservation."

"I cannot agree with you," Joazar snapped.

"Nor I with you. Put it to a vote. A voice vote will suffice.
The damage has been done."

Joazar glanced around at Annas who sat immobile. He said
coldly, "Very well. I will step down and call for the vice-president, Annas, to conduct the vote in whatever manner he
deems proper. You may proceed, Rabbi Annas."

Annas sat up slowly, scanning the judges' faces. "We have
before us an unusual situation. I am sure that each of you has
given the question your fair appraisal. Because of the hour,
I will call for a voice vote. A vote of 'aye' will mean the Nasi's
testimony shall stand, a vote of 'no,' that the Nasi's entire
testimony will be struck from the record and disregarded."

Justus smiled, seeing from Annas' pompous manner that
he felt superior to the other judges because of his dual position
as both high priest and vice-president. He knew that the vote
would do him little good, for regardless of how it went, the
damage had been done: the scribe might strike the statements
on the papyrus, but even the fairest judges could not erase
Joazar's testimony from their minds. Still, the vote might give
him an indication of how the judges were feeling about him.

"Nathan, call the roll," Annas commanded.

"But, sir," Nathan said, "I thought you said this wasn't to
be a roll-call vote."

Annas flushed. "Oh yes . . . all those that believe the testimony should be admitted will say 'aye.'"

A loud chorus of 'ayes' seemed to rock the room.

"All right. Now, all those who feel that the statements
should be struck will vote 'no.'"

Again there was a roar, and the vote seemed the same to
Justus; in fact it had sounded as though all the judges had

voted both times, and this would mean that Annas could rule either way he chose.

"The vote is more 'aye' than 'no,'" Annas said, not waiting to consider the matter. "The statements of the Nasi are accepted, as he has qualified the same."

He bowed in the direction of Joazar, whose pleasure at the ruling was betrayed by a slight smile as he nodded and said, "The bailiff will bring in the next witness."

Doras spoke up. "Sire, may I and my committee approach your throne?"

"For what purpose?"

"It concerns other witnesses."

"Very well, but hurry."

Justus sat forward, intent. Why did they hesitate to call other witnesses? They had plenty of others. He watched as Doras and two more judges of the preliminary examination committee approached Joazar. Joazar seemed disturbed, and when the three judges neared the throne he asked, "What's the trouble? Can't we get on with the trial?"

"Sire, we have no other witnesses," Doras whispered as Justus strained to hear.

"What?"

"It's true, Sire," Abba answered. "The couple who just testified are the only competent witnesses against Justus."

"But I thought he killed twenty-five children. Surely you can find more than two witnesses."

"No, Sire. There were twenty-eight children killed, all told. The defendant killed eight children and two adults. His men killed the others."

"Why can't you make more than one case?" Joazar raised his voice in anger.

Doras answered, "Because we need corroborating testimony. We have one witness only to each of the other crimes.

We might get some general testimony, but we cannot establish a crime except in one case — and even that is weak."

"What about testimony that he directed these other men to kill . . ."

Theophilus interrupted, "That's his defense. If we attempt to do that, we'll be building a defense for him, because old Ismeal is obviously trying to establish that Justus was only acting under orders. No. I'm afraid that might lead to certain acquittal. Then too, we'd have to face the problem of not putting his companions on trial with him, and that fact alone might give some of the judges grounds to vote acquittal, for his companions are not Jews — besides, they are unavailable."

"Why didn't you tell me all this earlier?"

"We tried to, but we didn't have an opportunity."

"That's a lie!" Joazar's eyes flashed anger.

Doras answered, also angry, "Regardless of what you say, Sire, we tried."

From where he sat Justus heard this whole discussion, and he wondered what effect Joazar's anger at the judges would have on the trial's outcome.

"Now, let me get this straight," Joazar said, "are you saying the Zadoks are the only ones who can fulfill the Law's requirements of having two witnesses to the crime?"

"Yes, Sire," Doras told him. "We have only one witness to six of the others. One family was completely destroyed by the defendant, but those crimes can be attested only by circumstantial evidence — which, as you know, is insufficient."

"Humph," Joazar snorted, glancing at Justus.

"Again, Sire," Theophilus interjected, "if we throw these unprovable acts into evidence they will fail. And as to the murders by Justus' soldiers, if we pursue those acts we may give credibility to his only defense of his having acted on Herod's orders. For, if Justus is accountable for the murders committed by his men — when *they* are not being held accountable — then

128

some judges may feel that King Herod, not Justus, should be on trial here."

Joazar sat silent, plainly contemplating his next move, and Justus felt that he could read the old man's mind. What the committee had said was true; it was better not to get the Sanhedrin embroiled in other legal questions. Objectionable testimony, if introduced, might divert the judges from their real purpose. It was true that this prisoner could be convicted in one case and get death, just as if he were convicted in all of the murders.

The committee stood silent as the Nasi debated, and Justus looked at the judges who were whispering among themselves, obviously wondering what was taking place in the huddle at Joazar's throne. He thought it was unfair to him for his judges to be in a secret conference in open court.

Suddenly the committee bowed to the Nasi and returned to their assigned seats; then, all eyes in the hall were turned on Joazar. As the Nasi rose, a hush fell over all the judges, and Justus sat frozen.

Joazar spoke slowly. "The committee have announced that they wish to rest the prosecution at its present stage. They ask that the Sanhedrin give consideration only to the charges of John Zadok and his wife against the defendant for the murder of their son, Jonathan Zadok."

Justus sat rigid, thinking, "What's happening, why have they changed? Do they feel they have my conviction clinched? Why is Joazar so angry at Doras and the other two judges?"

His thoughts were interrupted as Joazar turned to him, solemnly, "The defendant, Justus, may now testify."

Justus trembled. Joazar had taken him too much by surprise, and though he had waited all day to testify, now that the time was at hand, he hesitated. He needed advice but there was no one to turn to.

"I said, you may testify if you desire," Joazar repeated.

"Sir, I am not sure of the procedure," Justus said.

Joazar cleared his throat. "You may make such statements as you deem proper to your defense. You can then be questioned by the judges on any matter concerning the offense for which you now stand charged."

Justus asked cautiously, "Do I have to testify?"

"No. And if you do not, the judges cannot question you. Further, your failure to testify is not to be considered as evidence against you. Does that answer your question?"

"Yes, I think so. May I have a moment to consider?"

"Yes. We have no wish to rush you in this serious matter."

Justus nodded and looked up at the judges, who stared back at him as he wondered if his case was in shape for a rational defense, and as he debated whether or not he should attempt to lay the blame on Herod. But actually, they already had that before them, and if he testified he might get confused and make statements bringing in the other killings. "Yes," he thought, "if I tell about Herod, I'll definitely have to lay all the other deaths before them." Suddenly he remembered once hearing a Roman senator say, "If you have a client who may make a poor witness, and he can add nothing of value to his defense, it's best for him to keep silent. If he should falter on cross-examination, he would destroy himself . . ." and in a flash he decided. "Sire, I respectfully decline to testify."

Joazar looked stunned, obviously amazed at Justus' failure to fall into the trap of cross-examination by judges who could fire loaded questions till a defendant convicted himself.

"Very well, then," the Nasi said. "Do you have any evidence —is there any witness whom you wish to call in your behalf?"

Justus thought of Nicolas and Hezron, but he knew they were out of the question. He'd have to take his chances as things stood now.

"Sire, I have no witnesses to call in my defense."

Joazar looked at the court. "Does any judge have witnesses

to call to testify for the defendant? Does any judge have evidence to give in behalf of the defendant?"

"Yes, Sire," Ismeal cried. "The testimony of both Sarah and John Zadok!"

Joazar looked irritated. "Do you mean you want to recall them to testify for the defendant?"

"No. I mean, the testimony they have already given."

The judges all looked at Ismeal in apparent astonishment, and Justus let out a sigh.

"That damned old fool," he thought, "arguing for me and against me, he'll get me convicted for sure."

XIII

Joazar smiled slightly now as he spoke. "Although it's an unusual request, I'll approve your motion and the scribe will record that all of Sarah and John Zadok's testimony is now entered as if Justus had called them as witnesses." The Nasi looked hopeful of having no further trouble with Ismeal. "There being no other evidence, I rule the evidence against Justus is closed. We will now hear arguments. But remember, no argument may be made against the defendant until one is made in his favor."

"Sire." Eleazar stood up.

"You may proceed."

"We have before this senate a most unusual case. We have heard testimony of the terrible, senseless slaying by this defendant of the boy, Jonathan Zadok. But we have *not* heard evidence of a murder. A homicide has been committed—not a murder." Eleazar paused to let his statements take effect. "Every killing is not murder, just as every act of sexual intercourse is not rape. Now, before you protest that the killing in evidence is brutal and should be punished, let me say I agree: it was both brutal and senseless. But then, any killing of a human being is barbarous. However, in this case a sentence of death by this senate would amount to premeditated murder —unless the defendant is guilty beyond any shadow of a doubt. We must therefore be extremely careful in deliberation lest we, given the power to judge our fellowman, fall into error. We must remember the Torah admonition: 'A judge should always consider that a sword threatens him from above, and destruction yawns at his feet.'" Eleazar paused in his toothless, halting harangue, then continued, "But why do I say these things to you, the honored and wise judges of our nation? Well, first, the testimony clearly shows that at the time of the slaying the defendant stated he was acting on the orders of his commander, Herod the Great. Because the killing took place as he made this pronouncement and because it was introduced into evidence by Sarah Zadok, a prosecuting witness, her testimony must stand as evidence for the defendant. I am sure that Rabbi Ismeal had this in mind when he formally introduced her testimony as evidence for the defendant to emphasize his point. But what does it mean, as far as we are concerned? It means that Herod—not the defendant—is the guilty party. The King should be on trial, not this defendant."

The old man raised his voice. "Now, what would have happened if the defendant had refused to carry out the King's orders? He'd have met with certain death for insubordination or treason—probably without a simple hearing. Then, isn't it true the defendant *had* to carry out his commander's orders? You know it is. A soldier must carry out orders; discipline is his way of life. And death is the product that a trained soldier dispenses. Regardless of how cruel or gentle a soldier may be in his personal life, when it comes to orders from his superior officer he has no choice but to carry out those orders. The defendant obviously acted on orders in killing the child, and is, therefore, not personally accountable. Homicide, yes, but not murder. It may not sit well upon our collective conscience—but

—we have no choice save to acquit this man. I move that he be acquitted."

The old man sat down, and Justus' hopes soared. If the judges followed Eleazar, he could be acquitted. He was glad that he hadn't testified, but he was afraid some of the other judges might see it as evidence of guilt.

"Sire."

"Yes, Rabbi Urias?" Joazar answered.

"The learned Rabbi Eleazar sounds convincing until we look closely into the facts of this case. The defendant stands accused of murder. We have heard how he entered the home of John Zadok and stabbed the child to death. He murdered that child in its mother's arms—and never since I've been a member of this senate have I heard of a colder, more in-humane crime. Never since our people left Egypt has a Jewish child been so cruelly murdered by a soldier. And that act calls for us to judge this man severely—without reserve or pity. We should not be swayed by speeches, by tricks, or the Law's technicalities. If, by our vote, we convict this defendant, we will be upholding God's law; if we do not, we stand to make a farce of God's spoken word. Rabbi Eleazar seems to insist that Justus should be excused for the murder because he said he was acting on Herod's orders.

"But what evidence have we before us that Justus acted on Herod's orders? None, except that which comes from his own lips, for Sarah heard no one say it but him. And no one else has said he was, so do not be misled. A person who can destroy an innocent child will contrive any cunning ruse to escape punishment. And that is obviously what the defendant sought to do in telling Sarah he acted for Herod. Remember, too, there is no external evidence that he acted on Herod's orders. We have only his word, and since when is the word of a killer reliable when his own life is at stake? No, I say, it is subject to the gravest doubt. Furthermore, according to the Nasi, Herod has said he did not order the child's death.

"If we accept Eleazar's theory, we will, in effect, license murder, for then any evil person, in order to escape punishment, need only say the King ordered him to commit a given crime. In addition, if we accept Eleazar's argument, we will lose all control over punishment for crime. There would be no crime except the King's crimes; and Herod follows the maxim: *'The King can do no wrong.'* No, I say we cannot accept this attempted excuse."

Justus had watched intently as Urias spoke, hoping to get an indication of the Sanhedrin's reaction to this fierce argument. It was plain that Urias had their full attention, but he could not sense their feelings for or against him, though he did see several nod in approval as Urias sat down.

Then, as he sat raptly attentive, several other judges argued the case, five for him, four against him, each repeating, in slightly different terms, the points advanced by Eleazar and Urias. Each sprinkled his passionate pleas with Torah quotations, and each claimed that God's Word sustained his position —but how could God be on both sides?

Justus took hope from the fact that those who argued for his acquittal did so apparently believing he was innocent under the Law, while those against him tried to play on the judges' emotions.

"Sire."

"Yes, Rabbi Ismeal," Joazar answered with a slight grimace.

"Before I go into what I feel is the most important reason for this defendant's acquittal, I must first say I fully agree with Rabbi Eleazar. There are ample grounds on which to base an acquittal of Justus; there is sufficient evidence that he acted on the orders of Herod. I, of course, do not question the fact that this soldier killed the child—that is fully proven. It has been argued that when two people conspire to kill a third person and, by plan and agreement, the killing is carried out by only one of the two, then, under our laws of principal offenders, both conspirators are equally guilty. I agree with that law, and recognize it as a good one. However, it does not apply in this case. Why?"

He waited as if for an answer from one of the younger judges, then went on, "It does not apply because of the relationship between the defendant and his King. At no time does a soldier have control over his superior. He must follow his commander's orders—in this case, Herod's. Suppose, for a moment, that Justus had been a slave, ordered by his master to commit the crime of theft. Would he be guilty? Of course not. Why? Because the slave had no choice *except* to carry out his master's orders. Now, is there any great difference between the captain of Herod's guards and a slave? I think not. And if the rule applies in a case of theft, it also applies in a case of murder. The defendant should therefore be acquitted."

Ismeal cried out the last words, his voice reaching a crescendo, then, pausing, he scanned the judges' faces.

"Now, I come to specific grounds for acquittal. Our Law is absolute in demanding a verdict of not guilty. Of course, I speak of the antecedent warning. If there is one distinguishing feature of the jurisprudence of our nation and people, it is the antecedent warning. No other system of justice has such a rule of criminal procedure. At the risk of offending some of my wise brothers here, let me review the meaning of this warning. It simply means, no person charged with crime, of any degree, may be convicted unless competent testimony shows that just before the crime was committed, the offender was warned: first, that the act he was about to commit was a crime; second, as to a certain penalty of punishment. Further, the warning is not effective if time has elapsed between the admonition and the committing of the offense. In other words, the warning and the criminal act must occur at the same time.

135

"Now," Ismeal continued, "the Law goes further in stating that the warning is of no effect unless the accused acknowledges the admonition, expressing a willingness to continue with his criminal act regardless of the Law and the punishment. In other words, to be guilty the defendant must turn to the person warning him, and say, 'I am aware of the nature of the act I am about to commit — of the rules of the Law applicable thereto and of its inevitable consequences.' And, unless he so states in those or similar words, this court cannot consider the condition of the antecedent warning as having been complied with."

The old man raised his head. "Now, was an antecedent warning given in this case? No. There wasn't a semblance of one. The warning serves three distinct purposes. First, to protect the would-be offender against his own crime by a timely warning; second, to aid in establishing criminal intent at the time of the accused's trial; third, to aid the Sanhedrin in establishing the proper punishment for the subject crime."

Ismeal paused once more, cleared his throat with a muffled cough, then continued, "How does this basic rule of Mosaic and Torahic Law apply in this case? What evidence is there of a warning? There is exactly *none*. Not one word. You heard the question I put to both Sarah and John Zadok. There was no warning by either of them — no admonition. There was no reply by the defendant that he knew the nature and consequence of his acts. Thus, the defendant should stand 'not guilty.'"

Justus sat amazed, mulling over this law about which he knew nothing. If Ismeal was correct, he should be found not guilty. Well, it was true no one had warned him, but in his heart he knew that it wouldn't have made any difference, because he would have had to carry out orders regardless of the Law. And anyway, he'd always considered himself above the Jews' laws — except those that Herod had forced him to obey.

"I know some of you may feel that in this particular case we should forget about the law of antecedent warning," Ismeal went on, relentlessly, "but can we cast aside one of the basic tenets of the Mosaic law, merely to punish a man whose act has shocked us? I say, as judges we cannot apply this Law simply as it suits our fancy. If it is the Law, we must follow it. There are no contingencies — it is either the Law or not the Law. Not one of you can question the existence of the antecedent warning in our code; because of that Law I must vote for acquittal, and if you, too, follow the law of God, you will vote 'not guilty.'" Ismeal ended with slow, deliberative speech, stressing his pleas by pointing a skinny finger at Justus. "Perhaps God will punish this man, after our acquittal."

Justus fought back a smile. Their God did not worry him; now there were *two* reasons for acquittal, for surely even the angriest judge could not ignore the Law as outlined by Ismeal, and he was all the more thankful that he, in ignorance of the Law, had decided not to testify.

His muscles tensed as Altazar rose to speak, for he was sure that this man would be against him, and he wondered if Altazar could counter Ismeal's point on the antecedent warning.

Altazar immediately attacked Ismeal for attempting to free an obvious murderer. His mouth poured forth streams of adjectives describing Justus as a typical Roman killer — a man, born a Jew, who had been trained by the Romans in the art of murder.

"Ismeal," Altazar cried, "tries to say this man should have been warned of the nature and consequences of his foul deeds. What good would that have done? You know that this type of man feels he is not only above our laws, but all laws. Why, even the Roman gods decree that it is proper to murder. And what Roman ever stopped because of a Judean law? None. The Zadoks could have talked all day and never stayed this man's sword. He acted from malice and avarice in wielding the death blow. The rule of antecedent warning does not apply in his case, for it was designed to protect the sons of Israel—not these foreign dogs who fatten on our land. The defendant says he is not a Jew and does not consider himself under the jurisdiction of our laws. Then take him at his word. Do not allow our fair and generous laws of God to apply to this infidel. Death should be the only verdict that we as protectors of our people should vote, in obedience to God. Vote death, and thus tell all his kind that Judea metes out a proper punishment for murder. If you free Justus, you will be telling every mother in Israel that her child can be murdered, and we will do nothing about it. Our people have entrusted the punishment of crimes to our hands. They look to our verdict—and we cannot turn our backs on them or our God!"

Justus' hopes for an acquittal grew dimmer by the moment. Although Altazar's argument was general and did not specifically offset Ismeal's outline of the law of antecedent warning, he saw that the judges had sat strictly attentive, weighing every word of this man's speech. Then, as another judge rose, he knew that the case had boiled down to a matter of hate versus the Law.

If the judges could set aside their prejudices, he had a chance—if they could not, he would die.

XIV

Joazar spoke softly. "If there are no further arguments, I will call for a vote. Nathan will call the roll."

The moment of decision was finally at hand; the defendant's fate was now in the hands of the solemn judges. Unconsciously, Justus' hand moved to the Christ coin that hung from his neck, and as he gently fingered the gold pendant, he silently asked for mercy.

"Rabbi Jonathan," Nathan called.

"Based upon the premise that no antecedent warning was

given, I vote not guilty," the Rabbi said, and again Justus held back a smile, seeing that Joazar could not hide his disappointment at the youngest judge's vote.

Jonathan seated himself, and Nathan called, "Rabbi Ben Heron."

The Rabbi rose. "The servant is not culpable for his master's crimes. I feel the defendant acted on orders and is not personally liable for the death. I vote not guilty."

Again hope swelled in Justus' heart and its beat seemed audible to him as blood rushed to his brain. The first two votes had been for acquittal, for two different reasons.

"Rabbi James."

"There is joy in the destruction of the wicked," James cried out. "I vote guilty!"

Then Justus remembered. In the vote on the ancillary hearing to determine if the Sanhedrin had jurisdiction, Jonathan, Ben Heron, and James had all voted in his favor. Now James had voted to convict him; and he was disturbed, too, because James had evidently disregarded the arguments in his favor, merely quoting the last line of the witnesses' warning as his grounds. Without a doubt James had cast his vote of guilty solely on the basis of how many other judges would follow his lead.

Justus kept track of the votes by repeating the running total over and over. Under the rules every judge had to make a short statement explaining the reason for his vote. The atmosphere of the hall was taut with excitement as the judges cast their votes, and Justus tensed with each one, though he tried to hide his reactions. Sweat ran down his legs and his whole body had a clammy dampness about it.

The ballot mounted, with the votes falling into three basic categories. There were those who voted guilty on the basis of prejudice, and though they gave varied reasons, few were based on the Law. Another group voted not guilty on the basis of

Justus' having acted on Herod's orders, while the third based their not guilty vote on the antecedent warning. The vote mounted on both sides — guilty — not guilty — and the lead shifted back and forth as Justus' life swayed in the scales.

Urias cast the sixty-sixth vote — guilty; then only five votes remained. Now it was thirty-one not guilty, thirty-five guilty. Justus sighed as his life seemed to be slipping away. He needed four precious votes to assure his freedom; two more votes of guilty would finish him.

He looked at the judges who had not voted, thinking that Joazar would vote guilty, but that Ismeal and Eleazar would undoubtedly vote for him since they'd argued for his release. But they could still change . . . they had before. The next two votes were critical ones, and he had to be found not guilty on both. Only Levitas and Ben Levi remained uncommitted.

Justus was now covered with sweat. His throat felt desert-dry and his body numb as his hand again unconsciously clasped the Christ coin.

"Rabbi Levitas," Nathan called.

Slowly Levitas got to his feet, his breastplate catching the light of the hall's torches. He cleared his throat as he waited for the judges to turn in his direction.

"The antecedent warning came to this senate from the Torah; the Torah came from Moses, who took it neither from the mouth of an angel nor the mouth of a seraph, but from the King of Kings of Kings. I cannot ignore His words that require me to vote not guilty," he cried.

"Now Ben Levi stands between life and death for me," Justus thought. Ben Levi had voted against him at the ancillary hearing. Would he change this time?

As Ben Levi rose in response to Nathan's call, Justus noticed that Joazar quickly stepped to Nathan's side, looked at the scribe's tally sheet, then returned to his throne, and that Ben Levi was angry at Joazar for stealing any part of his moment.

His fat body puffed as his small eyes darted over the judges' faces.

Justus cursed his luck. Why couldn't it have been another judge who held his life in his hands? How could he get a fair vote out of this fat pompous fool? He sat on the edge of his chair, his head bowed, unable to look up as Ben Levi cast the most important vote in his long career as a judge.

"I vote . . . on the basis that the defendant must have been acting on orders when he killed the child. If he were not, he would certainly have killed the parents. He *must* have been acting on Herod's orders. Also, the requirement of the antecedent warning was not complied with. I believe this is the most cruel, unfeeling man I have ever heard of, but the Law must be followed. Regardless of my personal feelings, I must vote not guilty."

Justus raised his head, and tears streamed down his cheeks as the tension drained from his body. Thirty-three now for acquittal, and thirty-five for guilty. With Eleazar and Ismeal yet to vote, he was positive he would obtain the two necessary votes. Eleazar quickly voted not guilty, and Ismeal and Joazar stood with equal votes. A single vote of acquittal between the two would free him . . .

As Ismeal slowly rose, Justus saw the old man's face break into a toothless smile, and in an instant he felt nauseous, for in that face he thought he saw Ismeal telling Joazar that his vote would be for conviction.

"No, it can't be," Justus thought, "not now . . . he led the argument for my acquittal." But Ismeal had voted different from his argument before, and remembering this, he suddenly whispered, "Oh God, let him vote for me."

Then he heard Ismeal say in a clear voice, "Sire, I have already argued why I feel we must acquit the defendant. By my vote I feel that I add to the protection of the Great Sanhedrin, because when we fail to follow the Law, this court shall die soon after. I vote not guilty."

Justus shivered and fell back. He had been acquitted. He had kept count of the votes, and now the look on Joazar's face told him his tally had been as correct as that of Nathan's scribes. He had done the impossible. He felt like running to give old Ismeal a hug but restrained himself. He looked toward Ismeal, and when their eyes met, he smiled his thanks, but the old judge scowled and turned his head away.

Now, without waiting for Nathan to call his name, Joazar sprang to his feet and launched into a vindictive speech against the judges who had voted not guilty, while the rabbis sat in shocked surprise, appalled that their Nasi had lost his composure.

Joazar ended his mad tirade at last. "I can do no more than cast my vote of guilty. If the total vote is guilty I will take pleasure in it—but I know that the defendant, by your vote, will be set free. I object—but I concede there is nothing more that I can do. The scribes will confirm the vote."

Justus sighed and whispered "Thanks" to some unknown benefactor, as Nathan reported that the vote had been checked and verified.

"There are thirty-five votes of not guilty," the scribe on the right reported. Then, in response to Joazar's question, the scribe on the left reported thirty-six votes of guilty.

Joazar rose from his throne, his face still flushed with anger. "There not being a majority plus two votes, the defendant must be acquitted. The case against him is closed. I have said I think this is a miscarriage of justice, but, as your Nasi, I have no choice except to free the defendant. May God punish him for his sins against our people. Tarfon, open the doors so that this beast may slink from our presence."

Justus remained in his chair, his wet eyes fixed on the Nasi, as Tarfon moved to the heavy doors. When the doors stood open wide, Joazar pointed. "Go! And may the demons of hell forever give you no rest."

Justus got up slowly, and all the judges' eyes followed him as he walked out the massive doors into the setting sun. He was happy about the acquittal, but his heart was indeed heavy with repentance for his deeds, and the Nasi's words beat like wild birds' wings in his head, *"the demons of hell . . . no rest . . . no rest . . . no rest . . ."*

XV

Justus glanced over his shoulder as Tarfon closed the massive doors to the Sanhedrin courtroom. When he heard the bolt slide into place with a heavy thud, he threw out his chest and arms, and the cool evening wind billowed his robes. The fresh air felt clean in his lungs as he drew it in deeply, exulting.

"I'm free!" he said aloud, still unable to fully comprehend the old judges whom he could hear shouting behind the door as they prepared to adjourn for the day. "Free!" he said again, and ran down the long row of steps toward the Temple gates. But as he crossed the inner courtyard and passed the Court of Women, he quickly brushed past worshippers and priests preparing to close the Temple for the night and suddenly realized that, in spite of his acquittal, he was still in danger. If he were recognized by any slain child's parent from Bethlehem, an attempt would be made on his life, now that he was unarmed and without the throne's protective power. He automatically felt for his missing knife and sword, seeking their comfort and safety, and he grew increasingly nervous as his eyes constantly darted about surveying the crowd, searching for a hate-filled face.

The sun was nearly gone as he entered the almost deserted street, and he decided to walk at a normal pace to avoid attracting attention.

He would have to get word to Mariame immediately, and he wanted to do it himself, so as to see her radiant face. From what Nicolas had said, she must have been half out of her mind with worry. But no, he could not go to the palace, for even though he slipped by the palace guards, Aizel would report him to Herod if he caught him with Mariame. Then Herod would probably kill her. No, damn it, he would have to leave the country.

"If I can get back to Rome," he thought, "I will have friends who can help. Caesar knows Herod is mad, and he will help me. He would never let Herod kill me. There is the Roman garrison at Caesarea, and if I can get there safely, perhaps I can bribe my way aboard a ship . . . hell, I'd go as a galley slave just to get out of reach of the Tiger's claws."

As he passed a man leading a goat he tripped over the rope in the dim light, and the man yelled, "Damn you, stop mumbling, and watch where you're walking . . . you almost broke my animal's neck."

"I'm sorry," Justus said. "You're right, I didn't watch where I was going."

Suddenly he decided to return to his house. Perhaps his treasures were still there. Maybe the Sanhedrin hadn't stripped it, and maybe Herod's men might also have waited to be sure he was dead before dividing his wealth. Anyway, he would go to his house, then flee and send word to Mariame that he was safe. Perhaps after he was settled somewhere, he could send for her.

As he turned into the house and opened the door, he was surprised that the lamps were lighted. The room was just as he had left it. But who had lighted the lamps?

Cautiously he moved about the room, taut to defend himself from a possible hiding assassin. He found one of his daggers in a table drawer, and slowly edged the bedroom door open a little. He could see no one inside, but his nerves tensed

144

as he pushed the door back and sprang into the room, ready
to strike a death blow if necessary.

Then he heard a woman scream, whirled, and saw Mariame
behind the door. Her hand was at her mouth ready to ward off
a blow, as Justus dropped the dagger and stepped toward her.

She flew into his arms, moaning, "Oh, Justus, I had almost
given up hope . . . oh, my love, my love." Tears streamed from
her limpid eyes as Justus covered her mouth with his, and she
clung to him, molding her body to his.

He whispered against her face, "Mariame, Mariame,
I thought I'd lost you. I thought all was ended. But the Sanhedrin acquitted me. Imagine! Thank the gods you're safe.
I was so afraid that Herod or the Sanhedrin may have harmed
you because of me."

She spoke into his ear. "We must leave at once. There is no
time to waste. Herod has gone mad. He swore he'd kill you if
the Sanhedrin didn't." She pulled away from his strong grasp.
"Please, let's go! I have horses waiting in back of the house."

"Wait . . . let me . . . there is still time . . ."

"No, please" she cried softly. "There is a lifetime for that.
Herod's guards may be on their way here now. I'm surprised
they weren't waiting for you at the Temple."

"All right," Justus said. "Look under that bed — there should
be treasure there in the saddle bags." He began to gather up
other items about the room, including his spare sword.

In five minutes more they were on their way out the door,
laden with the leather pouches of money and jewels, then he
remembered it was exactly here that he'd been arrested by the
Sanhedrin's police. "Wait," he said. "I will see if it's safe." He
placed the saddle bags by the door, stepped outside, and
cautiously edged himself around the corner of the house. The
horses were tied to a rail near the rear court, and as he turned
the corner he thought he saw a glint of metal in the moonlight.
Then he glanced left and made out, partially hidden in the

145

shadows, the outline of a Roman-style helmet. Yes, a trap was set to be sprung, and he was the rabbit. He slowly stepped backward, easing his foot to the cold ground, his back to the wall. Then he heard the clanking of armor to his rear, and whirled around, sword drawn, body crouched, ready to fight.

Out of the darkness a soldier, sword in hand, moved silently toward him; he heard footsteps in back of him, and as his head snapped around he saw them on all sides. Herod's men!

"Drop your blade," a voice said. "We don't want to have to have to kill you, Justus. You haven't a chance with us, but you might have with the King. Be sensible, and drop your sword."

"I can't," he called. "I can't trust you."

"Yes, you can. You have no choice. Drop the sword, come with us peaceably, and we will forget the woman. Act now, before she comes out . . . or it will be too late."

Justus' sword struck the rocky ground with a dull metallic thud as he held up his hands and walked toward the faceless soldier.

XVI

Nicolas approached Mariame in silence, and she saw at a glance that he was gravely concerned, for his eyes were troubled under bushy gray brows. The old man stopped, slowly eased himself into a chair next to her, and watched as she folded the cloth which she had been sewing. He cleared his throat with a deep gutteral growl. "Mariame, Herod knows you were with Justus the night the palace guards captured him. I don't know how he found out, but I suppose one of the guards told him. He has informers everywhere—some that even I don't know about."

Mariame looked up. "I have done nothing wrong, Sire."

"No, I suppose you haven't. But Herod looks upon you with favor . . ."

"And I, upon him with disgust!"

Nicolas cleared his throat. "I'll pretend I didn't hear that."

"You need not. I will tell him myself." Mariame looked up, defiant, her eyes blazing.

The old man raised his thin hand. "Calm yourself. I come not as Herod's advisor but as your friend." He touched her hand in assurance, but Mariame was not convinced. She knew this old man was loyal to the King, and that he was a real power behind the throne. Still, Nicolas had always been a friend to her and her father, and it was he who had been largely responsible for her father's presence here in the court. She had known him all her life; she looked upon him as a kind uncle, but how could anyone be sure where Nicolas' true loyalty lay—with the King or with his friends?

She attempted to smile at Nicolas, but she knew that her smile did not show complete trust in him, for he shook his head at her. "Mariame, I have known you since you were a child . . . perhaps even before you can remember. I have watched you with pleasure as you have grown into a beautiful woman. I come as a friend—believe me. Forget for the moment that I am the King's chamberlain."

Mariame nodded. "All right, Uncle Nicolas. But why does it matter that I saw Justus?"

"You were going to run away with him, weren't you?"

"Yes, I was. I knew Herod would kill him if the Sanhedrin found him not guilty . . . I heard my father say so. I knew Justus would have to flee from Judea, and it is true I was there when he was captured. He could have fought his way out of the guards' trap, but he feared for my safety."

Nicolas looked at her as she wiped her eyes. "Then the reports were true?"

"Yes, they were true. Oh, God, if we hadn't delayed for a moment we might have escaped."

"But why did you want to flee with him? Do you love him enough to give up all of this?"

Mariame looked up. "Yes. At first I only wanted to get away from the palace life—from Father and Herod. But when the Sanhedrin arrested Justus, I missed him so much I thought my heart would break. Oh, yes, I love him enough to go with him anywhere."

Suddenly she threw herself at the old man's feet. "Oh, Nicolas, he's going to lose his life because of me. He could have escaped if it hadn't been for me." She wept for the first time since Justus' arrest, releasing her pent-up emotions.

"He knows that you love him," Nicolas said, as he stroked her hair. Her sobs subsided, and she raised her head. "Oh, can I see him? Please! I've tried to bribe the guards, but they are too frightened to chance it. Uncle Nicolas, you can arrange it, can't you?"

Nicolas did not answer, and she cried out, "Oh, if you don't help me, what am I going to do?"

"That is why I am here," the minister said. "Your father has also heard you attempted to flee with Justus—and you know how he hates the boy. Also, Aizel is heartbroken for fear you will run off and leave him."

Mariame looked into the old, lined face trying to think clearly as Nicolas went on, "You know, your father intends to offer you to Herod in marriage. He plans to make the marriage contract soon, and Herod will accept. I know he will, for he has already discussed the matter with me. I have tried to discourage him, but I am certain he wants to marry you."

Mariame froze. "My father has gone ahead with this without my consent?"

"You are a grown woman, Mariame. You know how these things are handled."

"Yes, but he promised me that he wouldn't."

"Your father is an old, sentimental man. We both know he

148

has always dreamed of your marriage to a king—or at least a prince. When you attempted to run off with Justus, he said you had broken your word to him, and that this released him from his promise not to make a marriage contract with the King. He is not going to chance your flight with another soldier—or with Justus, if he lives," Nicolas sighed, shaking his head. "Frankly, I do not approve either of your father's action or his reasoning, nor do I approve of Herod's marrying you. He is four times your age, and this marriage would add nothing to the throne."

Mariame sobbed. "Herod! The throne! Doesn't anyone care about me, or how *I* feel?"

"Of course they do. I do. But your father honestly thinks that he is acting in your best interest."

"Oh, God," Mariame said. "Why can't my father understand? Why can't he? He claims to love me, yet he would sell me like a common whore."

"Hush, now," Nicolas said. "There may be a way, but we must be extremely careful. You must tell no one—not a single person, not one soul. You cannot give a hint, or the plan will fail."

Mariame looked up hopefully as the old man looked off into space, apparently laying plans, calculating possible risks involved, and hope sprang to life within her. "Oh, I promise I will be cautious. Help me—please, Uncle Nicolas."

The old man did not speak at once but sat stroking her long hair, seemingly lost in thought; then he tilted her chin in his hand, looked deep into her eyes, and spoke slowly. "Yes, I will try to help you. Herod is ill; his moods change from day to day, but generally he will behave in a rational manner for two or three days in a row. I can almost predict his behavior in advance. There are exceptions, of course, but generally—for some reason unknown to his physician—his illness runs in

149

patterns. You know him very well, so perhaps you too have noticed this."

Mariame nodded. It was true the King seemed to have fits of depression that lasted several days at a time. Everyone in the palace knew this and did their best to avoid contact with him during those times. She sat tensed as the old minister continued. "Now, if I can succeed in getting Herod to hold Justus' trial while he is in a good mood . . . he may spare the boy. If so, there will be a severe punishment, but perhaps not death."

Mariame shivered. "Oh, God, can't you bribe the guards to let him escape?"

"No!" Nicolas snapped. "If I attempted to bribe any guard, he would report me to Herod, and Herod would let the guard keep my bribe, but he would give the informer a bonus of the same amount for revealing my plot. And then even I would not be safe from the Tiger's claw. No, this will require the utmost cunning. Justus is no ordinary prisoner, and he has personally disobeyed his King. He was Herod's most trusted guard, and Herod will make of him an example to be remembered. He has been delaying the trial at my suggestion, but he will not wait much longer to have his revenge — or, as he calls it, his 'justice.' Now. If you love Justus, and want to avoid the King's bed, you will have to follow my instructions to the letter."

"I will," the girl cried. "Oh, Uncle Nicolas, I will."

"Good. And remember, no one is to know *anything*. Not Justus, not your father, not *any*one. For if you talk, I shall deny everything and wash my hands of this whole affair."

"I promise. I will tell no one."

"So be it. And now, a final word, Mariame; I make no promise, for there are too many factors to be controlled. All I can say is that I will try for you and Justus. I will tell you more at the proper time."

"When will that be?" Mariame asked, searching his eyes.

"I do not know — not yet."

"Uncle Nicolas . . . could you arrange for me to see Justus, even for a little while?"

Nicolas thought a moment. "Yes, I think that can be arranged. But only if you promise again that you will tell him nothing. Remember, I cannot promise you anything, so don't even tell him I'm trying."

"No, no, I won't. But, Uncle Nicolas?"

The old man touched her cheek with his frail fingers. "Soon. Perhaps tonight — if I can arrange it." He rose from the chair and helped her to her feet. "Stay calm — and be ready when my slave Umbla comes for you."

XVII

The dungeon cell in the Fortress Antonia was not unfamiliar to Justus, but in the past he'd always been on the outside looking in; now, as Herod's prisoner, he was on the inside. The cell's thick granite walls seemed to close in around him, leaving him breathless. A single pitch torch with a pungent odor cast a flickering light over the man who sat on a straw bed, damp from the sweating walls and floors; he lay still and thought about his fate. If he should ever get out of this situation, he'd never serve as a royal bodyguard again. A soldier, yes; but never again as the Tiger's personal executioner; you were damned if you did and damned if you didn't, with that maniac Herod.

Herod knew that he'd failed to commit the murder in the desert and that in all probability the infant he'd allowed to escape had been the Christ Child. On the other hand he'd followed Nicolas' instructions not to involve Herod in the Sanhedrin trial; Herod had been brought into it by the judges and their questions, never by him. Still, he had to admit that he'd disobeyed Herod, and he didn't yet know why.

In the single week since his arrest he had tried, without success, to get a message to Nicolas. Although the Tiger's lesser guards had always been under his personal command, they now refused to help him in any way, and he knew that, aside from a fear of Herod, the men were taking revenge on him for his harsh treatment of them in the past. They taunted him with vile language and gloating laughter, and he cursed them for their ridicule, which only increased their sadistic pleasure. They all felt certain that Herod would sentence Justus to death and that he would never escape to carry out the threats of reprisal he flung in their direction.

Brooding, Justus suddenly looked up, alerted by the scraping sound of the cell door on the floor, and stared at the King's minister.

"Nicolas! Did you get my message?"

The old man shook his head as Justus stood up. "No. I just came on my own—as your friend."

"Can you get me out of this awful place?"

"No. I'm afraid that's impossible. I've already tried. I lied to your guards to be here now."

"But why am I being kept here? I've done no wrong."

Nicolas sighed. "You know as well as I do: you disobeyed the Tiger. He has ample grounds on which to punish you— either for insubordination or desertion."

"Am I to have a trial?"

"Well . . . if you mean will you get a fair hearing, like the Sanhedrin's, the answer is *no*. I don't know how the King will handle the trial. But I know it will be a brief one, held to appease the Sanhedrin and to ridicule them for letting you go free."

Justus clenched his hands. "Talk to him for me, Nicolas. You can change his mind if anyone can. I have done as you said.

I didn't tell the Sanhedrin about the Christ Child, and I've always done what he asked . . . except for that one time in the desert. I still don't know *why* I failed him there. Maybe I was just worn out and bewildered after all the killing that day. But please, old friend, talk to the King. Please Nicolas. See, I'm begging for the first time in my life, but it is *for* my life and I'm not ashamed."

Nicolas spoke slowly. "Justus, during the time you've been attached to Herod's court, I have looked on you with favor, knowing you were always faithful and loyal in carrying out your duties. In spite of your violent nature — your often cruel and ruthless behavior — I have loved you almost as a son. And, too, both of us are strangers in this land, living off it, directing its people who hate us, so perhaps that is the bond between us . . ."

"Then, you will help me?"

"I have already, my boy."

"You mean, you talked to some Sanhedrin members — interceded with them?"

"No, because if I'd tried to help you in that way, I would only have assured your conviction. No . . . I knew their law of the antecedent warning. While the Sanhedrin's rules and laws are highly developed, and perhaps the most humane criminal jurisprudence in history, the antecedent warning will eventually render their system of criminal law totally ineffective. Theirs is the only system holding that 'ignorance of the law is an excuse for crime,' and I knew they'd have to apply it in your case. Also, I knew old Ismeal would as usual require the judges to follow the Law — even though there was a chance that Joazar could get enough support to obtain a verdict of guilty . . . . But no, I did not attempt to influence the judges directly."

"Then . . . how have you helped me?"

"In two ways. First, Herod wanted to have you maimed as soon as the Jews released you, in order to prove to them that you were not acting on his orders in slaying the children of

Bethlehem. I advised him not to; then, when he suggested having you murdered, I advised him against that as well. I told him that the Jews would interpret such action against you, without a trial, as proving he was implicated in the children's murders. He took my advice in each case—so, twice I have saved your life."

"And now?" Justus waited breathlessly, almost afraid of the answer.

"Now, I have persuaded Herod to hear your side of the story. If you can convince him, he may spare you."

"And when will he see me?"

"Soon, before he leaves for Callirrhoe to take the hot sulphur baths for his ailments. I am going with him, so perhaps this is the last time we'll be able to talk."

Justus rubbed his eyes. "What time is it, Nicolas? I can't tell night from day in here."

"It is late afternoon—near sunset," the old man told him.

As they talked on together, Justus' mind was filled with fears of the Tiger's vengeful plans. He sensed that his chances of escaping Herod's wrath and possible death were slim.

In the end Nicolas sighed and embraced Justus, telling him in a choked voice, "Son, I wish you well. I will see that certain matters are taken care of. Remember to be very cautious. You still have an outside chance of success with the King, if you handle yourself correctly. Meantime, I have a surprise for you. I shall shortly send you a good meal—enough for two people."

Justus said, "Thank you." The old man smiled and left the dungeon cell, the massive iron door slamming behind him.

Justus tried to think of some reason to give Herod for his failure in the desert. But, always as he attempted to think of some logical explanation for his actions, he came to a dead end. He could not find, anywhere in his mind, a reason for his having spared the Christ Child. Even though he knew his life now hung in the balance, he could think up no believable story to tell the Tiger, since he couldn't explain his conduct even to himself. He rubbed the Christ coin in his hand, wondering why he, the best soldier in Judea, had failed to carry out his sovereign's orders.

Suddenly the windowless cell door opened and a huge black slave owned by Nicolas stepped into the cell, carrying a heavy straw basket.

"Why, Umbla, what are you doing here?" Justus asked.

The slave set down the basket and spread a linen cloth on the damp floor.

"Sir, my master has sent both food and clothes for you. Here is a fine meal, with wine from the King's own cellar." The black man continued to spread out the food as though he were setting a place for Herod himself. Justus watched, smiling a little.

Nicolas had once offered Umbla his freedom, but the man had preferred to stay on with his master, and Justus had often thought it was really Umbla who owned Nicolas, for the black did not hesitate to tell the minister how to eat, sleep, and dress. Over their years together the two had come to love each other — in spite of Nicolas' threats when the old slave made him eat certain foods or take unpleasant medicines . . . and Nicolas always found a way out of these threats, continually giving the slave a second chance, warning him the next time would be the last. Actually, without Nicolas, Umbla would have nothing at all to live for, and without Umbla, Nicolas would be lonely.

Justus sat down and reached for a bottle of wine, but the black jerked it out of his reach as Justus roared, "Damn you, Umbla, give me that bottle!"

"No, Sire. Not yet. Your guest has not arrived."

"*What* guest, you old goat?" Justus cried, but the words were scarcely out of his mouth when a shadow fell across his face, and he saw Mariame in the open cell door, her glistening black

155

hair falling around her shoulders. Her soft red robe picked up the torch light, giving radiance to her olive skin.

"Oh, Mariame," Justus whispered in disbelief, "How, my dear one?"

She did not answer as he rose and gathered her in his arms. Their lips met just as Umbla said "Goodnight," closed the cell door, and withdrew to stand guard outside.

The silence of the cell was broken only by their whisperings as they stood locked in each others arms. Justus had been in the arms of many women, but never before in his life had he experienced the feelings that surged through his body now. He felt weak all over, yet filled with exhilaration, as though he were soaring into space. His body came alive, responding to Mariame's. He could think of nothing except having her, completely, without reservation, in actual love.

"Oh, Justus . . ." she whispered, "I love you so. I had to be with you . . . to let you know, no matter what happens, I'll always be with you, somehow. Oh, God, if only I hadn't delayed you, you could have escaped. It's all my fault."

"No, Mariame, no." He hushed her with a long kiss, then spoke softly, lowering her to the pallet of straw. "Forget the past, my darling, and don't think of the future. We have each other now . . ."

He held her . . . kissed her, and when at last he eased his body onto hers, insistently, she responded "Yes, oh *yes,* . . . *oh, my darling, yes.* . . ."

XVIII

Aizel walked slowly into the room. "Where were you last night, daughter? You did not sleep in your bed."

"Does it make any difference to you where I was, Father?"

Aizel bristled. "Certainly. I am your father!"

"Yes, but I think you're concerned about just one thing with

156

me—a possible marriage to Herod." Mariame spoke coldly, "I know your plan to make a marriage contract with the King tomorrow."

Aizel stood speechless, plainly surprised that she knew this, and she wondered if she should tell him that Herod would no longer be getting a virgin.

"Don't try to change the subject," Aizel said. "I asked you where you were last night, and I expect an answer."

"I won't tell you anything." Mariame rose from the breakfast table, knocking over a glass of water in her agitation. "Admit it, Father! You have gone to the King and arranged for my marriage to him. You broke your promise to me!"

Aizel looked up at her. "I felt I was released from my promise when you broke yours. You were with Justus the night he was captured. You had promised me you wouldn't see him again, yet you tried to flee the country with him. And if I have spoken to Herod about a marriage, it is for your good. *You* will be *Queen of all Judea*, my girl—think of the women who would give anything on earth for this opportunity!"

Mariame walked slowly toward the open window. To the west she could see a large thunderstorm moving toward the city, its dark clouds warning of violent winds and rain. She did not turn to look at her father who stood waiting for her reaction to his statement.

She thought of last night, relived the rapture of her lover's thrusting body, the rough straw next to her bare skin, and touched her hair, wondering if it still bore evidence of her crude marriage bed. Justus was the only man in the world she wanted. She knew that after last night; there was no question as to his wanting and loving her. He was no longer only an escape from her father's plans for bartering her to Herod; she was deeply and completely in love. She smiled a little, recalling her lover's violent passion and his tenderness. No matter what happened now, she had been awakened into full womanhood.

She had heard that a generous giving by both a man and woman must be the very foundation of love. If that was true, then she had experienced everything that body, mind, and spirit could conceive of as true love.

Her father came over to where she stood and touched her arm. "Mariame, I will not ask you again about last night; I think I know what happened. You seem grown up today — a woman rather than a too-romantic girl." He looked out at the darkened sky. "There is a rising storm now in Judea. This country — our way of life — is changing because of violence. Like that storm out there, with all its destruction, it will serve a useful purpose. The storm will bring rain to our fields and leave the country green after its force is spent. Herod and his violent reign will pass, and there will be peace." She stood rigid, unspeaking, as Aizel began again, "I know how you feel. No young girl wants to marry an old man, but this union will serve to raise you up to where you belong. Herod will die soon — and you will ascend the throne as Queen of Judea."

Mariame bit her lip hard to keep from lashing out at Aizel. She wanted to slash at him, to hurt him as much as she could, but there would be no point in that, for this morning early, Nicolas had sent word to her by Umbla to be ready to travel at a moment's notice. She had packed several boxes of clothes. Then she had unpacked everything — filled two large leather pouches — one with clothes, the other with jewels and gold which would be needed if Nicolas could effect an escape for Justus.

She turned and said to her father, "There is no use arguing with you. I have told you time and again that the very thought of lying with Herod sickens me. I will never marry him, and that is that. Now go. I can't bear to discuss this any longer."

Aizel patted her shoulder. "You are just depressed this morning. Storms always did affect you . . . you used to hide from the thunder and lightning when you were a child. We will talk again about your future, when the storm has passed and the air is cooler and clearer."

As the old man turned and shuffled toward the door; his bent head and stooped shoulders suddenly seemed to his daughter symbolic of his mind's condition. For the first time she realized, with a shock, that Aizel had grown senile. He was unable to understand that she could not bring herself to lie down beside the diseased, repulsive Tiger. His failing mind had blotted out all thought of that. He could only see her now, with the romantic eyes of second childhood, in the black robes of Herod's widow — as Judea's triumphant queen.

XIX

Justus raised himself from the bed as the cell door scraped open. He straightened the clothes which Umbla had brought him and stood up. As the two grim guards watched, he fastened his tunic, thinking of Mariame, remembering.

The soldiers were brusque in instructing him that the King was waiting, and he sensed by their downcast eyes that they could not help feeling sorry now that their former comrade must face the irate King, and possible death. He could also understand that they had allowed themselves to be bribed by Nicolas so their former comrade in arms could spend his last night in the arms of a beautiful woman. He knew he would have done the same for one of them.

As he neared Herod's audience room in the Fortress, the corridor reeked of that putrid smell Justus had almost forgotten.

The chamber which he now entered was used when the Roman Army commanders visited Jerusalem, or for audiences with possible trouble-makers, when Herod needed to have his military men near at hand. The old fortress, built by the Hasmoneans, was the strongest and tallest building in all

159

Jerusalem. One wall was adjacent to the Great Temple, and there was talk that Herod sometimes climbed its high walls to spy on the Temple priests. One wall of the Fortress was a part of the city wall, and the top portals of its battlements rose some two hundred feet from the base. Herod had named it Fortress Antonia in honor of Mark Antony,* an old friend, and he had refused to change the name after the love-sick Roman's death. The Tiger had lived here during the construction of his palace, and he loved the rough old building, which gave him some sense of security.

Herod stalked into the room, his drooping stomach painfully evident, with Nicolas in his wake. Justus looked at the floor, fearing to raise his eyes to the King. The room was silent except for the sick king's heavy breathing as he seated himself on his gold-encrusted throne. He said, as Justus strained his hands in the leather thong the guards had bound too tight, "So, you don't like being tied like an animal. Well, that's what you are. Why did I ever put my faith in you?"

Herod suddenly screamed in rage. "Look how you've repaid me for all I've done for you! You disobeyed my orders, you've embarrassed me in front of the Jews, and you've had me accused of murder! Damn you to hell, Justus! I would not put it past you to be scheming to run to Rome and tell Caesar I sent you to murder those children. Speak, now! What have you to say in defense of your treachery?"

Justus kept his eyes on the stone floor. "Sire, I regret having caused you pain. But you must know, the Sanhedrin arrested me for disposing of one of the children of Bethlehem — as you ordered me to do."

Herod sat silent, as Justus went on. "I did only as I was ordered, Sire. The Sanhedrin acquitted me of murder — and I never once mentioned your name throughout the trial."

* Herod the Great: 73 B. C. — 4 B. C.; Mark Antony: 83 B. C. — 30 B. C.

"That's a lie! You brought me into the trial. *I* know. I have heard that you said you were acting on my orders!"

"I did not tell them you ordered us to kill the children so as to be sure the supposed Christ was destroyed. I could have, but I wanted to keep you out of it, Sire. I did the best I could. I did not testify. I did not mention you. You know that I have always been loyal to you."

"The hell with what you did or didn't do at your trial," Herod shouted. "You disobeyed me in letting the Jews' Christ escape! You allowed a threat to my throne to exist. Furthermore, your foolish disregard of duty may cause the Jews to revolt, if they hear a Christ has been born and has been taken to Egypt. You *knew* the importance of your mission and what it meant to me. I trusted you. Now, God only knows what repercussions your disobedience may cause. By letting the so-called Christ live, you may have caused untold dangers to all Judea and the Roman Empire. You may think that you merely let a child escape, but I tell you that far-reaching—disastrous—events may stem from your action." Herod stopped shouting. He waited a long moment, glaring at his prisoner. "What do *you* think I should do to punish you, Justus?"

In a low voice, Justus answered, "I don't know, Sire."

"Then I will tell you. I think you should be crucified to show the Jews that I believe in punishing the wicked, but Nicolas believes that might cause trouble." Herod looked at Nicolas. "So, Minister, what should I do to punish this traitor? Should I have his disobedient hands cut off at the wrists?"

Nicolas answered quietly, "No, Sire, I think a sound beating would suffice. I think that Justus will carry out your orders in the future. Remember, this was his first mistake."

Herod snorted. "I have no use for any man who fails me. He is a traitor to his King. How could he be trusted again?" He turned to glare once more at Justus. "What do you say to a hundred lashes at the post?"

161

Justus raised his head. "I will accept whatever punishment my King decrees. I know that I failed you, Sire."

Herod looked at him. "Why *did* you disobey me, Justus?"

Justus shook his head. "I don't know, Sire. I know only that when I raised my blade to kill the child, my hand was paralyzed. I could not thrust home the sword."

"You mean, something supernatural took hold of you?"

"No, Sire. Nothing supernatural that I know of . . . I . . . can't explain what happened. Nothing like that had ever happened to me before. I felt no qualms in killing the other children, but I could not kill that child in the desert."

"Then why didn't you let that dog Mundus or Tactus do the job for you?"

"I cannot answer that either. All that I honestly know is that I could not let any harm come to that child."

Herod scowled. "Didn't you think about consequences? Didn't you know you'd have to face me for disobedience?"

"I didn't think about that—at the time; somehow it didn't enter my mind."

"Ha! You thought I'd forgive you, didn't you?" Herod snapped. "And maybe you thought, too, if this *was* the Jews' Christ, you could ingratiate yourself with him in case of revolt. That is true, isn't it? You wanted to be on both sides. Tell the truth, Justus. Tell me the whole truth."

"I have, Sire. I truly did not consider anything like that. All I know is, I couldn't slay the child, and I felt no disloyalty to you. I am a soldier, trained to carry out orders, and I admit I failed in this assignment. Why, I don't know. But I can't believe the child will ever trouble you. Those people were on their way to Egypt. If the child was the Christ, he will not return to threaten your throne."

"Be that as it may, what punishment can equalize such disobedience?"

Justus spoke humbly, "I will gladly submit to the lash if you so order, my King. I have learned my lesson. Such a thing will never happen again."

"I know it won't. I'll damned well see to that."

Justus knew that Herod was toying with him, wanting to see him grovel and beg. He also knew, from having watched others, how great a mistake that would be, for Herod took a sadist's pleasure in taunting those who were helpless. He stood silent, his face expressionless, as the Tiger continued.

"Nicolas thinks that I should spare your life—that your past service warrants a reprieve. So, against my better judgment, I shall follow his advice. I order that you be given fifty lashes with a weighted whip; then, if you live, you shall be banished from my kingdom." Herod belched and fouled the air around him. "You, guard. Strip him. I want to watch this devil suffer for all the pain he has caused me!"

Justus almost smiled as the guard pulled his dagger and began to cut the tunic from his body. He knew that he would suffer agony now and for days afterward, but at least he would be alive, and that meant he'd see Mariame again. All was not lost; he would live.

As his clothes fell to the floor, another guard began to unlimber a heavy lash, and he realized that Herod must have planned this punishment beforehand.

The guard began to tie his hands around one of the two columns dividing the room, and Justus tensed himself for the ordeal.

"Wait!" Herod shouted. "What is that thing that hangs from his neck? Bring it to me!"

As the guard lifted the chain with the gold Christ coin from around his neck, Justus knew that it would throw Herod into another rage, and he held his breath as the guard placed the pendant in the Tiger's pudgy hand.

"Damn you!" Herod screamed, and his face went suddenly purple. "Now I know you are in league with the Christ and his followers! Now I know why you protected the child. You are his spy, set against me. You wear his pendant — his safe-keeping medal!"

Justus stood silent, shaking within himself. No explanation could possibly calm this madman.

Herod leaned forward, eyeing his minister. "Ha, Nicolas, I told you. See, he is a traitor! This proves his allegiance is to the Christ, not me." He stared at the old man. "I should punish *you* for speaking up for him. I'll not listen to your pleas for him any longer. Here is the proof of his guilt!"

He held the coin out, and as Justus saw the light reflect off its surface, he knew that he was doomed. The King stood up now, and his fat, swollen belly rose and fell with each curse word he hurled at Nicolas and Justus.

"Damn . . . damn . . . damn! When shall I ever live in peace? Will I never feel secure? Here, guard, hang this damned thing back around his neck. He will need it where he is going. Justus — like the prophesied Christ — shall die a criminal's death. If I don't live to kill this false Messiah, my sons will . . . . Now I shall attend, personally, to this traitor."

Justus' hands unconsciously tested the bindings as the guard dropped the thin gold chain around his neck. He noticed that Nicolas stood stone-still, his head bowed, silently weeping.

"Ah, now!" Herod pounded his fat right fist into the palm of his left hand. "You, half-Jew, I shall punish you as the Jews punish idolators and blasphemers by stoning. You are guilty of both crimes. I decree this death! I find you guilty!" The cords of the Tiger's short throat stood out — purple. "Guards, take him to the highest wall of Antonia that overlooks the valley below. You will stone him — then throw his body over the side so that the rats and vultures may have their fill of his traitor's guts! Take him away with that damned coin around his neck. He will learn that the only safe passage it will give him will be to death!"

XX

The muscular guards pulled him to the open door that led to the wide sentry walkway atop the fortress. Justus began to twist and turn, fighting to free himself from the strong hands tugging him toward destruction. He tried bracing himself to keep them from pushing him through the door, but with both hands tied behind him, he could get no leverage.

It was raining now; and a cold wind whistled through the valley below the walls of the fortress. Low flying clouds blacked out the late afternoon sun, and lightning forked the sky with jagged tongues of fire, adding an eerie glow to the brown and black colors of the countryside.

The soldiers cursed as they struggled to get him outside; suddenly catapulted into the storm, he felt his nerves quicken to the rain pelting his naked skin.

"Damn you, stop fighting! One of us will fall over the wall," one guard shouted above the roar of the wind.

"Hit him on the head!" another cried.

"No!" shouted a third. "Bring up those spears; that will quiet him," and still another shouted, "Grab his legs! Throw him!"

Justus felt himself being lifted by his tormentors and arched his back, twisting, attempting to bite the arms of a captor. His body fell to the rough stone floor with a dull crash, and a soldier jabbed him with a spear, breaking the flesh on his right shoulder. Blood ran from the wound to mix with puddles of rain on the floor, while the other guards encircled him with their long, pointed spears.

Justus struggled painfully to his feet and stood staring wild-eyed, as the soldiers braced themselves, ready to plunge their spears into his body, and the silence was broken only by the rain and the flap of the guards' wet uniforms in the wind.

Suddenly Herod cried from the open door, "Damn it! I told you to *stone* him!" His shriek rose above the roar of the storm. "Must I do everything? Hand me a stone!" He held out his hand to the guard who'd accompanied him to the tower, and reaching into a leather bag, the man placed a jagged rock in his outstretched hand.

Herod slouched into the rain, his fat fingers closing around the stone's uneven edges; as he moved toward the soldiers who held Justus at bay with their spears, the guards separated to make a path into their circle.

Justus' eyes were like a cornered animal's, as he saw approaching death in the form of the cruel, fat, little man moving toward him. Herod's clothing sagged with water, his hair hung in strings over his forehead, and his beard sagged under the weight of the rain. His red lips spewed forth obscene curse words, and Justus crouched, bending his knees, while the Christ coin swayed in the wind. Then Herod hurled the stone, and Justus tried to dodge, but his foot slipped on the rain-slick floor. The heavy stone dug deep into his scalp, and he staggered as the blood ran into his eyes.

Justus blinked and shook his head; through a red mist of numbness, he saw Herod reach for another stone, then, as he stared at the cruel King, his body froze. It was as if he were standing off to the side, watching this thing happen to him; Herod became a blurred figure through the blood and rain. He felt a second crashing pain and then in a flash of lightning he saw the Tiger's face, reflecting a sadist's satisfaction, suddenly blur again. Justus' knees buckled; he fell headlong through a sea of blood face down on the cold stone floor.

He could hear voices above the roar of the wind and the surging rain, as he felt himself being lifted. There came a clap of thunder as he felt his body rise higher; then, the wind rushed past his ears as he fell, and he knew the end was only seconds away. He tried to brace himself for the impact; he tried to summon a scream from his dry throat. His body bounced off the side of the fortress wall, and as its ragged surface tore into him, his mind whispered, "Help me." His body whirled through the air, down toward the valley below; then with a sickening thud he landed, and all was darkness.

PART III

XXI

MARIAME paced the floor distraughtly, awaiting news from Nicolas. Her clothes were packed in two large leather bags, along with all her money and jewels, including the large pearl and diamond ring given her by Herod on her last birthday. She was eager to flee the palace and the King, but most of all she wanted to be with Justus, if he should escape execution. She thought of going to the Temple to pray, but she was afraid of missing the courier from the Chamberlain, who had told her to pack and wait for instructions.

When her slave, Ebana, ushered Umbla into her apartment, she asked at once, "Do you bring word of Justus?"

"No, my lady. My master, who is now at the Fortress Antonia with the King, has instructed me to conduct you from the palace."

"But what of Justus?"

"I know only that he must see the King."

Mariame directed Umbla to get the leather bags she had hid under her bed, and as he lifted them to his shoulders, Ebana returned with her own cloth bag of possessions.

Mariame said, "No, Ebana, you mustn't take this risk . . ."

The slave interrupted. "I shall go with you, mistress. I would be slain for certain anyway, for permitting your escape."

"Of course—how could I be so stupid," Mariame said. "It is better that you should come."

Umbla told the women he would place their bags in a wagon and that they would leave the palace as though setting out for

171

the Temple, then meet him on the north side of the market, where he would have a small two-wheeled covered wagon waiting.

Mariame and Ebana left the palace separately, and once outside the grounds, they hurried to the edge of the market where they found their escort perched on the driver's seat of the wagon, with its rear end hidden from the street. The women climbed into the wagon bed, then Umbla closed the canvas cover and clucked to the horse. The wagon rumbled over the cobbled streets of Jerusalem. When the noisy city was far behind them, Umbla stuck his head through the canvas curtain. A cold wind was blowing, and Mariame, hearing a clap of thunder, asked, "Why are you stopping, my friend?"

"My master told me not to tell you until we were out of the city, but I'm to take you to the Inn of the White Camel where rooms have been prepared for you."

"I see. And will Justus also come to the White Camel?"

"My master plans it so, my lady. I'm to return to the palace, after leaving you and Ebana at the inn. The King and my master will be at Antonia for Captain Justus' trial—and I beg you not to worry—my lord is the greatest man in the world. With his help you and Captain Justus will escape."

Umbla turned and started the horse once more, and though the thunder shook the wagon and rain beat hard on the canvas, the storm could not dispel Mariame's high-hearted hope of again being with her love. At the inn the travelers entered by a rear door, and Umbla led the women to an ornate apartment.

"These are the innkeeper's rooms," he told them. "My master says you will be safe here, but you must keep the doors and windows bolted and allow no one to enter except at my master's orders. Now I must return to the palace."

"Thank you, dear Umbla," Ebana said, "But do come back soon. I don't like this inn. It is a place of prostitutes, and I am afraid for my mistress when the city's whoremongers arrive tonight."

"There is no need to fear," Umbla said again, but a shiver passed through Mariame, and she quickly moved to bolt the door after the black man had passed through.

As the slow hours melted from the tall white and red-striped time candle, she went repeatedly over the chancellor's plans for Justus' escape.

Nicolas would contrive to have the King hold the trial at a time when the Tiger was not in a bad mood, in order that he might persuade the King merely to give his prisoner the lash, then banish him from the kingdom.

"My love will suffer," Mariame thought, "but he will live. And I shall give him so much love and care that he will soon forget the lash-cuts on his back."

Still, with each flickering of the candle's flare her steady concern increased. She refused to eat and grew irritated at Ebana's firm insistence that she do so. The cold rain beat against the shuttered windows, and even if she had dared to look outside, Mariame could not have discerned a horseman in the rain-dark, windy courtyard. Finally, as the time candle melted to a puddle of wax and winked out, she knew that too much time had passed. She tried to tell herself that Justus and Umbla were waiting till dark to travel, and when she voiced this hopeful, querulous surmise, Ebana answered quickly, "Oh, yes, that must be the reason they have not yet arrived. But they *will* come, my lady. We would have heard from the chamberlain otherwise."

Now a drunken Roman, staggering down the hall, shouted for a whore, pounded on the heavy cedar door, and bawled, "I know you're in there, Sarah. Let me in. I haven't got all night."

Then came the unctuous voice of the innkeeper. "No, no, brave warrior; Sarah is not in there. Those are my quarters—

and please, do not disturb my wife, for she is as mean as an asp. Come, sir, I have a new Egyptian girl, just arrived this morning, who was trained by the Temple priests in the subtle arts of the flesh. Come with me and learn from this fair sorceress how Cleopatra charmed Mark Antony."

The warrior cried, "So be it. Lead on, landlord."

Almost an hour passed, while Mariame and Ebana strove to reassure each other. Mariame was so tensed with anxiety that she did not hesitate when she finally heard a knock at the rear door. She slid the bolt and opened the heavy cedar door; then the black man stepped into the room, speaking quietly, "I warned you to be sure it was I at the door, my lady. I could have been anyone."

"Oh, no. Don't scold," Mariame cried. "Just tell me: is Justus with you?" Her hand flew to her mouth. "No. Oh, God, no. I can see it on your face. He is not with you . . . my love is . . . dead, isn't he? Umbla, tell me the truth."

She waited, spine stiffened, while Umbla related what Nicolas had told him about Justus' trial—of Herod's sudden rage on seeing the Christ coin—of the stoning, and Justus' body being hurled from the fortress wall. Finishing sadly the big slave said, "Alas, my lady, my master says Captain Justus is surely dead—no man's body could survive such punishment."

"Then, where is his body?" Mariame whispered. "I want to see for myself."

"Oh, no, my lady. The King has given orders that no one is to move it, on pain of a similar fate. Besides, he is certainly dead . . ."

Mariame cut in, crying, "*No!* I cannot believe it; you must take me to him, Umbla. I must know for myself."

"My lady, I cannot take you there. The King has already issued an order for your arrest—and my master has plans for you to flee to Antioch, where there are Jews who will hide you. Then, tomorrow morning, the King and the whole court, including your father and my master, will set out for Callirrhoe where the sick Tiger will take hot sulphur baths—thus my master wants you to flee tonight."

"To hell with your master—and Herod, too!" screamed Mariame. "I *will* see Justus decently buried. His body shall not be left to be devoured by vultures and jackals."

"But, mistress, the *King* . . ."

"*Take* me there, I said! I will leave for Antioch only after I myself have seen to Justus' burial, then I'll go anywhere— why not? There is nothing left now for me in Jerusalem."

Ebana said slowly, "Umbla, it is useless to argue with her, as you can see. We must do as she says."

The black man answered, "Very well. I will drive you to Jerusalem, but I will not help you search for Justus' body, for if I were discovered with Mariame, my master's life would be endangered."

✦

The rains had slackened as Umbla drove toward Jerusalem. When they were near the city, he drew to a halt and told Ebana, "Drive toward the northwest side of the Temple area. I know you are determined to go on, but I beg you—do not use a light or make a noise, lest you be heard by the guards patrolling the tower walls. Also, you will have to travel on foot from the place where you tie the horse. After you find the body, keep the wagon and travel on to Joppa. Many grain ships land there, and you can buy passage with reasonable safety. Please leave as soon as possible, and . . . do, for your own sake, be cautious."

Mariame thanked him; then, as Ebana gave the horse his head, Umbla disappeared in the darkness. About a mile from the sheer granite walls of Fortress Antonia they tied the animal to a small olive tree. Far off they could see pitch torches, lighting each end of the fortress ramparts, and as they walked closer, a lone sentry appeared like a silhouette on the great wall. The cold rain beat down as they struggled in slippery clay, and their clothes hung heavy about their legs, while they slipped and stumbled toward the fortress. Mud covered Mariame's slender legs; her leather sandals afforded little traction, and she felt chilled to the marrow. From time to time, she could see the guard atop the rampart as he neared a pitch torch. Each time he disappeared he stayed in the tower for a longer time; the rainy, pitch-black night hindered her, and she realized this was a blessing, for if she could not see the ground, the guard could not see her and Ebana, and the rain and wind would mask whatever noises they made.

They reached the wall below the place from which Umbla had said Justus was thrown, but they could not find his body. Mariame lost track of time as they tried to find him—first at random, then by searching in a criss-cross pattern.

"Alas, my lady, he is not here," Ebana said at last, holding Mariame's hand for support and balance against the slippery footing.

"He is—he must be. Nicolas would not lie. We will not stop if it takes all night," her mistress ordered. "Look sharp now. Keep your eyes open, girl."

Suddenly Mariame tripped over an object and fell forward, sprawled in the mud and clay; and as she sat up she realized she had tripped over a human leg.

On her hands and knees she crawled back, feeling about her.

"Ebana, I think I have found him . . . yes," she almost cried as she felt the muscular leg. "Oh, Justus, my own darling, what have they done to you? Oh, merciful God, why?"

Ebana knelt, and they felt the cold body, straining to see through the darkness.

"Shall we move him?" Ebana asked.

"In a moment," Mariame groaned. "Let me have one moment . . . Oh, Justus, I loved you, more than I ever told you.

176

Forgive me, darling . . ." Her hands found the beloved face, and she kissed the cold lips; then with her face near to Justus', she heard a low moan and tensely whispered, "Ebana, *he is alive*. Here. Feel his heart. He is breathing."

Ebana whispered back, "Yes, yes, my lady. It is true."

They tried to lift the man's great body; then strove to get their arms under his shoulders, but the mud, rain, and blood made him too slippery to hold. Finally in desperation Mariame removed her outer garments; they tied the robe and cloak around and under Justus' arms, then tied knots which they could hold at either end.

As the rain stung her half-naked body, Mariame said through chattering teeth, "Now we can drag him."

When at last they reached the wagon, they had even more difficulty hauling the heavy man into the wagon bed. After they had finally gotten him in, the slave fetched towels from Mariame's traveling bag, and after drying herself and Justus, Mariame lay down, covering them with all her clothes and the towels.

When they had traveled some leagues, Ebana asked over her shoulder, "Where shall we go, my lady?"

"To a physician, of course."

"But . . . which one? We know only the palace physicians."

Mariame thought for a moment. The slave was right; and panic seized her as she asked, "Think, Ebana. Have you never heard of any others?"

Ebana was silent. Then she said, "Yes, I have heard the soldiers speak of one named Ben Bag Bag—but they say he is a frightening, malformed monster."

"What does that matter, if he can be trusted. Can he?"

"Well, I have heard he secretly performed an abortion on the wife of Herod's cousin Saturnia, who was pregnant by her black slave, and she survived."

"Where can this man be found?"

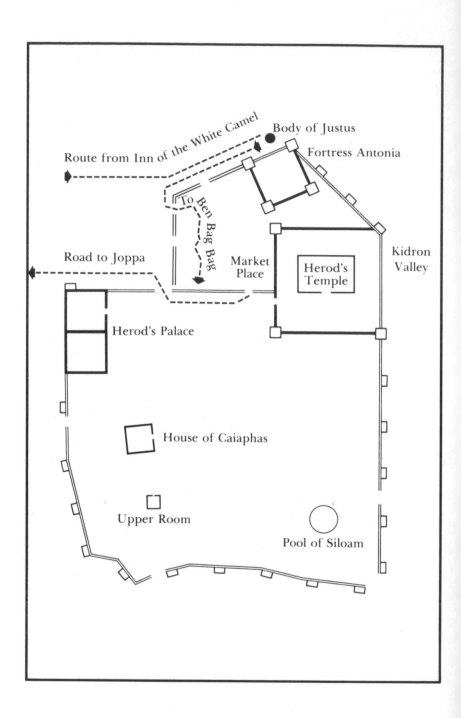

Route from Inn of the White Camel

Body of Justus

Fortress Antonia

To Ben Bag Bag

Road to Joppa

Market Place

Herod's Temple

Kidron Valley

Herod's Palace

House of Caiaphas

Upper Room

Pool of Siloam

"I have heard his office is near the Dung Gate."

"Then, turn us in that direction — and make haste."

It was near dawn when Ebana led Ben Bag Bag to the wagon. The big man carried Justus into his examination room, and Mariame followed, clutching her wet clothes about her.

The women gasped as they saw the mangled body in the light of a torch. "Oh, God, it is hopeless," Mariame cried. She rushed to the table, and her loose clothes fell to the stone floor as she kissed Justus' torn face.

The grotesque physician felt for a pulse, his eyes on Mariame's breasts. "Let me see what I can do," he growled. Mariame looked up at the large man, then instinctively gathered the robe about her body.

Ben Bag Bag said, "He is somehow still alive. Go in the next room, rid yourselves of that blood and grime, and leave me alone with him."

XXII

The giant man, who Mariame had retained for an exorbitant fee, was in every way as extraordinary as his mammoth appearance might lead one to expect. His skill as a physician was outsized, too. He was, perhaps, the only physician in Judea who could even come near dealing with the mass of wounded flesh and broken bones that now passed for the Roman stalwart, who had recently served as head of King Herod's corps of bodyguards.

Ben Bag Bag was aptly named. The physician's huge body gave his robe the appearance of an overstuffed feed bag, and he moved with a slow, lumbering walk. No one — not even he — knew his actual age, and few of his patients would have guessed that he was years younger than he looked.

Ben Bag Bag's weight was enormous. From his earliest memory he had realized that he was much taller than other children. As he grew older he continued to grow in height,

179

but when he reached puberty his body seemed to explode with huge layers of fat that covered his muscles. He became self-conscious of his difference from other boys and withdrew into his shell of softness, relinquishing any chance for a normal life, for once he admitted to himself that his outsized body was abnormal, his mind and personality became abnormal, too.

His father had been a butcher, and because of his size the boy was drafted to help kill and dress the animals for market. The butcher marveled at his son's skill with a knife, his quickness in learning the tricks of dividing an animal in such a way as to lay out the greatest number of salable cuts. Thus Ben Bag Bag soon knew the location of all the parts of a body, and with his father's help he learned the purpose and function of every vital organ. He began to wonder if the human body was like that of a sheep, a goat, or a cow, and as his curiosity grew, he became possessed of a consuming desire to learn as much as he could about human anatomy. At first he did not consider becoming a physician; nevertheless, he performed crude experiments on small animals to learn as much as he could about the function of living things and how to repair live flesh.

By the time he was 17 he had opened the belly of a sheep, and, after examining it, had sewed it back up without killing the animal. The sight of the blood had had no effect on Ben Bag Bag, nor was he moved by the animals' tortured outcries.

Because of his great size he was called, at 18, to serve in the army of Herod the Great, who was concerned about a Zealot's uprising in Samaria. After two weeks of training, the officers in charge realized that Ben Bag Bag was so clumsy he would be a danger to himself and to other soldiers in the battleline. He was assigned to the army physician who had seen the ease with which he had carried a fellow soldier in an exercise, and the physician asked that Ben Bag Bag be assigned to him so that the man could carry the wounded and help hold down those men who needed limb amputations.

By the time the young giant was 25 he had absorbed all this physician's knowledge of medicine and anatomy. While he continued to grow in size, becoming extremely clumsy in movement, his ability with a surgeon's knife had grown as well. His skill in operations and amputations was simply astonishing, and after the death of his superior, he became chief army physician.

Ben Bag Bag liked his work and was always pleased to learn that a battle would take place, thus offering him an array of new cases upon which to test his skills. He cared no more for those unfortunate men brought to him for repair than for the sheep he had dissected in his father's butcher shop, and he would have made the army his life's work except for one slight mistake.

In attempting to save the life of a Roman general, Decius Ariaman, who had been seriously wounded in a skirmish with some Bedouin warriors near the Syrian border, he had failed to heed the general's threats and pleas. A lance which had shattered the bone of the right wrist had also lodged in the general's chest, and by the time the mortally wounded man had been brought to Ben Bag Bag, there was little doubt as to the seriousness of his condition. An ordinary soldier would have been left to die on the battlefield, but because Ariaman was a general, his lieutenants thought they should try to save his life, reasoning that some day they, too, as officers, might lie wounded and be at the mercy of lesser men than themselves.

In a lucid moment General Ariaman had ordered Ben Bag Bag not to take away his hand, realizing that his life as a soldier would be ended without that hand. He actually threatened to kill the physician if he should cut off the hand, and, unfortunately for Ben Bag Bag, the general neither died nor forgot his threat. The physician performed a near-miracle as he closed the chest wound, but in order to save the general's life he had removed the hand. He had never been so skillful as while cutting the useless hand from the strong body, and he even congratulated himself on his excellent work, believing that when the patient recovered, he would be richly rewarded for having saved the general's life.

He was in for a surprise when General Ariaman summoned him to his tent one night and asked coolly, "Didn't I tell you I'd kill you if you cut off my hand?" He held up the stub, bound in white linen bandages, and Ben Bag Bag answered, "Yes," thinking the general was joking.

"You know that I keep my word?"

Ben Bag Bag nodded.

"Well?"

"I had no choice, General. You would have died."

"But look what you've done to me! I am dead now," the general shouted, thrusting the stub at Ben Bag Bag.

"But, sir, poisoning had set in. I had no choice — I had to amputate."

"You had no choice, no! Only a direct and simple order from your general. Yet, in spite of that order you proceeded toward an end which you, personally, sought. Well, I intend to punish you as you have punished me."

Ben Bag Bag stirred. He could see that the general was deadly serious.

"But I saved your life," he said in a low, unbelieving voice. "I saved your *life*, General!"

"You destroyed it, and I told you I would kill you if you amputated my hand. But I shall not give you the pleasure of a quick death. Instead I shall prove to you that a man's life *can* be destroyed by cutting off his hand. A warrior without his sword hand is a dead warrior. A physician without his knife hand is a dead physician. You will remember that General Ariaman is a man of his word!" The general motioned for his guards to seize the monster of a man, and four of them sprang upon him.

Ben Bag Bag screamed all the vile names he knew at the soldiers as he fought a losing struggle; then his hand and arm were placed on a wooden block, and General Ariaman, without much accuracy, plunged his blade into the upturned palm. A searing white flash streaked across the giant's mind as pain enveloped him; then in the seconds before he lost consciousness, he wondered if the sheep had suffered as much pain when he'd operated on them, and now he realized how much agony his amputees had experienced.

General Ariaman called for Ben Bag Bag's assistant, and screamed as the guards hauled the limp hulk from the tent toward the physician's tent, "Now, damn you, you'll see what it feels like to live and feel dead inside. You will never work as a physician again."

But the general had reckoned without Ben Bag Bag's assistant, who had learned his lessons well from a great master. This man removed the physician's hand at the wrist, and, though the amputation was not as technically perfect as Ben Bag Bag's removal of General Ariaman's hand, it was still a most successful operation.

Ben Bag Bag swore he would some day kill Ariaman, but he secretly knew that his oath could never be carried out. After a year of wandering almost as a beggar, he found a patient — a wealthy farmer who had been thrown by a horse. He set the farmer's broken leg and cared for him with such skill that the injured man felt constrained to reward him richly; and so Ben Bag Bag reentered the world of medicine.

The grateful farmer had given him money enough to go to Jerusalem, so he set up an office there in a small rented house. But at the start of his practice, even the most diseased and crippled creatures looked upon this one-handed behemoth of a man with jaundiced eye, so Ben Bag Bag did not press for payment of his fees until his practice and reputation had begun to grow. Gradually his patients had learned that his true ability had nothing at all to do with his appearance.

Later he spent a small fortune on a set of surgical tools constructed on leather sheaths that could be fitted, glove-like, to the stub of his right arm. In all he had seven different knives and one set of clamps made into sheaths; after a difficult period of adjustment, he regained sufficient use of his right arm to become an outstanding surgeon. He was happy in his work — and he had made a liar out of General Ariaman.

XXIII

"Will he live?" Mariame asked.

Ben Bag Bag stared at the mummy of a man who lay on the hard bed. "Do you want the truth?"

"Yes."

"Who knows what is the truth?" The man heaved a sigh that shook his monstrous jowls. "All I can do is give you my opinion based upon experience. I call myself a physician. I suppose I have treated as many sick people as anyone in this country, but it has always been on a trial-and-error basis. Some of those whom I thought would die, lived; some whom I thought would live, suddenly died. Why, I didn't know. I never will."

"But will he live?" Mariame's eyes pleaded for an answer.

"I have done what I can — what I think is right — but I must be honest with you: I have never seen any patient in such a condition."

"Then, you think he'll die?"

The fat man shrugged. "Young woman, what I am trying to say is, I honestly don't know. If I say he will live, it will do nothing except make you feel better for the present. I tell you that I can only guess as to his recovery. I have done all that I know how to do. Why is it that people always ask the same question: 'Will this patient recover?' How many years have

I sought a sufficient answer to that question, which I have never found. No! I will not try to predict what the final results will be in this man's case, for if I were to say I thought he would live, and he died, I would be faced with the unanswerable questions, 'Why? What did you do wrong?' . . . . And those are questions I could not answer any more than I could answer if I were asked 'Why did he live?'"

Mariame spoke quietly. "Are you afraid to tell me the truth, physician?"

"You wouldn't listen. You haven't been listening. All you want me to say is, 'Yes he will live,' and this I cannot do. Place as much trust in me as you can — and leave the rest to God."

"Then you refuse to answer me directly?"

Ben Bag Bag looked at her and shook his head in disbelief that this young person could be so persistent in demanding an answer he did not want to give. He said, "I shall remain, for the present, silent. Perhaps in a few days I can give you an answer, but for now I shall be as silent as a tomb, and my silence is not to be interpreted by you as any opinion whatsoever concerning this man's recovery. You understand?"

Mariame nodded, looking wanly at the mummy on the bed.

"Very well. Now, I want you to keep these bandages tight. I don't think he'll stir or try to loosen them, but if the drugs wear off, who knows? His pain without drugs would be unbearable, therefore, you must give him a small amount of this amber liquid every hour."

Mariame stared at the vial.

"What is it?"

Ben Bag Bag sighed. "What do you care? Just follow my instructions. Should he begin to scream, give him a little extra of this. If the drug continues to work, he will appear to be in a deep sleep. But he may even talk and laugh — and if he laughs, you can be sure the drug is working."

"How long must this routine continue?"

185

"Until he is either dead or alive. He is neither at present. Now, the oil in this jar must be heated slightly—not enough to burn the skin—before it's applied to the bandages on his head, legs, and arms. Heat some flat stones to the same temperature and gently apply them to his lower back. But I caution you: be gentle; do not move his body at all, if you can possibly help it. Do you understand all this?"

Mariame nodded and Ben Bag Bag looked at her slave who also nodded.

"I will be back tomorrow. In the meantime you might arrange to have an offering made at the Temple. He will need it—and you will, too." The big man smiled and picked up his large leather bag. "Remember now, no more questions. I will do my best to save him, but don't annoy me with foolish womanly curiosity."

Mariame watched as her slave, Ebana, let Ben Bag Bag out the door; then she turned again to examine Justus' bandages.

As he left the house where he had ministered to Justus, Ben Bag Bag glanced sidelong at Mariame, wondering what kind of woman she was. He knew that she must be of noble birth or rich, because of the way she spoke and gave orders to her slave. But there were many things he wanted to know about her, for Ben Bag Bag wished to see more of this beautiful young woman. *"Well, love and sorrow are closely akin,"* he thought. *"Perhaps she will need the comfort of a strong and healthy man when this patient dies."*

XXIV

Mariame watched the small cloth absorb the strange, sweet-smelling mixture of herbs that Ben Bag Bag had mixed with olive oil. She wondered how long it had been. Her hands were stained with the purple-brown medication she had been applying with utmost care and regularity to his mummy-like bandages. Her body, just short of exhaustion, seemed to sense the lateness, and she moved as in a dream. *'How long can this nightmare continue,'* she thought. *'Why can't he respond . . . why doesn't he speak?'*

She applied the purplish cloth to Justus' forehead . . . then suddenly the feel of heavy fingers on her shoulder caused her to start. She almost screamed as she turned and looked into the bloodshot eyes of Ben Bag Bag.

"You frightened me," she told him, rising from the chair by the bed. She could smell the stale odor of wine, and as Ben Bag Bag took a step toward Justus' bed, she noticed that his always clumsy walk seemed even more awkward than usual. She took a quick step toward the giant, afraid that he might stumble and fall upon Justus; then fear took over as the monster found his balance and halted near the bed. The massive body, magnified by the blood-red robe that loosely encased it, wove in a slow arc as Ben Bag Bag strove to focus his eyes on his unconscious patient. Mariame's gaze shifted to the grotesque leather sheath that had replaced the missing hand, and she stood motionless, sweating, afraid to speak.

The giant wiped his wine-wet beard with his stub. "How is my purple mummy?"

Mariame stepped quickly back toward the table, placed another wick in the open oil lamp, and lighted it, unable to summon words.

"Answer me," Ben Bag Bag shouted as the light of the lamp doubled. "I *said*, how is he?"

"I . . . can see no change."

"Well, I can. He looks purple to me." The monster staggered, shaking his head to clear it. "A purple patient! I am the only physician in all Judea with a purple patient. Have you done everything I told you to?"

187

"Yes."

"What about the drugs?"

"I have given them as you instructed."

"A purple patient," Ben Bag Bag mumbled again as he half fell into the chair by the bed, its rough goatskin seat creaking under his weight. "Do you have any wine in this house?"

"No," Mariame lied as she edged toward the table near the wall behind her.

The man's eyes narrowed. "Don't lie to me, woman. I want wine!"

"There is none," Mariame said. She retreated until she felt the edge of the table touch her buttocks, almost bawling, "My slave has gone out; she will bring some shortly."

"When will she be back?" The reddened eyes slowly surveyed the room and came to rest upon her, appraising her body.

Mariame's right hand searched the table top behind her until at last she felt the cool metal of the kitchen knife that lay between the supper plates; then with her eyes fixed on the drunken giant she gripped the knife's wooden handle and felt, for the first time since this monster had entered the house, some degree of safety.

"I know there is wine here," the man said. "Don't save it for the purple patient — it will be vinegar before he's able to enjoy it. My purple one would want you to give me his share."

Fear rose again within Mariame — not for herself, now that she had the knife, but for her helpless Justus.

The stub of the giant's right arm again made a slow swipe at his lips as his eyes moved from her eyes to her feet, then back to her eyes. She could read his thoughts as he mentally disrobed her, and she felt naked beneath his lustful gaze.

She knew that Ben Bag Bag's knowledge and skill were the only things that were keeping Justus alive, and that she would have to keep him appeased, for she was afraid to seek out another physician who might go to Herod. She could tell from his silent leer that Ben Bag Bag also knew of her dependence upon him, and she felt trapped, even with the knife in her hand, so she eased it back onto the table. If she stabbed Ben Bag Bag, she would, in effect, be driving the knife into Justus' own heart, so she must not even offend him in any way, much less attack him.

"Why does your medication stain his skin that peculiar shade of purple?" she asked, and the red-rimmed eyes unconsciously darted to the bandaged patient.

Ben Bag Bag laughed softly. "What do you want—a live lover whose body will be purple a few weeks, or a clean, dead lover? The color comes from Egyptian herbs that aid in healing and prevent corruption. If he developed pus in those wounds it would be fatal—just as it would have been for you, if you'd tried to stab me with that knife a moment ago. Tell me, why did you drop the knife?"

Mariame raised her head. "Because I realized I would not need it."

He smiled at her, showing his big, irregularly-spaced teeth for the first time.

"You realize, of course, that my fee is high. How long do you think you can afford me?"

"Until he is well."

"And what if I told you I'm going to double my fees? How would you pay me then?"

Mariame knew what he was up to now, and she answered, "I'll get the money," thinking, *'how long will it be before he offers to exchange his skill for my body?'* She felt ashamed that this repulsive monster could even think she would pay the price he was demanding with this searching stare. If she still had the palace guards near, no one except Herod himself would dare suggest such a proposal . . . but that was before. Now she had fled the palace and had only her wits for protection. She was alone, without friends in Jerusalem, and she was facing the very thing that she'd sought to escape when she had quarreled with her father; only this time the threat was immediate and serious. She did not know if she would be able to evade the wine-sodden animal standing before her, so she said, "Please . . . be patient. My slave Ebana will return shortly with some wine."

Ben Bag Bag brushed that aside. "Answer me!" he shouted. "What would you do if I *tripled* my fee?"

"What could I do . . . except pay you?"

"Come here," he said and opened his hairy arms. "I will show you how your problem can be easily solved."

Mariame recoiled, shaking her head as she backed away. "No, please. You are drunk now. Leave me alone . . . please."

"Do you want your lover to die?"

Again she raised her head. "If his life ends . . . I shall end mine."

"Ho, you don't mean that. I know women. Look at it this way: I have kept him alive all of this time; if it hadn't been for my treatment, he'd be dead. I have given him my best, and now you shall return the favor to me. He would never know . . . look at him. He has a chance for recovery, so don't throw it away."

She said, "I couldn't. I love no one but him. And besides, I could never be unfaithful to him."

"But he would not know."

"No—but *I* would."

"Well, now is the time for you to decide," Ben Bag Bag said again.

"Leave me alone," she said, and burst into tears. "I can't . . . you must see that."

The giant looked at her. "Woman, I can walk out that door and never return, and if I do, he will die. Well . . . he is already prepared for the grave. You could give him an Egyptian burial. You could fill his veins with embalming fluid, and he'd be a perfect mummy."

"Oh, no!" she screamed. "Stop it! Stop it!"

190

The scream seemed to calm Ben Bag Bag momentarily, as though she had reached behind the screen of alcohol to his brain. Then all at once the door flew open, and Ebana stepped into the room, a long dagger shining in her slender ebony hand. She was ready to spring on Ben Bag Bag. She did not know Mariame's reason for screaming, but the fact that her mistress appeared to be in danger from this creature was reason enough for unsheathing the knife.

Ben Bag Bag took a step backward as he saw the glint of the steel blade, for though he was three times the size of this young woman, he guessed from the scar on her right cheek that she had fought with knives before.

"Wait," he said as Ebana took a step toward him. "Wait. It's all a mistake."

"Yes, Ebana, wait!" Mariame cried. "He meant no harm. It was simply a misunderstanding. Ben Bag Bag, please. I want you to return tomorrow — sober — will you?"

Puzzled by the change in her, the giant nodded. Then as she smiled at him, he smiled back like a child. "Yes," he said, "I will return tomorrow."

Mariame smiled and spoke calmly. "Ebana, open the door for this great physician. He is always welcome here."

XXV

The man, encased like a mummy, opened his eyes. His pupils contracted to the dancing light in the open oil lamps, and he tried to turn his head, but the tight binding at his neck and head prevented that. He started to speak, then hesitated as he tried to raise his right hand to tear away the head binding, but again he was hampered by a sheath of linen that held his arms rigid against his body.

"What has happened?" he thought. *"Where am I? Why am I trussed up like this?"*

He tried to move his left arm, but that too was firmly fixed in place, and panic flooded his brain as his eyes moved to his chest. In the lamp light he could see that his body was wound in purple-stained linen, and he thought, *"I am bound for burial, but how can that be? It can't—unless someone who thought me dead has prepared me for the tomb."*

Again his eyes searched the small room in which he lay alone and silent, and a sickening feeling assailed him, leaving him helpless and weak. He tried to calm himself, but he could only think, *"What has happened? How did I get here?"* Sweat stood out on his forehead as he tried once more to move his arms; then pain shot through his whole body as he succeeded in moving the right arm a mere fraction of an inch. His eyes rolled toward the ceiling, where in the flickering light of the small lamp the rough-hewn cedar beams seemed to bend and weave. He could now smell a sweetish odor that half-blotted out the putrid smell of stale sweat, and he let out, in a loud sigh, all the air in his chest. He wanted to scream, but he only began to pant in quick, short spasms; then, unconsciousness blackened his mind, and once again he became unaware of himself.

He had no idea how long he had been awake. He couldn't remember opening his eyes, yet the ceiling seemed to be slowly coming into focus. Sunlight streamed through the small window above the bed, and the long narrow shaft of light, in the shape of a perfect rectangle, was clearly defined by the haze of smoke from a flickering lamp. This time he didn't try to shift, knowing that any movement would set off a series of sharp pains. As his mind cleared, he wondered again where he was, and if he had wakened first a night or a week ago.

He shut his eyes to think, but his mind seemed blank; then a door's iron hinges gave off a cry of age, and he heard soft footsteps on the hard stone floor. He kept his eyes closed, reasoning that these footsteps could belong to an enemy, and his heart beat loud in his ear. He wanted to hold his breath, but he knew that it would be futile to try, so he breathed in soft, quick breaths instead, while the footsteps came closer, deliberately nearing the bed. He knew that this unseen someone was looking at him, and, feigning sleep, he heard breathing and knew the person was coming close to stare into his face. Then a hand reached for his head and a quiver of fear ran through him, until a cool hand touched his cheek. It was soft, and he thought as the hand stroked his head, *"Who can this be?"*

"Justus," a soft voice whispered. "Oh, Justus, my dear one . . ."

The cool hand left his face; he could hear the soft weeping of a woman; then the hand, wet with tears, returned to his face, and he knew that he could open his eyes at last.

She was not looking at him as he opened his eyes, but as the sunlight poured through the window, bathing her face in brilliance, he saw . . . *Mariame!* Then she slowly turned her face, and seeing him conscious, dropped the jar of medicine she had been holding. She stood transfixed, scarcely believing what she saw, then kneeling beside the bed she whispered, "Justus, Justus, oh, Justus, at last. . . . Thank God!"

He could not hold back the tears that flooded his eyes. His vision was blurred, and he blinked his eyes to clear them. "Mariame," he whispered, seeing the purple-stained hands and the face that looked years older, as she stooped to kiss his lips.

XXVI

Justus closed his eyes, reliving his punishment. He could see the rain-soaked Tiger with the stone in his upraised hand and almost feel himself being lifted again and thrown over the high wall. His body tensed and twisted; he screamed aloud, and

Mariame sat stunned as he let out a cry of pain that shook the dishes on the table next to the bed. She stood up and bent over him, pleading, "Don't Justus, don't! You are safe. I'm here. You're safe!"

His eyes opened, and he looked at her, thinking, "I am safe; we are alone, and Herod is gone." Fear drained from him as cold sweat soaked his bandages, and he smiled into Mariame's face. That lovely face looked tired, changed, but the hand brushing his forehead was soft, soft, and oh, so gentle . . . .

"Justus, you are safe," she whispered in a motherly tone, "and we are both free now."

"How can I be free when I am like this?" he asked giving his head a slight nod toward his feet. "I'm a mummy. I can't move. Were most of my bones broken?"

"Some of them, yes, but you will heal in time."

"Yes, but when? I don't even know how long I've been here —or where I am. How did I get here?"

Mariame hesitated and then decided this would be as good a time as any; she proceeded to tell him of her journey to the Inn of the White Camel and her search for his body. "It is a wonder that you survived our rough handling—we even dropped you when we attempted to place you in the wagon," she said diverting her eyes from him. "Thank God, you were unconscious of pain."

"You make it sound as if your treatment was worse than the Tiger's," he said half smiling. "I didn't feel a thing. The last I recall is Herod throwing a stone at me and his men lifting my body . . ."

"Don't, Justus—please, don't," she said, wanting to ease the terror that flashed across his face. "Then, we brought you to the physician."

"What physician?"

"His name was Ben Bag Bag."

"Where is he now?"

"Gone."

"Will he return?"

"It is a long story . . . we will manage. He told me what to do before he left."

"But where am I?"

"We are in Jerusalem. After the physician treated you, I rented this house. Though it's in the slums, I thought it would be safe."

"How long has it been since Herod . . ."

"Three months."

"*Three* months?"

"Yes—three months."

"Three *months*," he whispered. "How can that be possible?"

"You haven't been unconscious all of that time," she said, stroking his brow. "In fact, you've had quite a few good days. We have talked of this before. You have had nightmares and fits of rage since we ran out of drugs, but you *are* getting better."

Justus lay silent. He could not recall anything since the stoning, yet she had talked to him since then. Had his mind been damaged? Was he insane or was all this a cruel dream?

He said aloud, "If I am getting better, why am I bound in this tight cocoon? I can't move an inch."

"Because your bones were broken. Ben Bag Bag named them all—in the legs and arms and back. He said when you landed you must have hit in an almost sitting position and that's why your legs were so twisted; also, because your backside hit the ground, your vertebrae were pushed together. He had to straighten your legs and arms again, and that's why he used the mummy wrappings. He said it was a trick he'd learned in Egypt."

"When is this Ben Bag Bag going to remove the wrappings?"

"He isn't."

"What? I have to live like this? I'd rather be dead!"

"No . . . it's just that, Ben Bag Bag won't be coming back."

195

"Why?"

"It's a long story. I'll tell you some day. Can I get you some broth now?"

"I'd rather have wine."

"Food or broth would be better for you."

"Not the way I feel. Can you imagine what a shock this is to me—how it feels to wake up from death? I thought my life was finished when that bastard Herod stoned me; now I find I'm only half dead. I am prepared for the grave, yet I still breathe—still feel pain. What does a man have to go through? Only drink can answer the questions running through my mind now. Give me the wine, please."

"No!" Mariame said. "I have seen you drugged most of these three months. Now is the time for you to face the truth. There is no turning back for you or me, for when you went over that wall a part of me went with you. I could not turn my back on you then; and you must not turn your back on me now. We will live with this thing together. You're not going to escape into wine if I can help it."

"But the *pain*, Mariame."

"I have suffered pain, too—and my pain will continue as long as yours continues. Together, the two of us will purge ourselves of pain and of the past—without living in drunkenness."

"Please, Mariame."

"No!"

"The physician would give it to me," he said firmly. "I have seen many badly wounded men—and the physician always keeps them half drunk."

"You no longer have a physician," Mariame answered. "I am your physician now, and you'll have to follow my orders."

"But where is this Ben Bag Bag?"

"Dead."

"Dead? . . ."

"Yes. It's a long story. I'll tell you some other time."

"No. I want to know now."

"Did you ever know Ben Bag Bag?"

"No . . ."

"Well, he was a horrible man—a huge, bloated giant with his right hand cut off at the wrist. But he was the only physician I could find to care for you. At first I was thankful for him; then I became afraid he would let you die. I could tell by the way he looked at you."

"But he treated me, you say."

"Yes. But as time went on he wanted to let you die, and I couldn't let that happen. Then . . . he started wanting me, and you can't imagine the disgust I felt, knowing he did. It was almost as bad as Herod—though nothing could be that bad!"

"All right, what happened?"

"Well, first he said he was going to triple his fees. I gave him everything we had; then, when the money was gone, he suggested I become his mistress. He said that if I didn't he'd let you die." Mariame paused, looking away from the face on the pillow. "I became convinced he would poison you, and I couldn't let him."

Resentment swelled now in Justus' breast. He said, "Then, you agreed . . . how else could I be alive?"

She turned to face him. "No! How could I? I said that he was almost as horrible as Herod."

"Yes? And then what happened?"

"I . . . got rid of him."

"How?"

"I sent him to Nicolas. Jerusalem was all alive with rumors that Herod was on his deathbed, that his soldiers had captured the Temple priests, and that all the principal men of the country were being kept under guard in the hippodrome in Jericho. The Tiger ordered his guards to slay the influential Jews upon his death so that the country would mourn when he died; then the rich families took up a great collection for the physician

197

who could cure Herod, because it was the only way their loved ones could escape death."

"Yes, yes. And?"

"Well, I told Ben Bag Bag I knew Nicolas and could get him into the palace. I also told him that if he could save the King's life, he'd become the richest man in the country."

"So he went?"

"Yes, he knew the risks—the odds that Herod might die anyway, but Ben Bag Bag wanted to pit his skills against those of the court physicians . . . and, of course if he succeeded, he would have riches, power, and Herod's respect as well. Anyway, the idea intrigued him."

Justus grimaced. "I can see how it would. Go on."

"Well . . . I sent Ebana to Jericho with Ben Bag Bag. Nicolas, she said, was surprised to hear what had happened to you and me, and he regretted that he couldn't help us because since he'd befriended you, his life was still in danger. He even sent word for us to change our names and flee the country."

"So . . . what about Ben Bag Bag?"

"Nicolas let him attend Herod, and of course the other physicians were furious and jealous, but the monster seemed to help Herod. Then, just as he seemed to be recovering, Herod took a turn for the worse and on his deathbed denounced Ben Bag Bag as a spy of the Zealots. Once again he ordered the prominent Jews still being held in the hippodrome to be slain —and died that very night."

"So. The Tiger is gone at last. Did the guards kill the priests and the others?"

"No. Herod's sister Salome changed her brother's orders and had them freed." Mariame hesitated. "But she was too late for Ben Bag Bag. He died at the King's bedside. Herod's son Archelaus stabbed him in the back."

Mariame finished speaking, and Justus was silent for a long

198

moment, then he said in a whisper, "Oh, Mariame, my love, forgive me for doubting you, ever."

She dropped to her knees by the bed and with her soft fingers, wiped the tears from his cheeks. "It's nothing," she sighed. "Only get well, my beloved, that's all I ask now."

XXVII

Gradually Justus learned to accept the facts of his future existence. As months replaced months, becoming years, he realized that he would never again be an active military man — indeed that he must live the life of a cripple — and this knowledge caused him more acute mental suffering than the physical pain which stabbed at his body.

Ben Bag Bag's medicine had prevented infections of his open wounds; Justus marveled at his late physician's obvious skills. He had often seen wounded soldiers die of infections and fever, yet through Ben Bag Bag's unconventional treatment, he, who had been more severely injured than any man he'd ever known, had escaped these hazards and survived.

Furthermore, Ben Bag Bag had even solved for him the problem of bed sores — by constructing a pallet of sheep skins. The physician cut the wool to a quarter inch in height so that the fleece supporting his patient's body allowed for circulation and prevented the blood's becoming stagnant in those parts of the body touching the bed's surface.

The physician also claimed the sheep's skin contained a healing oil to keep the skin soft, and Justus told Mariame one night, "It must be true, because I haven't felt any sores under the wrappings."

He would never forget the day his bandages were removed. The pain was severe; the operation took twelve agonizing hours. Mariame had not wanted to remove the bandages, but Justus had argued so long and loud she'd finally given in. Without

Ben Bag Bag's advice, she had no idea as to the proper time for this ritual, but Justus had argued that broken bones usually knit within a few weeks' time, and since he'd been bound for months, it would do no further good to keep him swathed from head to foot.

So Mariame and Ebana, working as a team, slowly cut and stripped away the purple linens. Despite the excruciating pain, Justus marvelled that the handicapped giant could have bound him with such uncanny skill.

When at last he lay amid a pile of scraps and pieces of soiled linen, he looked upon his naked self for the first time since his punishment. His skin was a dark purple, yet it was soft and smooth. Here and there across his body he saw the long pink scars from once open wounds, but all had healed smoothly except for one jagged chest scar, edged with small patches of proud white flesh.

His eyes came to rest on the gold coin, that still lay on his chest, its shining surface untarnished by Ben Bag Bag's strange purple medicine. Slowly, painfully moving his hand, he grasped the coin in his fist.

He longed to destroy this emblem of all his sufferings, but though he squeezed the pendant until it all but cut his skin, he could not muster the strength to break the slender chain that held the coin. Resentment against this object which had caused him to be stoned raged within him, yet try as he would, he could not bring himself to remove the pendant. So he swore to wear it until he was well—as a constant, bitter reminder of that inexplicable act of folly in the desert which had brought him to this pass.

When he examined his legs, he screamed aloud—not because of the pain of running his hands over them, but because of their grotesquely twisted shape. Knowing that he was paralyzed from his waist down, he wanted to die.

In spite of all that Mariame or Ebana could do or say, he

cursed his fate and cried until he slept in sheer exhaustion and bleak despair.

XXVIII

A year dragged by; each day was a burden scarcely to be borne. He brooded, ate, and slept without meaning or purpose, adrift on a sea of pain.

If he had tried once to walk, he had tried a thousand times—each effort ending in miserable, painful failure. It puzzled him that his legs, which he could never move, contained such execrable pain. Even his toes would never respond to his sweating efforts; finding he could not balance himself, he cursed and shattered his crutches on the stone hearth of the fireplace.

Finally, seeing that his twisted legs had started to atrophy, he cursed his rotten luck. Wishing Ben Bag Bag had let him die, he would shout at Mariame, "This is not living . . . I'm a vegetable! Look at me! I can't walk. Look at this useless body—a mound of pain."

Mariame had learned to live with his complaints, but one afternoon she too all but gave in to despair. Justus fell from the chair to the cold floor and shouted, "Damn you, why don't you kill me? I am useless . . . free yourself . . . free me." He sobbed and banged his head on the stone floor.

Mariame looked at him, not daring to move. She knew that any attempt to help or comfort him in these fits of despair would only increase the resentment against his condition. She looked down at his half-finished plate, realizing the meal she'd so carefully cooked—because it was his favorite—would be sadly wasted. Tears filled her eyes as she replaced the meat on her plate and straightened the cup that had tipped over as Justus hurled himself to the floor.

While he continued to curse his body and his condition, she

remembered how, as a child, she had sometimes deliberately hurt herself to make her father suffer. She had tried to retreat into a world of pain, knowing her pain would cause him pain that would in turn bring sympathy for her. The victory she had gained had been sweet, and she wondered now if Justus' success in causing her pain eased his own exquisite anguish.

When he had first realized he was crippled for life, he encased himself in a shell of despair. His mind refused to accept the obvious, but the ever-present suffering constantly reminded him of his fearful injuries.

His despair and shame increased as Mariame helped him perform the necessary body functions. The strong military man of his youth was being destroyed. His former arrogant independence gave way to an ignominious, complete dependence on a woman.

"Justus," she finally said, "you must recognize and accept our situation . . ."

He cut in, shouting, "Damn you, do you think I don't know?"

She answered softly, "Yes, I think you do. But what good will it do either of us for you to go on brooding about your injuries."

"What do you expect me to do?" he cried.

She rubbed her hands together as though trying to remove the last pore-deep vestige of purple stain from Ben Bag Bag's medicine. "You can stop feeling sorry for yourself."

Justus turned his face to the wall, but she went on severely, "Don't turn your back on me. I'm asking you to face facts. You're not a child."

"No, I am not. I'm a baby. You have to bathe and clean me like an infant. I'm completely helpless."

"Yes . . . as helpless now as those children in Bethlehem were," she snapped.

Justus lay silent, but though she immediately regretted her

outburst, the words of apology she wanted to utter stuck in her throat.

Suddenly, Justus turned his face. Great tears streamed from his eyes that pleaded with her, begging for mercy, asking forgiveness, and she ran to cradle him in her arms. They clung to each other like children seeking protection and safety; then, as in the past, whispering words of love, they forgot their sorrows for an hour.

The thin line between love and hate had narrowed during the years of adjustment. Mariame had become so tied to Justus that she could not have left him even if she had so wished. She was tired of drudgery. She often longed for the luxuries of the old life, but she knew that she could never go back. In Justus' dependence upon her she had found a deep satisfaction she'd never known before. It was as if the mother instinct had grown within her, until she now felt for her helpless lover the emotion a mother might feel for an afflicted child.

On the other hand, Justus, in seeking some measure of independence, had strained his body and mind near the breaking point; but there was no escape from the situation. He was a cripple who must accept help from her.

He could see her aging quickly before his eyes, her face beginning to line—her youthful, lovely body wasting away. He felt he should drive her from him for her own sake; he pleaded, cried and cursed her. Yet, she stayed on, always attentive to his smallest needs, serving him without a sign of complaint. In his humiliation, his helpless anguish, he tortured himself and her saying, "You were going to marry Ben Bag Bag, weren't you? Oh, I know . . . you thought he was rich. You were going to desert me or have him give me poison."

Mariame grew sick of the baseless accusations and finally screamed at him, "I love you, Justus. Oh, why can't you understand? I could have been Queen of Judea, but I didn't want Herod! When I heard you'd been stoned, I could have gone back to the palace, but I went in the night instead to find your body. When I found you alive, I could still have turned to the palace, but I didn't. When I went down into the valley to search for your body, I turned away from my father whom I loved, too. I chose to live with you, and my choice literally killed him. You know quite well Herod threatened to throw him out of the court when I disappeared, and the Tiger realized there'd be no marriage contract. My choice caused my father to commit suicide, and that meant I killed him as surely as if I had cut his thin old wrists myself. My father bled to death because I went down to that valley for you. My God, Justus, what *else* can I do to prove my love?"

"You know what you can do. You can save what's left of your life by leaving me."

Mariame whirled around, "And have you waste away, brooding over what was and can never be again? No! I won't let you take the easy way out. An old prophet once said: God has arranged each man's life so that he walks part of the way and rides part of the way."

Justus groaned. "Then I have a long, long ride ahead of me."

"Yes, you do. Just as I have a long, tedious walk in store for me. But you're not even letting me walk . . . you're trying to make me crawl."

She burst into tears, and Justus looked at her, consumed with remorse and regret. She was aging so fast. Her black hair had lost its lustre. Her ragged clothes hung loose on her wasting body; her face was now lined, and all the sparkle was gone from her lovely eyes. Her destructive ordeal would surely continue while she stayed with him; no matter how he pleaded with her to leave him, she would remain; and the worst thing was that he could not bear to think of her going. All through his youth, as a soldier, he had sought and found only sexual satisfaction, but this relationship had changed his outlook. Sex was denied him now, but he had reached a plateau of loving that had no relation to the heights and depths of physical passion.

The facts of her sacrifice impelled him to insult her—to scream epithets of tormented jealousy at her—in a mad determination to drive her from him. But inwardly he cringed at the thought of her possible departure.

Mariame had insisted on his using the name "Joseph Barsabbas," for Herod's hatred lived on in his sons, who were little better than the Tiger. Mariame feared that one of the princes would discover their whereabouts and order Justus' death.

She especially feared Archelaus, the King, whose mind was almost as deranged as his father's had been, for Jerusalem was rife with rumors that the Romans were having trouble forcing him to bend to their will.

Then, too, there was the constant fear of being recognized. There were countless Jews who would never forget Justus' cruel acts as captain of Herod's guards. There was always a possibility that someone from Bethlehem would identify him, either by name or by looks—and there were men in the town who would risk their own lives to slay him.

She insisted that Justus stay always inside the house, and so, in addition to every other handicap, he had become a prisoner of her fear.

He had grown a huge beard that made him look like a pious rabbi, and she had dyed his light hair glossy black. He dressed like a Jew, as well, and thus, with his crippled body—his scars —and the beard—even his closest friend could not have recognized this Joseph Barsabbas as Justus, the ruthless, handsome captain of the dead Tiger's guards. Still, there was the fear in Mariame—and so the two people lived with it, bickering in drab despair.

As for poor Justus, each time he saw the Magi's coin gleaming on his chest, he would recall the woman and child in the desert, and ask himself, *"Why did I spare them and thus destroy myself? Why? Is there an answer — or must I live with this burning, torturous question as long as this pain-racked body lasts?"*

"Is the Christ Child alive today," he wondered, always telling himself, *"No . . . he couldn't be, or the Zealots would certainly have revolted. Maybe Antipas has been successful where I failed . . . . Oh, I should have killed all three of those people that day in the desert. Why couldn't I drive my blade into that child? Where is Mundus — that evil Roman bastard — and where is the Christ Child's gold?"*

XXIX

One clear, sunny day after 5 long, painful years of hiding, "Joseph Barsabbas" went, out of necessity, into the streets. The last of his and Mariame's money had dwindled out, the rent was due, and there was almost no food in the cupboard. Even Ebana was gone, having died of overwork and tuberculosis 2 years earlier.

There was no employment for Mariame, who had neither training nor skill in any trade. She would have done anything — perhaps even become a street woman — to care for Justus, but she knew that would have killed him, so she never mentioned her willingness to make such a sacrifice.

Finally, it was Justus who reached the decision that she guessed he'd had on his mind for years. He would go into the world again and become a beggar.

And so she helped him prepare by drawing a sketch of the cart he wanted built — a low platform with three-inch wheels. It was to have a wide leather belt nailed across it to strap himself onto it with his useless legs folded in front of him. He could propel himself by using two blocks of wood held in his powerful hands.

Mariame did not argue against his decision, but she was

concerned about it. The danger—however slight—of Joseph's being recognized as Justus was frightening. She also feared that his pride would be shattered by the ignominy of asking for alms.

A carpenter, whose wife was a friend of Mariame, constructed the crude cart, and though it lacked the finish Joseph had visualized, she was pleased, for it was sufficient to allow her to pull him to the city's gates.

Justus woke early on the day he would start his new life, and after a small breakfast, he lifted himself clumsily onto the cart.

The two people were silent as she pulled him over the rough streets, the tiny wooden wheels jarring his spine. Justus-Joseph's mind reached back to a day when he had driven a chariot, pulled by two white horses, into Rome. He remembered the feeling of triumph as he'd entered Caesar's palace that first time. He'd held his head high like a prince of the blood; now he must hold it at a painful, ugly angle to look up at the faces of common folk on the street. He had felt tall and triumphant in his handsome Roman uniform; now he felt shame while passersby looked down upon him as they might at some insignificant animal.

Mariame left him at the city's gates, knowing that this was something he must face alone. Joseph, the beggar, watched her walk away, head down. He knew that she was blind with tears, for he saw her stumble as she slowly climbed the narrow, ascending street.

He reached under his mantle and removed the small clay bowl. The sun was warming the air, and farmers and merchants had begun to enter through the vast city gates. There were poor men leading donkeys, but now and again a mounted rider would pass, and each time Joseph marveled at the animal's size for, seen from his position, it looked much larger than life. He ached inside, realizing he would never be able to sit astride a good mount again—feel his feet in the stirrups, his thighs

207

against a strong, smooth saddle. Instead, he was reminded of his permanent, pitiable condition by a sharp pain as he moved his leg on the little cart.

He sat silent all morning. No one dropped a single coin into his bowl, and he wondered if he would fail in this venture, even as he'd failed to become a general in the Roman army.

"I must succeed at this," he thought. "I must collect some money to feed Mariame and me."

And so for the first time, bitter with shame, he looked up into the eyes of a stranger and said, "please," as he held out his little bowl. The tall skinny merchant did not even acknowledge his presence; Justus, now "Joseph, the beggar," wondered why? Suddenly he realized the man had no way of knowing whether he really needed money or was just a lazy, malingering scoundrel who found it easier to ask alms than to work, for indeed, such had always been his own attitude as an arrogant soldier.

Mariame came in the middle of the afternoon with a piece of bread and some water. She smiled at him timorously as she sat on the ground beside him, afraid to ask if he had been successful.

Joseph volunteered, "I will learn. Those fellows down there aren't doing much better than I." He pointed to five other beggars around the gate and added, "I suppose it takes time — but I will learn."

Mariame squeezed his hand. "Of course. Like everything else, it takes time to learn all the tricks — and then, too, there are always bad and good days in any work."

Joseph asked her to come back at dark, and when she left him, he sat there, patiently waiting.

Suddenly, a husky Roman soldier rode through the gates, and Justus recognized him as Cassius who'd been in charge of the post at Caesarea.

"Justus" started to speak, but "Joseph" warned that he

should not, and fear took over as Cassius stopped in front of him. The eyes of the two men met for a split second before the beggar shifted his eyes.

He shook the bowl twice, and the Roman slowly reached into a small leather bag at his waist and drew out a coin. Then, with his eyes still glued to the almsman's face, he dropped the coin in the cup.

The Roman started to speak, then, as the beggar nodded his thanks, he noted the twisted legs, and rode on, head averted, while Justus grasped the coin and muttered in a soft voice, "God bless you, Cassius, friend."

He fingered the copper coin thoughtfully. It wasn't very much, but at least it would buy some food. He smiled, feeling proud because he could be of some help to Mariame. The copper coin represented his only collection, yet, he could not hide his pride in his small success.

Mariame thanked him profoundly. It was not the money that made her happy, but the fact that he was plainly elated over his first day's success as a beggar. Her greatest fear had been that he would come home empty-handed, and go into such a fit of depression that he might never regain any confidence in himself.

She bought a chicken from a farmer who did not want to carry the skinny bird back home, and that night as they feasted, Justus/Joseph for the first time in years seemed to forget his pain.

As Mariame cleaned the dishes he told her how he had blessed Cassius, the Roman, and asked, "Why did I do that?"

Mariame smiled. "Because you sincerely wanted to thank him. You wanted to give him something in return for his gift . . . and asking God to bless him, you gave him the ultimate gift."

"Could that be true—even though I do not believe in God?"

Mariame shrugged. "You have said that time and again,

Joseph, but sometimes I wonder if somewhere within you there isn't a spark of belief? I heard a rabbi say once that God is within all men, because He created man in His image. This rabbi said that by his actions man brings out the part of God that is in him. Perhaps this Roman's gift was the spark that kindled the light of God in you."

Justus was still puzzled. Mariame was a devout woman; she did not strictly follow the dietary laws, but she went to the Temple often to make offerings, however small, and her belief had remained unshaken by the tragic turn of events in their lives.

She was a Jew, faithful to her God; her faith gave her strength, and he wondered if living with her had somehow been changing him.

As though reading his thoughts now, she said, "Joseph, you are changing. You can't see it, but your whole personality has changed over these past few years. You are not the same person as Justus, the arrogant captain. He was a cruel, hard, self-centered man. That man is dead, and Joseph, the living man, has feelings for others — not just himself. Time has changed — is changing — you. Though you are crippled, you are a greater man today than the calloused, heartless military captain who went on that bloody mission to Bethlehem."

Justus fingered the coin that hung from his neck. He said simply, "Thank you, Mariame," realizing that she was right . . . he *was* different. The process had been slow and painful, but he had changed and was still changing.

He recalled the woman in front of the Bethlehem synagogue, crying, "May the Lord cause you to suffer for this deed!"

God had answered her prayer; he had suffered beyond his wildest imaginings, but he had changed inside where now a spiritual man had emerged to replace the lecherous, greedy hedonist who had served the Tiger, intent on nothing so much as his own selfish gain.

XXX

As the time of the Passover neared, Herod Antipas held a lavish banquet for the Procurator, Pontius Pilate, who had returned to Jerusalem from his headquarters in Caesarea to assure himself that the vast crowds of pilgrims paid proper respect to the city of Rome and the Empire.

Reasoning that there might be trouble from rabble-rousing Jews who still refused, after 92 years of Roman domination, to accept the rule of the Empire, Pilate had ordered his best troops into the city.

He was determined to maintain the glory of Rome, even though he had to move carefully lest Herod Antipas report some impudent action of his to the Emperor Tiberius, who had ruled the Empire for 16 years.

Conversely, Herod Antipas, eager to free himself of the Procurator, planned to handle the rabble with care, not only because Pilate could report him to Rome, but because there were still many Jews whose lot had not improved under his rule. Herod Antipas and Pilate, therefore, had one thing in common: the Jews could destroy them both in a revolt.

Antipas' spies had been alerted to seek out subversives, and Pilate's paid informers worked overtime reporting even the slightest rumors to the Procurator.

Joseph, the beggar, knew that the Passover pilgrims would be generous, and savoring the atmosphere of the Passover, he found that he yearned to participate in the worship of God, yet the Jews' religion somehow fell short of the need he felt within himself. He could not accept the faith of the Pharisees and Sadducees, with their senseless and to him revolting temple sacrifices, so he found himself asking forgiveness for his unenlightened past life. He always ended his prayer with a plea for complete recovery from his injuries or of merciful death and release from his incessant pain.

211

The sun was hot, and his ragged garments were saturated with the chalk-white dust of the road. An unruly gray beard all but covered his face, and his straggling gray hair hung in his pink-rimmed, watery eyes. If he had bathed, he might have made a better appearance, but he had found that his collections decreased when he looked too clean; and if he presented a picture of a slovenly derelict, a victim of helpless poverty, it was a truthful picture.

Only one thing could have identified this hapless wreck as the once handsome Justus and that was the coin under the filth of his clothes, still gleaming on his chest, only the genes and chromosomes within his warped body remained the same. The mind, spirit, and psyche of the man who had been Justus had changed completely.

Half awake, the beggar closed his eyes and thought of Mariame, as he had done each day throughout the past 12 years . . .

"I don't know how I've survived without you," he said to her. "Twelve years . . . it seems a thousand. I don't know why God took only you; why didn't he take me, too, since you'd become a part of me? I am thankful to Him, it was quick, and there was so little pain for you . . . but, oh, Mariame, there were so many things I wanted to tell you . . . so much in my heart that was never said. When your health began to falter, I was so concerned I couldn't think. I didn't know you'd go so quickly—I didn't have time to ask your forgiveness for the terrible life I gave you—too quickly for me to tell you I loved you more than human language could express. You—who could have been Queen—living the life of a beggar's wife with me! I loved you, Mariame, and I still love you . . . if the soul exists after death, I pray we meet again that I may tell you all the things in my heart . . . ."

"Justus . . ."

He heard the soft voice, but did not open his eyes, thinking he had not heard aright, for no one had called him Justus for more than 30 years.

Yet again the voice called, "Justus . . ." and he heard but kept his eyes closed, afraid to confront some enemy who had tracked him down.

The soft voice came a third time, "Justus . . . don't be afraid. Open your eyes." Slowly he opened his eyes, lifting his head. Before him stood three men, and he looked into their faces but did not recognize any of them.

The tall man in the middle wore a white robe that set off his olive skin and deep blue eyes. One of his companions was fair, and dressed in a dark blue robe; the other wore a dark red mantle that blended well with his nut brown skin, and each of the strangers had long flowing hair and short beards.

The man in the middle must be the leader, though youngest of the three. He had such a serene look about him that Justus' fears were allayed, yet, because this stranger had called him by his old name, he remained silent, thinking, *"How could this one know me? He must have been just a baby when I stopped using that name . . . it's been over 30 years. . . ."*

The man spoke again, softly. "Justus, fear not. I have come to thank you."

"Do I know you?" Justus whispered.

"Yes . . . from a long time ago."

Justus looked puzzled, and the tall man's companions showed even greater surprise. One of them started to speak, but the leader held his hand up to prevent it.

"Who are you?" Justus asked, painfully raising his arm to shade his eyes.

"I am Jesus of Nazareth."

Justus blinked. "Should I know you, sir?"

"Yes. Though perhaps not by name."

"Then . . . how?"

"Years ago, on a cold morning in the vastness of the desert, you made a choice to protect Me and My parents."

"It was *you?*" Justus whispered. "*You* were the child?"

"Yes," Jesus answered.

His darker companion then asked, "Master, what do You mean?"

The man raised his hand once more. "Simon Peter, you and John are witnesses. Here sits Joseph Barsabbas, once known as Justus. He has proof that I am the Son."

Justus shifted his weight on his little cart, thinking, "*How can He know so much about me?*" His heart pounded and his throat felt curiously dry.

"I do not understand," John said, glancing from Jesus to the beggar at His feet.

"No, but you will. This brave man for years has worn a pendant. It has always been with him, regardless of fearful hazards and sad conditions, since he became a part of My Father's plan. He wears a gold coin on a chain—a gift of the Magi."

Justus moved his hand to his chest and felt the coin through his dirty tunic, asking himself, "*What power does this Man have? How can He know I am wearing the coin?*"

"A gift of the *Magi?*" John asked. "Master, what is that?"

"It was a gift from three Wise Men of the East who came to Bethlehem at My birth. Justus has worn it since a few days after that night."

Jesus turned to John, then, seeing the puzzled look on Justus' face, He added, "Although you did not understand, My friend, the pendant was a reminder that you had come in contact with Me, Jesus of Nazareth, the Christ. Our lives touched in the desert. You did not understand, but you have been seeking Me, and your search is now fulfilled."

"Please, may I see the coin?" Peter asked.

Almost as in a trance, keeping his eyes on Jesus, Justus slipped the coin from beneath his tunic and placed it in Peter's hand. As Peter examined the coin, with John looking on, he wondered if he should give the coin to Jesus.

Jesus spoke again, as though reading his thoughts, "Justus, I wish you to wear the coin all your days."

Unconsciously Justus nodded as he took the coin from John, and then he whispered, "You are truly the Christ?"

"Yes."

"But . . . what do You want of me, Master?"

Jesus stooped and placed His hands on Justus' shoulder. "Only love and allegiance. There is a place in My Father's kingdom for you."

"But . . . I have heard of Your teachings. Surely one who has lived a life such as mine . . . there is nothing that I have not done . . . I have robbed and lied and *murdered* . . . ."

"I come not to punish you," Jesus said, "but rather to give you freedom from the past. Follow Me, and I will show you the way to a new life. My Father's kingdom waits for all His children and just as all the birds and animals of the world are His, so are you. Just as all the grains of the desert sand are known to Him, so even are you. I, too, know you—and through Me He offers you everlasting life."

John shifted on his feet, staring, as his Master continued.

"And there is more: when you were baptized by John who came before Me, you signified that you yearned to wash away the sins of your former life. Since then, your life has hung in the balance—waiting."

Justus swallowed hard. "But . . . if you know I was baptized by John, do you also know *why* I was baptized?"

"Yes. You were more interested in other matters. Repentance was secondary in your mind . . . but when you asked forgiveness, you were sincere."

Justus nodded. "Yes. I was seeking relief from my body's pain. I would do anything to rid myself of pain . . . even if it meant my death. But as John bore me under the water, I forgot my pain, and for some reason I asked forgiveness for all my terrible past life. I didn't really think about my body till later."

"Yes. Without regard to your disability and pain, you made a plea for forgiveness of your sins. And where there is repentance, there is forgiveness. My Father and I love you and grant you life and salvation."

Justus smiled, and his heart was suddenly filled with happiness that he had pleased this soft-spoken Man whose eyes smiled into his own.

"What can I do?" he asked.

"You will learn in time. There has been a plan for your life that began before time was measured. That plan is not yet complete."

Justus, not taking his eyes off Jesus, shifted his crumpled legs. He said, "But what can I do with my body in this condition? Since You seem to know my innermost thoughts, do You also know the pain I suffer from this twisted, broken body?"

Jesus looked grave. "Yes. Your pain is My pain, even as your hopes are My hopes, your life, My life. My Father's children are all My brothers and sisters; if My brother suffers, so do I; I also love My brother, even as My Father loves His Son."

"You . . . can love someone like *me*? A person who has lived the life I have?"

"Justus, if a shepherd loses a lamb from his flock, does the shepherd reject that lamb when it returns?" Jesus looked at John and Peter. "No. He welcomes the stray lamb back with joy, thankful that it has found the way to his arms again. Thus, too, My Father welcomes the sinner returning to His fold."

"But isn't this different?" Justus murmured.

"No. You are the lamb, and I am My Father's shepherd. Through Me He welcomes your return, and through Me your sins are washed away. You are received with His love, for the Son welcomes you for the Father."

Justus sat in amazement, filled with awe and a wondrous

happiness. This was the Messiah for whom the Jews had waited; the Messiah of whom John the Baptist had spoken, the Man grown from the Child Herod had bade him kill.

Jesus raised His hand. "John, I want you and Peter to hear this. Justus is, as I have said, a part of the plan. He will carry My Father's message to the ends of the earth."

"Master, what do You mean?" John asked. "Is he to be one of us?"

"*That* you will know when the time is right. *Justus will know* when My Father tells him."

A tremor swept through Justus as the Christ continued, "Justus, you shall be healed. It is ordained that your body shall again be straight and strong."

Justus whispered, "Thank You, Master," and the tears rolled down his scarred cheeks into his dusty beard as the comforting voice went on.

"You shall be healed — first, out of love; second, so that your purpose in life may be fulfilled. All your past life has been merely a prelude to that which is to come. You shall walk again with a strong, young body, gathering into My Father's flock the stray lambs of the world."

"I will do whatever you ask. I shall do it with pride that I serve the true Christ, and because . . ."

Jesus interrupted. "No. Do not follow in the Way because I heal you, and do not seek followers through talk of miracles. Do not awe others with the fact that you are healed. Walk with love; live in humility before My Father, then those who come to Me and to the Father because of you, will do so only through love."

"I think I understand," Justus said. "I shall not talk of my healing in order to persuade others to believe in You."

Jesus nodded. "I may not see you again, but I shall be with you, Justus. Now go to the place where you were baptized; wash the pain from your body and from your bones. You shall walk

217

again. John and Peter will welcome you upon your return to Jerusalem."

Jesus turned to Peter and John and continued, "When Justus returns to Jerusalem you will not recognize him, but he will greet you and identify himself with the Christ coin and by the words spoken here today. When he has done so, it will be My wish that you and the other nine accept him as your brother."

"But Master, there are twelve of us," Peter said.

Jesus looked gravely into Peter's eyes. "There is a purpose to all things. What will be, will be. There will come a time when you will know — and understand fully."

He turned to Justus, who sat stone still, scarcely able to contain the joy consuming him. Leaning down, Jesus kissed Justus' cheek.

"I leave you now," He said. "Come Peter, come John; let us prepare for the Passover supper."

Justus' eyes followed Jesus and the two apostles until they were out of sight. He was still entranced by the wonderful words Jesus had spoken, and for the first time since his stoning, he felt an urgent desire to live. He could not quite believe that he would be whole again, but if it should come to pass he would have only one regret: that Mariame could not have lived to see the day.

The afternoon sun was descending behind the higher buildings, when he began pushing himself toward his room. As he struggled over the rough street he felt the urgency of his mission, and as his thoughts centered on Jesus' promise of healing, he prayed that this would be his last trip to the gates on his little cart. He was not even conscious of the dusty road as he struggled on, all but oblivious to pain, toward the experience awaiting him.

PART IV

XXXI

JUDITH was standing in the door of her small house as he approached. This thin old woman had sheltered and fed Justus/Joseph throughout the past 5 years. After her last husband had died, she had rented rooms; and Joseph, the beggar, had come to her by chance. Though she could have gotten more money from another renter, it pleased her to mother a grown man, because all the men in her life before had been too heartily self-sufficient to have need of her. Her husbands had all taken mistresses, and Judith had felt unloved.

Caring for the beggar gave her a sense of purpose—a reason to go on living. He looked on her as a foster mother, and she looked on him as an invalid son. They argued and shouted at each other on the slightest provocation, so now, as he neared the doorway where she stood, she called, "Why are you coming home at this time of day?"

"There are things I must do," Justus told her.

"Oh, yes? Well, what's important enough to bring you home from the gate on the eve of the Passover? Did you collect enough to retire? Did some rich pilgrim fill your cup with gold?"

Justus said quietly, "No, but I did receive a wondrous gift."

"What was it? Let me see."

"I have only part of it . . . ."

"Well, let me see what you have."

"It's something you can't see, Judith. Anyway, the main part comes later."

"Oh, so you have only a promise? Pilgrims always make promises they don't live up to, and what good is that? Look at

221

me. I've had plenty of promises in my life, and see what they have gotten me. A broken-down house with a broken-down renter who must be crazy with sunstroke! Broken promises. Hah. That's how I lost my virginity and disgraced my family."

Justus did not answer, and Judith looked down at him, storming, "Don't be a fool, man. Go back to the gate. You can take in more today than you may all the rest of the year. You might even get some gold."

Justus spoke firmly. "No. I know what I'm doing. Go and find Silas. Tell him I need him at once — and that it will be worth his while."

Judith sniffed. "What's in it for me?"

"If you don't go, I'll make you wish you had," Justus snapped in his old military voice, then he added, "I promise you, I will reward you in some way."

When the woman had gone, he scuttled into his bedroom and worked a stone out of the wall with his knife.

Behind the stone was a niche that contained a small leather bag which he removed and then replaced the stone. This had been his safe for the past 5 years, and though he guessed that Judith must have known about it, none of his cache was ever missing.

He counted the coins, placed half of them in a fold of his robe, and hid the sack containing the rest inside his tunic.

"I tell you the sun has driven him out of his mind," he could hear Judith saying as the outside door opened, and he pushed himself back into the living room, hearing Silas grumbling in his beard at the rasp in the old woman's voice.

"Look at him," she cried. "He *has* to be out of his mind . . ."

Silas glanced at Justus, wiped his broad hand across his mouth, and spoke in a deep voice. "Woman, can't you ever be still? If the man is crazy, it must be from hearing you shrieking all the time."

"It's all right," Justus said hastily. "Just leave us alone for a moment, Judith, please."

"Secrets, secrets," Judith snorted, as she whirled and entered her bedroom, slamming the door.

Justus spoke softly. "Silas, I must ask a favor. But I will pay you well for your trouble."

"What kind of favor?"

"I want you to drive me to the River Jordan."

"When?"

"Now."

"Oh, no, Joseph. I can't leave the city now. It's against the Law to work on a religious day . . . you know the Passover rules."

"I'll pay you well, Silas."

"I can't. I'd like to help you but I can't. You know . . ."

"I know you're not so pious as to forego this," Justus said, removing the money from his robe and pouring it from hand to hand. "All this, and more later, maybe."

Silas' eyes widened. "But I . . ."

"This is more than you could earn in six months." Justus weighed the coins.

"Where did you get that kind of money?"

"I've saved it, over the years. This is all I have, and I'll give it to you. Please, Silas. My life depends on your help."

"We-ll, if you put it that way. Give me the money."

"No. I'll keep it until we get there. You know *I* can't run off. I can't be so sure of you."

"You don't trust me, Joseph?"

"Yes, but I don't want to tempt you. Now go and get your wagon. I'll have Judith pack food and drink. And hurry— I want to be out of the city well before dark."

Silas turned on his heel in response to the order. He could celebrate later, and after all, this was a mercy mission.

"Surely God will understand," he said in a low voice.

Judith slipped out of her room as Silas closed the door.

"Are you really going away? Are you leaving me, Joseph?" she asked in a small voice.

"Yes, I must. But if what has been promised comes true, I'll return, Judith."

"But . . . suppose it doesn't?"

"It will."

"But you said 'if.' "

"I didn't really mean 'if'; I meant 'when.' It's just that it's such a wonderful thing, it's difficult for me to comprehend."

"Joseph, tell me what it is. I swear I won't tell a soul."

Justus shook his head. "No, it is better this way, Judith. Now, please pack food and water for Silas and me."

Tears were beginning to form in Judith's eyes.

"Oh, what shall I do when you've gone? I'll have no one to look after . . . no one who needs me, and I shall be so lost. Please come back, Joseph. I promise I'll treat you better if you'll only come back."

"I will. You know how I feel about you—how I love you," Justus said for the first time. "Now, dry your eyes, Judith. Things will be better soon for both of us."

Justus moved out of the room to keep her from seeing the tears in his own eyes.

"Are you going to be rich?" Judith called, placing bread, cheese, and meat in a rough goatskin bag.

"I am rich now." Justus took out his best clothes from a small box in his bedroom. "Not with money. But still, I am rich. You will see, soon."

The road stretched rough and deserted before the travellers. The only sounds came from the creaking of the leather harness on the small horse that pulled the two-wheeled cart and, now and again, the crunch of a soft stone crumbling under the wheels.

Justus looked back at the city over his shoulder. The last rays of the sun seemed to reflect off its limestone buildings in contrast to the countryside that glowed with the first flowers and the bright verdure of spring. Off to the north, small clouds were breaking up in the cooling air, and in the west he could see a low cluster illumined by the sun's great golden ball of fire.

"Why did you leave your cart in Jerusalem?" Silas asked. "Don't you plan to move about when we get where we're going?"

Justus did not answer at once. In front of Judith's house, as Silas had lifted him into the wagon and started to pick up the small cart, he'd said, "No, leave that here," ignoring the look on Judith's and Silas' faces.

Now he said enigmatically, "I was afraid to bring it."

Silas, of course, did not understand his answer so he asked, "Afraid? Why? What harm could have come of bringing your legs?"

"I can't explain except to say, I *had* to leave the cart. With it, I'd feel I was questioning the word of God."

Silas' interest quickened. "The word of *God?*"

"Yes."

Silas grunted. "What has God's word to do with a beggar? Maybe Judith was right. The sun has cooked your brain. Where and how did you hear God talking to you?"

"Today, at the gate. Through Jesus of Nazareth — His Son."

"I've heard of Him," Silas said, nodding. "I've heard He performs miracles. Have you really seen this Jesus?"

"Yes. Today, as I said."

"And did He perform a miracle?"

"I think He did, yes. I shall know later."

"But you're not healed . . . Is that why you're taking this trip?"

"Silas, there are things about this I can't discuss — not because I don't want to tell you; I do. It's just that there are so

225

many new and wonderful things in me . . . I can't understand them myself—much less explain them to anyone else. But I can tell you this: Jesus of Nazareth *is* the true Son of God. He is the living Christ."

"How do you know? I've heard priests of the Temple say He's a false prophet, and surely they should know; they've studied the Law. Of course, if He can really do miracles, He must be the Christ, but the priests said they were tricks and frauds. Anyway, if He were the Messiah He'd have already run the Romans out of Israel."

Justus smiled. "Then, you'd believe in Him only if you saw Him perform a miracle?"

Silas shrugged. "I'm not educated, Joseph. I don't know much about religion *or* the Law. So, sure, if I saw Him heal someone I knew who was blind, say, I would believe, regardless of what they said at the Temple."

"Have you ever heard His teachings?"

"Yes . . . I've heard some of His parables repeated."

"Well, can't you believe in Him from His teaching?"

"Are you trying to tempt me?" Silas glanced sidewise. "What sensible person could find fault in what He says? Sure, the Pharisees and Sadducees all say His lessons defy the Law, but everything I've heard that He's said gives hope to the little man—and God knows the little man needs some help. His word speaks of a good life, but somehow I don't think many will believe—or love—in the way He suggests. Still, I find no fault in His words, so I suppose I could believe in Him. Mind you though, I don't say I think he's the Anointed One. And a good miracle would go a long way toward convincing me."

Silas gave the horse a slap with the ends of the reins.

The night was beginning to cool, and the stars seemed near and enormous in the clear night sky. The air was still, and for a long time the two men sat silent, each lost in his own thoughts.

Finally, Silas asked, "Why do you want to go to the River

Jordan? I mean, why to the particular spot where the Jordan last intersects a creek before it enters the Dead Sea? There's nothing there, Joseph. It's not even a good place to fish."

"I know, but that's the place where John the Baptist baptized me," Justus answered.

Silas glanced round. "You were *baptized?*"

"Yes, about 3 years ago."

"Why? Did you believe in John? Were you one of his followers?"

"No. But I heard him speak in Jerusalem one day. His voice was full of promise. One of the other beggars told me he sometimes performed miracles when he baptized people. I didn't believe it, but I was willing to try anything to heal my body, so I hired a wagon and followed him to the place where we're going now. He baptized me . . . ." Justus hesitated, then decided to go on, "but when he bore me under the water, somehow, I failed to ask to be healed. All I asked was forgiveness of all my sins."

"Do you think he could have cured you if you'd asked? I mean, if he had the power . . ."

"No, I don't think so. I'm not sure he could have."

"But you think Jesus of Nazareth will? Why will He, when John didn't?"

"I know He will," Justus said flatly.

"Well, if He had the power, why didn't He do it in Jerusalem? Why must you make this overnight trip? I've heard that some have been healed merely by touching His robe."

Justus spoke calmly. "Silas, who am I to question the word of God? All I can say is, I feel His words consuming, directing me. I'd go anywhere, do anything He asked. Silas, this man is the Son of God. Believe in Him."

Silas could tell from his companion's voice that he spoke from the heart, and indeed there might be some truth in what he'd just said, for Joseph had always been level-headed. He said aloud, "I'll think about it. Anyway, I like the way He scourged the money changers out of the Temple. That took great courage. I'd understood He was a man of peace, but they say He was fighting mad that day. Now, if he'd just throw the Romans out of Jerusalem, He'd really be doing some good. That would be a real miracle."

As they neared the river, the sun was rising behind the high hills to the east. Spring flowers filled the air with myriad scents, and a light fog almost hid the narrow path that led off the main road.

"Wait," Justus commanded. "I think this is the spot, but it looks a little different in this light. Is the west fork ahead?"

"Yes." Silas' hand made a sweeping movement. "The road curves 'round to a fork over that way, and the fork empties into the Jordan below us. The Sea is off to our right, about 5 miles."

Justus looked all around to get his bearings. "Then carry me down to the Jordan. I'll take my things."

He gathered up his small sack containing his other clothes and some food.

Silas got down from the cart and went round to the other side. With difficulty and pain, Justus put his arms around Silas' neck as the man lifted his helpless legs. The dew on the grass soaked the bottom of Silas' mantle as he carried the helpless beggar down the rough path toward the sound of water below.

They came out of the underbrush onto a sand spit at the river's edge, and heard the soft music of water rippling over stones.

"Yes," Justus said, glancing around, "this is the right spot. Set me down here."

"What do we do now?" Silas asked. "It's just barely daybreak. Can we eat now?"

Justus surveyed the river, recalling his previous visit here.

228

He said, "Silas, you have done well. Here is your money. Now, I want you to leave me."

"Leave you?" Silas cried in disbelief. "I can't, Joseph. How would you get back? You'd die out here alone."

"Silas, you must. This is something only I can do. My Lord told me to come here, and here my new life will begin."

"Or your present one will end." Silas took the money from Justus' upturned hand. "However, if you have that much faith in Jesus of Nazareth, I don't suppose an argument from me would do any good. I only hope, for your sake, He truly is the Christ."

"Don't worry," Justus said. "You'll never see me begging again. I'll walk out of here into a new life in His service. I shall walk back to Jerusalem."

Silas looked down at the crippled beggar lying in the sand and touched his head. "I'll pray that He's the Messiah and that your promise comes true," he said softly; then he turned and trudged up the path.

As the sun rose higher Justus struggled out of his clothes, and when he was naked, he pulled himself painfully toward the water, his helpless legs and sliding body leaving a track in the sand. At the river's edge he stopped and dipped his hand in the cool water. He hesitated, afraid to test the Christ; then lifting his legs he moved them so that they stuck out into the water.

He could feel nothing but pain, so he looked down at the Magi's coin on his bare chest, and prayed, "Oh, God, if You can hear me—have mercy on this wreck that was once a man. Dear God, I know and love Your Son. He has spoken to me, and through Him I seek you, for I know He is Your Son. Forgive me, Father, for my former evil life. If You and Your Son can use me, I am Yours. And I come, not for healing alone. I do not understand all, but I know I must serve in Your Kingdom, and if healing my wounds will help, then I beg to be healed.

Lord, I love Your Son. I pledge allegiance, and ask to help Him, regardless of danger and hardship. Lord, please answer me."

Justus sobbed, pushing himself deeper into the water, and from the soft river bottom a cascade of small bubbles rose to the surface as his lifeless legs trailed in the mud and sand.

Lost in the morning's stillness, he wept with pain and joy, feeling that God must be somehow entering his heart.

The sun was growing hot, but as he tried to move his legs, nothing whatever happened, so he cried aloud, "Oh, God, am I being tested? Was there not to be a miracle?"

Sweat broke out on his forehead. He thought, "Could it be a hoax?" and then he screamed, "Satan, get out of my mind. There is no room for you. You cannot tempt me to disbelief. The Christ told me He loves me—that I am His brother and we shall win over you. The Son of God will win, and I am on His side. No. . . . God is on *my* side, because I know and love His Son."

He shouted up into the sky, clasping the Magi's coin, then suddenly a silence seemed to deepen over the river area. He began to feel his heart beat stronger and, for the first time in 33 years, his legs moved slightly, near the calm pool's surface. He let loose the root he had grasped and felt of his legs. They were numb, but he continued to pray as the sun reached its high point and started down. He looked at his skin and saw that it was wrinkled from the water; he had been in the river 6 hours.

He felt the water cooling his legs, and all his life passed before his closed eyes . . . the people he'd known and loved . . . Mariame . . . the evil things he'd done.

He prayed anew, "God, forgive me. I didn't realize what I was doing. Now because of Jesus, Your Son, I do know. I will live for You and for Him."

All at once he noticed that the birds had stopped their songs, and that a strange stillness had settled over the landscape.

He opened his eyes and saw that the sky seemed to have darkened; yet it was early afternoon and there was no cloud in sight. He turned to look over his shoulder, then in amazement he realized that his body had turned with ease.

He moved his legs. He looked at the water and moved his body a little. His legs had moved—they would respond to his command, and there was no pain in any part of him! He thrashed the water with his legs; happy, excited, he moved his body and his arms. There was no pain, and he could move at will. Jesus' promise had come true, just as he'd known it would! He pushed himself out into the river and swam.

As the sun began to brighten once more, he pulled himself out of the water onto the sand, lay on his back and looked up into the blue, clear sky, laughing, weeping, and thanking God.

XXXII

The buzzing of a fly awoke Justus; as he slapped at the pest he remembered where he was. The sun was touching the horizon, throwing long shadows of small trees and bushes across the sandy earth. In the distance he heard a bird call to its mate.

The warm sand of the spit had molded to the shape of his back as he lay looking at the tufts of white clouds above him; now the miracle of life surged in him as he freely moved his legs and arms.

He raised his arms and examined them, sat up and ran his hands down his legs, feeling the firm flesh; his knees were again perfect, and both his feet were flexible. Gone was the pain that had been his constant companion for 33 years. He drew his knees up under his chin and wrapped his arms round his legs; then, placing his chin on his knees, he bowed his head in gratitude once more.

After a while he raised his head and touched the Magi's coin. This was surely the Messiah's gift.

"He is truly the Christ," Justus thought. "Who can doubt He is the Son when He can do such things as healing a body like mine?"

He heard someone call. "Joseph! Where are you?"

Then as he looked up the bank where the voice seemed to come from, he saw Silas pushing his way through the brush. He did not know whether or not to answer, but before he could decide Silas saw him and called out, "Oh, there you are."

Justus reached for his clothing as Silas moved closer, unsure of what to do next.

"I was afraid something might happen to you," Silas said as he scuffed through loose sand at the river's edge, "so, half way to Jerusalem, I turned around."

Justus did not speak as he gathered his robe about him, and suddenly Silas asked, studying his face and body, "What has happened? You are Joseph, aren't you?"

"Why do you ask?"

"Because, look at your face and body. When I left you, your face was scarred and your body wrecked. Now . . ."

"Now?" Justus said, letting the mantle fall from his body.

Silas gasped. "No, it can't be." As he tried to back off in disbelief, he fell to the ground.

"Ah, but it is. Look!" Justus jumped high into the air and ran all around the awe-struck Silas. "Look what He has done for me! I am healed! Look at my legs! Look at my arms!" He shouted in happy abandon as he flexed all the muscles in his new body and then dropped on the sand next to Silas.

"I can see, but I don't believe it," Silas said. "You cannot be Joseph, even though you do look a little like him. Is this a trick?"

"You know it isn't!" Justus threw a handful of sand into the air, reached down and pulled Silas on to his feet. "Silas, He cured me."

"Yes, yes," Silas cried. "I can see now, truly. Let's go back to Jerusalem and tell everyone."

"No, not now; I want to stay here a while longer and thank Him. You go back now if you want to."

"No. We'll go back together," Silas said. "Take your time. Let me get us some food."

"There's some in that sack," Justus told him.

After they had eaten, Silas returned to his wagon. He brought a large bag containing sleeping robes and clothes and spread them around a fire they'd built from driftwood. Justus returned to the river. He bathed himself, shaved, then clipped his ragged beard and hair into the short neat style of his youth.

Silas watched with fascination as the man transformed himself from a beggar into someone he'd never known. And when the transformation was complete, he knew that Jesus, the Christ, had performed a miracle. Indeed, he was so taken by the miracle that he could not speak of it at all.

The next morning Justus went and knelt by the river. He dropped his hands into the cool water, gave thanks, and dedicated himself to helping the Christ. Then his mind flashed back over his life as a soldier. Now at last, he knew why he had disobeyed Herod—why he hadn't been able to slay the child in the desert. For the first time he knew, as few men have known, the purpose of his own future existence.

He understood that there was design in his life—that his years of agony had changed him from a cruel, arrogant soldier into a soul prepared for redemption. The metamorphosis was nearly complete. He was now ready to serve as a soldier of God. This was why God had renewed his body. Looking at the sandy banks of the river, he knew that "the sands of time" had cleansed him in preparation for the moment God would enter his body. Suddenly he realized that he had not only saved the Christ Child's life on that cold morning in the desert; in a sense he had saved his own.

They had decided to travel at night to avoid the heat, so, late in the afternoon, Saturday, Silas and Justus mounted the small wagon for the trip back to Jerusalem. When the horse gave his first tug at the shafts Justus turned and watched as they moved away from the river, trying to fix in memory the spot where he had found salvation and his future.

On the return journey Silas was unusually quiet. He still was not fully adjusted to the fact that next to him sat an entirely different man from the one he'd brought out to the Jordan 2 days before. There were questions he wanted to ask, but somehow he could not ask them. In Justus he saw the power of God, for here, sitting beside him, was living evidence that Jesus of Nazareth was the Christ for whom Israel had waited so long.

Yet, when the first light of morning appeared, Silas knew he could wait no longer.

He asked, "What are you going to do now, my friend?"

Justus answered, "I shall become a follower of Jesus of Nazareth, and do everything in my power to convince people that He is truly the Son of God—the Christ all men seek."

"Then, you will be one of His disciples?"

"Yes. If He will have me. At least I can be a witness."

"Will you convert men because you were healed by Him? If so, let me go with you. I can tell them I saw you healed—and that will make your story more dramatic."

Justus smiled. "Silas, do you believe in Him only because you know that He has healed me?"

Silas considered. "Well, yes. It helps to convince me. I can't put it out of my mind, since I know He did it."

"Ah, but you only know what I have told you—that it was

He who performed the miracle," Justus said, shaking his head. "I want you to believe in Him with all your heart, mind, and body, but not on the basis of miracles. His power is limitless — just as His love is boundless. He doesn't seek believers because of His power; He wants them to come to Him because of His love."

"Well . . . I truly can't separate my feelings. I'd like to, but I can't. Does that mean I'd be rejected?"

Justus thought a moment. "No. I'm sure He would not deprive anyone of His Father's Kingdom — not even great sinners such as I. If He will allow me to be His follower, then He will welcome you also. But you must believe in Him for Himself — not out of awe or superstition. If you truly believe in your heart that He is the Christ, then I know He will welcome you. But if you do not, you still will not be rejected, for He will continue to show His love. I know."

"But how do you know? You have talked to Him just once . . . ."

Justus spoke quietly. "Silas, there are things concerning all this I seem to know only with my heart. There are things I don't understand, yet I still know they are true. I only hope Jesus will teach me more."

"All right. But will you take me with you?"

"Who am I to reject you? How could I — of all people — tell you that you cannot follow the way to His Father? On the contrary, I beg you to accept Him and follow His teaching."

"Joseph . . ."

Justus interrupted, "No, please. Use my other name: Justus. It is my real name — one I haven't used in many years, but He called me by that name. And if Jesus chooses to call me Justus, I want the whole world to know me as Justus."

"Justus?"

"Yes. I abandoned the name, years ago, out of fear. Now I retake it, in courage and devotion. My name is Justus."

"Haven't I heard that name before?" Silas asked.

"Perhaps. Thirty-three years ago I was captain of Herod's bodyguards."

"Yes! That's it!" Silas snapped his fingers. "Bethlehem . . . you were the one . . ."

"Yes."

"Yes, yes. Now I remember. I had a brother living there at the time. If the Sanhedrin hadn't acquitted you . . . but, why did they, actually? I still don't understand why they freed you."

"It's a long story. I'll tell you about it some day," Justus said.

"But what happened to you? I know many people sought you, to kill you . . . but you could not be found. Did you leave the country?"

"No. I stayed in Jerusalem. Herod's stoning didn't quite kill me. However, I didn't go outside the house for 5 years because of my injuries, and I changed my name to Joseph. After that, no one recognized me."

"Is that how you became a beggar?"

"Yes."

Silas' next question was cut short, for now a man dressed in a white robe appeared in the middle of the road.

As Silas reined the horse to a stop the man asked, "May I ride with you?"

"Where are you going?"

"Only a little way."

Silas turned to Justus who nodded approval.

"Well, get in the back." Silas motioned to the bed of the wagon, and Justus watched as the traveller seated himself. There was something familiar about the man, but Justus could not remember having met him before.

As they started down the sloping hill into the Valley of Kidron, he turned to face the stranger and said, "You have a familiar look to me. Have we ever met?"

"Do you think we have?"

"I'm not sure . . ."

"Where are you going?" the stranger asked.

"To the city, first."

"And then?"

"I don't quite know."

"May I go with you?"

"Why would you want to travel with me?"

The man spoke softly, "Because I want *you* to travel with me — always."

Justus didn't understand the riddle of the stranger's answer. He asked, "Who are you, friend?"

The stranger smiled, "Don't you know me?"

"Sir, I've been trying, but I can't for the life of me place your face."

"Is it only by a face that you know someone?"

"No, but it helps," Justus said. "Are you playing a game with me? If I have failed to recognize you, I apologize for my poor memory."

"Your memory is all right," the man said. "You have not forgotten, nor will you forget. You will remember when the time comes."

"When will that be?" Justus asked, his interest quickening.

"Shortly. You have work to do and you must stand firm — unafraid."

"Oh, I have nothing to fear," Justus replied. "I have everything to live for, now, and nothing can change my destiny."

"No. Yet you will be tested when you reach the city," the man told him. "There will develop a serious question which only you can solve."

Silas turned to look at the man. "Mister, what work do you follow?"

"I am a shepherd."

Justus stared hard. "A shepherd? With problems that *I* can solve?"

"Justus, you shall lead lost sheep back into the fold," the man said, and then to Silas, "Please let me off here, my friend."

Silas pulled the horse to a stop, and he and Justus watched as the passenger climbed down from the wagon.

Then he held his right hand aloft, saying, "Justus, I shall see you again. Have faith, and do not become downhearted, for *I* have faith in *you*. Be assured, the city—and the world—await you."

Now, Silas whirled around as the horse suddenly began to trot, and he could not, by any means, stop the beast as it plunged ahead, snorting.

Justus looked at the man in the white robe who still stood on the edge of the road, his arm upraised; then a blade of sunlight cut through the trees and fell on the stranger's face, and Justus knew Him. He cried out, "Silas! That was Jesus!" Then as Silas wheeled round on the seat to look back, he mourned, "He's gone now. Look, He has disappeared."

Silas turned back to his driving. "Are you sure that He was Jesus of Nazareth?"

"Yes, yes. I'm positive!"

"Then, why didn't you recognize Him at once? I thought you said you'd seen Him before."

"I had, but I don't know . . . He looked different this time. I didn't recognize Him till after we'd started to move." Justus shook his head sadly. "Oh, I wish I could have thanked Him for healing me . . . and I had so much to tell Him. Why was I so stupid? I didn't think I'd ever forget His face after I'd seen Him in Jerusalem. Wait. Stop the wagon!"

Silas now managed to halt the horse, and Justus vaulted down and ran back to the spot where Jesus had stood. He found footprints in the dust where Jesus had alighted but could not tell which direction He had gone from the small clearing. He thought, "He will think me a fool for not recognizing Him," and continued berating himself as Silas returned with the wagon, asking, "Where did He go, Justus?"

"I don't know. *He just disappeared!*" Justus said and climbed back into the wagon.

"Justus . . . did you notice His face seemed to change?" Silas asked, low-voiced. "I didn't want to say anything about it, but He looked entirely different to me when He got out of the wagon than when He got in. I thought it was just the light, but now . . ."

Justus said, "Yes. Maybe He didn't want me to recognize Him at first. Maybe that's what He intended. I know He could change Himself . . . if He wanted to . . . He has the power to do anything."

"But . . . did you understand what He said to you? I was listening, and I sure didn't."

Silas gave the horse a slap with the reins as Justus spoke slowly. "I think I understood part of it, but He said I'd understand all at the proper time. I know He was telling me something important. When the time comes, I'm sure I'll understand."

The sun was beginning to warm the morning air as they passed through the city gates, and people were stirring. It was the day after the Sabbath, and the merchants had already spread their wares before their houses and shops.

When they neared the spot where the beggars usually sat, Justus put his hand on Silas' shoulder and told him, "I must leave you now. Please don't tell anyone about my miracle. Tell Judith that I will see her but that right now I have something I must do." He slipped the small bag containing the last of his money from his robe and gave Silas a small gold coin, saying, "Here, take this."

Silas shook his head. "No. It is I who should pay you because what you have given me can't be bought with money. I want to learn more about Jesus."

"Then you shall," Justus said, "and the more you learn, the more clearly you'll understand. Goodbye for now, but I shall see you again very soon, old friend."

"Goodbye," Silas said, "and good luck to you."

The horse gave a tug at the wagon, snorted with pleasure at the lighter weight, and galloped away.

Justus watched Silas turn the corner, then walked over to the beggars and placed a silver coin in each of their cups. All of them mumbled their thanks, but not one recognized him.

He wondered now how he could locate Peter and John. He thought of going to the Temple, then changed his mind, and began to wander the streets. It felt so good to walk again, and though his body was somewhat stiff from the ride back to Jerusalem, he felt refreshed. He recalled all his years in the city — the pain that had been his constant companion as he'd traversed these streets on his little cart. Now everything looked different; he no longer had to look up into people's faces — no longer breathe clouds of dust from being close to the ground.

His search for the two apostles was actually turning into a thanksgiving pilgrimage. He knew they would take him to Jesus, so that he could thank Him and apologize for not recognizing Him on the road.

The sun grew warmer as he continued his search, seeing things of beauty about the city that he hadn't noticed for years. He walked by the old house where he'd lived as a captain in Herod's guards and noted that its present owner kept it in good repair.

Finally, he moved on to the Temple and found a large crowd of people milling about before it. He hesitated, then walked into the Court of the Gentiles — the only place that he'd been inside the Temple. He still considered himself a Gentile and did not want to chance a death sentence for passing through the huge doors that led to the inner section reserved for Jews.

The Temple smelled of burnt offerings and slaughtered animals. Over the hum of people talking he could hear the sounds of cattle awaiting their turn to be offered to Jehovah, and the smells and sounds repulsed him.

He thought, *"How can these people turn a place of worship into a slaughter house? Surely Jesus, the Son of God, would not want to be worshipped with the blood and fires of sacrifice. Jesus spoke always of love; He said that all birds and animals belonged to His Father, so surely God would not have man resort to the cruelty of burnt offerings in worshipping Him."*

Justus started to leave the Temple, and as he turned he heard a money changer saying, "The priests were right. We'll have no more trouble from Jesus of Nazareth. Did you see Him? He was no more the Son of God than I am."

Justus grabbed the hawk-nosed man by his tunic, shouting, "What did you say about Jesus?"

The man strained to free himself. "I just said the priests were right. He has been crucified."

"Crucified?"

"Yes," the man said in a whisper as Justus' grip on his tunic tightened, "they did it on Friday."

"By whose order?"

"Pilate's. Please . . . I had nothing to do with it."

Whining as Justus released him, the frightened man knocked over his money stand. He scrambled around the stones searching for the scattered coins. Justus watched him, unseeing, and groaned, "It's a lie! This is Sunday— I saw Him this morning! I talked with Him!"

He rushed out into the street, headlong into pilgrims entering the Temple for the last time before returning to their homes after the Passover. "It is a lie," he thought, "a trick. They couldn't have crucified Him. I *saw* Him with my own eyes."

241

Outside the Temple a Roman soldier stood talking to a shop-keeper, and Justus walked up to him, asking in Latin, "Please tell me: Is it true that Pontius Pilate crucified Jesus of Nazareth?"

The centurion, apparently surprised that Justus spoke Latin, turned from the shopkeeper and answered, "Yes—although he takes no blame for it, for he ascertained that Jesus had committed no crime against Rome and washed his hands of the whole affair. Still the Sanhedrin ordered His death, and I saw Him die on the cross. Are you a citizen of Rome?"

"Yes," Justus answered. "Tell me . . . why was He killed?"

"I don't know," the young soldier said. "You know these Jews and their religion. Evidently some of the priests thought this fellow was falsely claiming to be the Son of God."

Justus turned on his heel. "He *was* the Son," he snapped, and disappeared in the crowd.

Tears streamed down Justus' face as he walked, muttering, "It can't be true; it can't. I *saw* Him this morning."

He began almost to trot; his body grew numb, and his vision blurred. He was sure the centurion hadn't lied—he'd have no reason to lie, yet his mind could not comprehend this situation. All his years of searching for something good in the world had ended just as he'd found salvation. The precious Jesus was now dead—just when he had found Him. But if He'd been crucified, who was the One he had seen this morning on the road?

Peter and John would know, but where would he find them? Frantically he roamed the streets, looking, seeking an answer.

At last, near the Fish Gate in the lower city he saw a large man in a black mantle, his face almost covered by a head cloth and called, "You, there!"

The man quickened his step, and Justus broke into a trot, telling himself, "It is Peter." He called out, "Peter, wait," but the huge man ducked his head, turned a corner, and disappeared down an alley. Justus ran to the corner. He looked down the long, shade-darkened alley, and the smell of wet garbage struck him in the face. The man he was pursuing must have entered one of the doors off the alley, he thought, and straining his eyes in the poor light, he called again, "Peter, where are you?" Then he moved forward, stopping at each door to listen for some noise that might betray Peter's hiding place.

After he'd examined four doors, he saw on the fifth's threshold a fresh wet footprint. He pounded his fist on the thick slab of cedar and called, "Peter, it is I, Justus." Then, receiving no answer, he called again, "I come in the name of Jesus of Nazareth."

Almost at once the door opened slightly. An eye looked out at him, and he said in a low voice, "You remember me — Justus. Please let me in, Peter. I must talk to you."

The door hinges gave off a screeching cry as the door scraped open and Justus saw only the blackness of an empty room. He took three steps into the darkness; then, before he could look around, his right arm was twisted behind him and he felt a thick forearm at his throat.

"Wait!" he cried before his breath was cut off, "I come as a friend."

But the pressure increased on his throat, and a light seemed to jump out of the blackness, quickly changing the blackened room into a spray of color. Three men stood before him and a giant held him at bay, but Justus felt no fear as his eyes searched the captors' faces.

John's was familiar to him, but the man gave no hint of recognition. Again Justus tried to speak, but no matter how he twisted his body he could not free himself of the hand on his mouth and the vise crushing life out of him.

Then in a moment of panic his free hand moved to his tunic, and he jerked at the tiny chain about his neck. It broke, and he held the coin out on his right palm.

His eyes pleaded with John, and as he slumped in the giant's arms the coin fell from his hand.

XXXIII

"Did you have to do that?" Justus asked, stroking his sore neck as they picked him up off the floor.

"I didn't recognize you," Peter told him. "I still don't, but John said to stop when he saw the coin."

"I am Justus, who talked to Jesus and John and you, last Thursday. I came here at Jesus' request. He said that I was to show you the coin as identification."

Peter spoke grimly. "Anyone can present a coin."

"Not one like that."

"No, wait," John said, "give the man a chance." He turned quickly. "If you are the man called Justus by the Master, what did He tell you? Repeat it in detail."

Justus knew that he was being tested in such a way that only he, Peter, and John would understand, so he retraced the conversation he'd had with Jesus, repeating without difficulty the exact words etched on his brain. He almost sang the words, recalling the joy that had filled him as he'd talked with Jesus. He saw that John was beginning to believe him, and even Peter was nodding his great head as he recited the marvelous promise of healing.

John interrupted to ask, as he ended his recollections, "And you were cured, as He said you'd be?"

"Yes—as you can see. My body is strong and supple. He cured me—just as He had promised."

Peter laid a huge hand on Justus' shoulder. "Tell us, did you have doubts that you would be healed?"

"No, not really. I knew that He was Christ. Some fear crept into my mind as I lay for such a long time in the waters of the Jordan, but when the sky darkened and the birds grew still, suddenly I knew that I was healed and that my faith had not faltered."

He heard one of the men gasp and saw a look of astonishment on John's face.

"What's the matter?" he cried, and John said, choking, "That was the moment our Master died on the cross."

Justus trembled. "Did you see Him die?"

"Yes."

"But I saw Him this morning on the road by the Kidron Valley. He rode in a wagon with me, and I talked to Him."

The men looked at each other in silence, and Justus waited for them to speak; then he insisted, "I tell you, I *spoke* with Him today."

"Are you sure it was the Master?" Peter asked.

"Yes. He called me by name."

Peter motioned to his companions; the four moved to a corner of the room to carry on a whispered conversation, and Justus waited, uneasy, as John argued with Peter.

Finally John led the group back to him and smiled as he handed over the Magi coin.

He said, "Now tell us, in detail, about seeing the Master," and Justus told them, not forgetting a word that had passed between him and the Christ in the early dawn. As he talked the men strained eagerly to catch each word as it fell from his lips.

When Justus had finished, he waited for their comment, but again the men remained silent. Then suddenly Peter cried, "It is true. It has come to pass. The Master has kept His word. Why did I doubt? Why did we fear? Don't you see, we have won. The Master is alive—this man's testimony confirms it."

Justus looked puzzled. "What do you mean? I thought you said He'd died."

John smiled. "This morning at daybreak, one of the Master's followers—a woman called Mary Magdalene—went to His tomb. When she arrived she found the tomb opened, even though the Romans had rolled a great stone across its entrance. She came for Peter and me; we too went to find the stone rolled away and the tomb empty. A little later, after Peter and I had departed, Mary of Magdala swore she had talked to the Master in the garden, but frankly, being afraid the priests or the soldiers had stolen the body, we didn't believe the Magdalena. We thought she'd had an hallucination—but you have confirmed her story. He has risen, indeed!"

"Yes," added the smallest of the men. "We thought you might have been a spy. That is why Peter treated you so roughly. Forgive us. From His words, the Master plainly meant you to be one of us. My name is Andrew, and this is Bartholomew. We are all brothers here, and we welcome you."

Justus smiled. "You mean . . . you will accept me?"

"Yes," John said, "and with the love our Master has for you—for He has honored you greatly with this confirmation of His rising."

"But . . . to die and then be alive again . . ." Justus said almost under his breath.

"Do you doubt?" asked Peter.

"No. How could I, of all men, doubt the Christ? I, who have seen and felt Almighty God's power? No. I know in my heart that His powers are limitless and that His love is unbounded."

"Then, you will stay with us?" Andrew asked.

"Oh, yes, yes. I want you to teach me all that the Master has taught you. I must learn—and you are the ones to teach me," Justus said. "Here is all of the money I have. Let it be used for the cause."

John put an arm about his shoulder.

"Come," he said, "let us eat together while we talk."

XXXIV

The place was too small to accommodate comfortably all one hundred twenty of them, yet, despite the cramped quarters no one complained, for they were safe here from the priests' spies and informers.

The old building had been used as a Roman army barracks during the construction of the Fortress Antonia; its thick stone walls were cold, but the high ceiling kept the flames of the seven wall torches from consuming the limited amount of fresh air that entered through the small windows near the ceiling.

This building was now owned by Nicodemus, who used it from time to time to store grain. The room was perhaps the largest in the city where a group such as this could meet in secret and be assured of privacy from the Temple priests and the Romans.

Justus stood with his shoulders wedged tight between two other men in the line that encircled the walls. People sat cross-legged on the smooth-worn floor, and the room was a patchwork of color from varying robes and head cloths. In the center there was a cleared circle about 10 feet in diameter.

The place was filled with a soft hum of voices as the crowd awaited the hour of ten. Justus recognized many men and women as believers he'd met throughout the past weeks, but there were new faces, too, and he wondered who'd called the meeting. He was here only because John had told him to come to discuss some important matters.

Suddenly the whispering died, and John began to move through the tight-knit group on the floor, making his way over a mass of feet and legs. When he reached the center of the room, the apostle held his arm aloft and began to speak.

"We are here today, as followers of Jesus, the Christ, to fulfill the Scriptures. Each of you has been asked here because you have come in contact with our Lord, and because your faith in Him and the Father has been tested. Some of you have been followers only a short time—some for longer periods. The length of time you knew and loved Jesus is unimportant. Your testimony to His being your Master is the reason for your being here. You come from many walks of life, and some of you do not yet know each other. Jesus has placed His love and trust in you all, and you must help carry on His work. Now I want to introduce some people—first, the person who loved Him most —His mother, Mary."

John indicated a woman seated on the floor, and Justus strained forward, but he could see only her back. He tried to move in such a way as to get a better view, but the room was too densely crowded.

"No matter how much we loved Him," John went on, smiling at Mary, "only she could give Him the greatest love of all. And because she gave us our beloved Jesus, we do her homage."

Again Justus strained to glimpse Mary's face, wondering if she would remember him, and as John continued to introduce people, his thoughts centered on her. What if she failed to recognize him? Surely she could not have forgotten the face of one who had saved her baby's life—but suppose she had?

He continued to argue with himself, wondering, "Why do these doubts come to my mind? Am I weak in faith?" The more he thought, the more uncomfortable he became, and he wished that he could glimpse Mary's face without being seen by her.

Now John was naming those who stood around the wall, and Justus tensed as John said clearly, "Next we have Justus, for whom our Lord told us the Father has always had plans." Justus raised his hand to acknowledge the introduction; his eyes were fixed on Mary's back, but she did not turn her head, as John went on, "Now that the introductions are over, let us turn to the business at hand. As I said, we meet today to fulfill the prophets' words. Our brother, Peter, will now take charge of the meeting."

Peter moved into the circle, and when he had reached its center, everyone again grew silent as he began, "My friends, the Scriptures' prophecy had to come true. You will remember that the Holy Spirit, out of the mouth of David, spoke of Judas Iscariot, and I now speak of him who, as one of us, acted as guide to those who arrested our Master — of Judas, who sold Him for 30 pieces of silver with which was bought a piece of land which will henceforth be known to all men as 'Blood Acre.'"

All the disciples stirred as Peter halted, then spoke again softly and slowly. "Yes, my friends, the money of this treacherous one purchased a small tract of land and thereby, unconscious of God's words, fulfilled a prophecy, for in the Psalms it is written: 'Let his homestead fall desolate; let there be none to inhabit it.'

"Those of us who have seen that wretched plot can testify that the prophecy has been fulfilled, for on 'Blood Acre' nothing can grow, and the land must lie barren.

"In the Book of Psalms is written that which has come to pass concerning 'Blood Acre' — and the same book commands us to take the next step in the great scheme of life laid down long ago by our God."

Justus wondered what was going to happen. He had not learned all the prophecies since joining the brotherhood, and now he waited with anticipation as Peter subdued the crowd's murmurs and went on, "Those same Scriptures state plainly, 'Let another take over his charge,' and thus, my friends, are we directed by the Lord to choose one to replace Iscariot."

Justus' eyes shifted around the room as the big fisherman continued, "Let us therefore select one who bore us company while we had the Lord Jesus with us, coming and going, until the day He ascended. One such must join us now, as a witness to His resurrection."

The group shifted and turned as each person thought about the one among them who might be best qualified to replace the tragic Judas, and as they searched each other's faces, Peter stood immobile. Then, after what seemed to Justus a long time, the big fellow held his hand up once more.

"I can see that you're thinking about who should be chosen for this task. I say task, because there will be times when doing the Lord God's work will be both trying and dangerous. The one selected will inherit enemies who shall seek his death, so let us choose with care that man who shall fight the Lord's battles and carry His message of love to the nations."

Justus felt sad. He would be so proud to serve, but he hadn't been with the apostles since they had first begun following their Lord, so he could hardly hope to be considered.

Peter was saying, "Now, in order that there shall be no question about our selection, I suggest we nominate those whom we feel could best serve. Then, by voting, we can make a final selection. Do I hear a nomination?"

James stepped forward. "Peter, I should like to nominate Matthias."

Peter looked all around the room. "Where are you, Matthias? I saw you a moment ago . . ."

Justus watched as a man rose from the floor. He had seen Matthias four times, but had talked to him only twice. He was a small man with a short black beard, who'd been a carpenter in a Galilaean village. His voice was soft, and he usually hesitated, carefully choosing his words. There were some who said he had been a true follower since Jesus had been baptized, but Matthias was a quiet man who rarely talked of his personal life — seeming content instead to listen while others talked of theirs.

Matthias seated himself, and Peter again raised his arm.

"Are there other nominations? Does anyone wish to put forward another name?"

"I do."

Justus looked at John who stood by the door with his hand upraised.

"Whom do you wish to nominate to take the place of Judas?" Peter asked.

"I nominate Justus."

Justus started, and strength drained from his legs. He could not believe his ears . . . surely he was not qualified to become an apostle. He could feel his face flush as the eyes of the group turned on him, and the men standing on each side of him gripped his hard shoulders. He could not believe it, yet Peter was even now acknowledging his nomination. He could do no more than raise a shaky hand in recognition of this great honor.

"Are there any further nominations?" Peter slowly searched the faces in the crowd, then after a silence he smiled, "So, you have spoken. The names of two brothers have been put forward, and I am thankful that there are two, for you must give this selection careful consideration. It is easy to approve a nomination if there is only one candidate; if there are two, your vote will be cast on the basis of contrasting qualifications possessed by the two candidates. Our task today will be difficult because both these men loved our Lord Jesus dearly, as He loved them. I know, for He commended them both to me."

Now Thomas stepped forward. "Peter, we too appreciate the obligation placed upon us. Jesus selected the original twelve of us personally. Now, according to instructions in the Scriptures, we must choose an apostle for Him. The burden of that decision weighs heavily on me, for I want to be sure we select the man Jesus would want."

"I agree," Peter said.

"Then, I suggest that we hear more of the background of

251

these honored two," said Thomas. "Mind you, it's not that I doubt they are qualified. I merely feel that all of us here should be fully informed before the voting takes place."

Peter nodded. "I see nothing wrong with Thomas' suggestion. Therefore, I ask that someone speak of each candidate's qualifications. Who will speak for Matthias?"

After a moment's silence, as the members looked around waiting for someone to rise, James spoke up. "I will say a word about my brother Matthias. First, I have known this man for 4 years. Like our Lord Jesus, he was a carpenter, and he is like our Lord in other ways. He is quiet and not in the least self-centered. Never since I've known him, have I seen him avoid hard work or shirk responsibilities. He has been and will be a splendid example of the way of life Jesus proclaimed. The person that we select must be one who, by example, will remove the blot of Judas, and Matthias is such a person."

Justus noticed that the crowd had listened well to James, and he wondered as his eyes shifted to Matthias, who had bowed his head, if someone would speak as highly of him.

"Matthias will work," James continued. "He is faithful to God, and he will be faithful to the brotherhood. I commend Matthias to you."

Peter cleared his throat. "Perhaps there are questions some of you may wish to ask that only the nominees can answer. If so, feel free to ask them."

"I have one question for Matthias," a stout woman said.

"All right, Edith, but you may remain seated. I know how hard it is to rise from this crowded floor." Peter smiled at the heavy woman.

Her face turned pink beneath her dark brown color as she relaxed from trying to raise herself. "I want to ask Matthias if he was a witness to our Lord's resurrection, and, if so, when? Also, I want to know if he talked to Him after the resurrection."

Peter smiled. "Edith, you certainly do ask involved single

questions. Matthias is fortunate you didn't decide to ask him more than one."

The group laughed a little. Most of them knew that Peter and Edith carried on a running joshing each time they met. These two felt great affection for each other and their gentle raillery, even at a time like this, amused the others, for everyone understood the great respect these two large people had for each other.

As the laughter died, Matthias rose and faced the fat woman. "Don't let Peter scare you, Edith. I think your questions are pertinent because, as I see the duties of an apostle, his function must be to assure unbelievers that in His death for all mankind our Lord Jesus was victorious over death. It will be the apostles' duty to tell others of His sacrifice, of the way of life He proclaimed, and about the future life He has promised. It is my personal belief that those of us who saw and talked to the Lord after He arose, were given that privilege and honor that we might bear witness to the resurrection, and tell about it with force and meaning.

"If, at the Master's death, many of us were lost and afraid, we have been found and made hopefully strong by His victory over the grave. Look about you. Does anyone here seem afraid?"

Pausing, Matthias seemed to be gathering words to continue. "No. I see us as a group of men and women whose fears and anxieties have fled. They will not return so long as we retain our belief in the Lord Jesus Christ.

"Now, as to your question, Edith, I saw Him at the Mount. I witnessed His resurrection and ascension just as many of you did. In that cool, clear evening I saw Him ascend into heaven on a single cloud in an otherwise cloudless sky, and He spoke to me, even as He spoke to some of you." Again Matthias paused, apparently sorting his thoughts. "Am I to repeat the words of our Master? They were words I did not understand, but He told me that one day the meaning would be made clear."

"What did He say?" Edith asked.

"He told me, '*Matthias, you shall be the mortar that will bind together the stones of my church. When a fissure develops in its foundation, it will be you who will mend it.*' Those were His exact words, as I remember them. And that was the only time I saw or talked to our Lord, after He arose."

Edith shifted her ponderous weight. "Can anyone tell me what our Lord meant? I'm afraid I have failed to understand."

James spoke again. "I am sure Jesus meant that we would all understand when the proper time came. For, if Matthias must await the proper time to comprehend, then it follows that we must too. And if He meant that we are to learn later, then I think we cannot question the meaning of our Lord's statement."

Justus stirred. His legs were beginning to tire but he quickly remembered that Jesus had restored him, so he thanked God for being able even to feel fatigue in those once shattered limbs, and thoughts of his healing continued as others questioned Matthias.

Perhaps Jesus had healed him for the sole purpose of his taking Judas' place. Somehow, the contrast between his life and Iscariot's fascinated him. He had been a cruel professional killer who had found the Christ, while Judas who had started out with Jesus, had ended up being a killer by proxy in selling his Lord to the priests. Their lives, starting at opposite poles, had crossed, and Jesus had surely given him back his body for one purpose: that he might replace the traitor.

The more he reflected on his healing, the more confident Justus became regarding its specific purpose, and he felt that he was at last understanding Jesus' special words to him.

His thoughts were interrupted now by Peter, who spoke in a loud voice. "If there are no further questions concerning Matthias, I will call for comments on Justus."

Justus looked all around the room. Who would speak for him? Who would lead the way? Time seemed to stand still, as silence enveloped the gathering. Then the boom of John's voice startled Justus. "I apologize. I thought that others might want to speak on behalf of this worthy man, but I see that you were waiting for me. Justus, do not think this delay on my part —or on the part of any other—was any reflection on you."

Justus smiled at John who moved toward the center of the room as he continued to talk.

His feeling of confidence began to come back, and he listened, enraptured, as the apostle spoke.

"I commend to you Justus, whom I met here in Jerusalem on the afternoon of our Last Supper with the Master.

"It was early in the afternoon and Jesus, Peter, and I were on our way to the house of Mark's father. As we neared the south gate of the city, Jesus said that He had someone to see. I thought that this was strange, but neither Peter nor I said anything. Then we came upon a beggar, dozing on a little four-wheeled cart that he used to move around on, for he was a hopeless cripple. Jesus awoke this scared, pitiful person and called him by his true name which was Justus!"

At John's statement the heads of everyone turned, and they looked at Justus, then back at John himself as he resumed his story.

"Yes, this same Justus whom we have nominated today was healed by Jesus, as you can see. Most of you have not known about this, and there was a reason. Our Lord told Justus not to talk about the miracle because He wanted Justus to gather followers who believed in Him and the Father, through love, and I think Justus has kept faith with the Master.

"I also think the Lord healed Justus for the purpose of having him become a teacher—perhaps even to take the place of Judas, for He told Justus to find Peter and me, and He bade us to welcome him when he came."

255

Justus nodded, with a slight smile, remembering his first encounter with Peter after the healing.

John went on, spreading out both arms. "The Lord Jesus told Peter and me that Justus would carry His Word to the ends of the earth, and as we started to leave Justus on that day, Jesus kissed him on the cheek." John paused. "Now, my friends, did He mean that kiss as a symbol? Remember that Judas kissed the cheek of the innocent Jesus to identify Him to the Sanhedrin police. Therefore, did Jesus, by kissing Justus' cheek, indicate that He was identifying Judas' successor? Frankly, I do not know, but I think He could have been."

John looked at Peter, who had seated himself at the edge of the circle, then continued, "The Lord said that this man had been with Him from the beginning. Justus wears a strange gold coin around his neck, that was given to the Messiah by the Magi at His birth. Jesus said that Justus had seen Him in the desert a few days after His birth. I know little of this—only what the Lord chose to tell us—but perhaps Justus will enlighten us further when he speaks."

Justus glanced at Mary who seemed about to turn to look at him; then she turned back to watch John, who went on to tell them how Justus saw Jesus on His return to Jerusalem.

Justus wondered if Mary would ever turn to look at him, and if she would recognize him.

John was saying, "I feel Jesus meant that Justus was to be made an apostle of His church. Therefore, I commend him to this brotherhood and state that I believe Jesus wished him to replace the traitor, Judas."

John sat down and Peter said, "Thank you, John. I, too, heard Jesus' statements to Justus, and you have repeated them correctly. Are there any questions from the brotherhood? If so, I know that Justus will try to answer them."

Justus tensed. There were endless questions that could be

asked, and he felt almost more nervous than he had during the trial by the Sanhedrin years ago.

Edith again asked the first question. "Did you see the Lord after His victory over death?"

Justus cleared his throat. Then he told about talking to Jesus on the way back to Jerusalem, and as he talked his confidence grew. He said, "I saw Him also at the Mount, and He told me I would soon know my purpose in life. He said that I was to stand firm in my understanding of His Word. But one thing I did not understand was His saying, '*In the end you will fight alone. Your loss will be the foundation of victory for Me. Time will justify you.*' So, like Matthias, I wait until the proper time to know the full meaning of all that He said."

Thomas stood up. "I'd like to know about the incident in the desert that John spoke of. Can you tell us about that in detail?"

Justus hesitated. "Thomas, I will be happy to tell you. But first, I want to explain that I will do so, *not* to enhance my chances in this election but only because you have asked." He then told the story of that fateful night 33 years earlier, leaving out nothing. As he talked he became increasingly engrossed in his recital, and his memory was as clear as though the events had occurred the day before.

Throughout the story he glanced now and again at Mary's back, but she did not look at him.

When he described his mission to Bethlehem and its purpose, he noticed the rapt attention of Matthew and Andrew. Each time he mentioned Herod the Great he could sense the bitterness that still stirred the hearts of Jews, for though only a few persons here could testify to the Tiger's ruthlessness, there was no doubt that all had heard of his treacherous rule over Judea.

Justus' voice weakened as he admitted to being in charge of the soldiers who had carried out Herod's orders. Then a low murmur ran through the room, followed by shocked silence; a hard knot formed in his throat, and he wept, confessing his part in the slaughter.

Every eye in the room except Mary's was on him as he told of the chase in the desert, and he could read disgust in those eyes.

"Oh, God, why doesn't Mary look at me," he thought as he told of sparing the child's life. Still Mary did not move, and he went on, summarizing his return to Jerusalem and his arrest.

He said, "I could go into detail in telling you of my trial before the Great Sanhedrin, but first I must say that the members conducted my trial fairly. They followed the Law to the letter, despite their personal hatred for me.

"Now, had those who judged our Lord followed the Law, He would be here today. From what I have heard, I know that His trial was illegal from start to finish. For example, before the Great Sanhedrin can convene in a criminal case, it must meet at the Temple at dawn of the trial day and ask permission of God to try that case. This they did not do with Jesus. Also, the Sanhedrin cannot convene at night, yet they met in the middle of the night. Thus two basic factors of the Law were violated by Caiaphas and the other priests. And there were other illegal aspects to Jesus' trial which I am sure you know about.

"In my case, I, who had killed innocent children, stood trial for murder. There was no question of my having slain the children, yet I was found not guilty. I was found *not* guilty on a pure technicality of the Law; yet Jesus, the most innocent person who ever lived, was found guilty. *Why?* What was the reason for this hideous miscarriage of justice?"

He could see that his statements were being considered by the brotherhood. Several nodded approval, some shook their heads in obvious regret, but of course he didn't know which of his statements were being weighed in these people's inmost thoughts.

He went on, "Since I came into contact with the Child in the desert my life has twice been spared—once by the Sanhedrin, again in the stoning by Herod. That did not kill me, yet, by all physical laws, I should have been dead." Justus paused, then continued the story of his trials before the Sanhedrin and Herod, and he could tell from the look in the people's faces that they were considering the trials and tribulations of his past 33 years.

At last he ended with the simple sentence, "This, then, is the story of my life."

Thomas spoke first. "I have several questions to ask. First, are you sure it was the Christ Child's life you spared in the desert?"

"Am I sure?" Justus answered. "No, Thomas, no one said, 'This is the Christ.' But when I saw Jesus, He as much as told me the Child was He."

"How did Jesus know of your actions?"

"How did He know anything?" Justus questioned. "He knew because He was the Son of God . . . and His words indicated to me that He was that Child in the desert. I have no doubt but that He was the Christ."

"Nor have I any doubt that Jesus was the true Christ!" Thomas snapped. "But if that baby was Jesus, then His mother should be able to say if such an event occurred. Mary, do you recognize Justus?"

Mary turned deliberately, resting the weight of her slim body on her left arm. Justus' eyes were fixed on her, and as she faced him, she let her head cloth fall to her shoulders. She looked at him, and he could feel all the eyes in the room; then, through the fog of the years, he recognized this woman. The face he had seen a thousand times in his dreams was before him, all but unchanged by time. Mary *was* the mother of Jesus, and Jesus *was* the Christ Child whose birth in Bethlehem the prophets had foretold.

Thomas' eyes suddenly shifted from Justus to Mary, and he asked again, "Mary, do you recognize Justus?"

The woman shook her head. "No."

"What?" cried Thomas. "You don't recognize him?"

"No."

"Then the story he tells is untrue?"

"No. The events, as he told them, did take place, but I do not seem to recognize this man."

"Could it be that the years have clouded your memory?" Thomas questioned, his face white with anger.

"Perhaps," Mary said. She rose and began to move toward Justus.

"Surely you remember me, Mary?" Justus cried as she drew close to him. "Do not deny me. I am the soldier who spared His life, and suffered for more than 30 years for that action."

Mary put her hand out to Justus' cheek, and her slender fingers moved lightly over his rough skin. Tears rolled down his cheeks as she continued to search his face with her sensitive fingers, then suddenly Mary touched the Magi's coin that hung from his neck.

"Mary," he whispered, "Oh, Mary, mother of God, tell them you recognize me — that I confirm the Scriptures."

"Forgive me," Mary said softly. "My eyes are growing weak, and I did not recognize you. It has been a long, long time, and this is the first chance I have had to thank you since that day, 33 years ago. Now I do thank you for saving my son."

"Then . . . you do recognize him?" John questioned.

"Yes. He is that brave soldier who let us escape. The coin that he wears around his neck is like the gold which the three Wise Men gave my son at His birth. Forgive me, Justus."

Mary returned to her seat, and Thomas said, "Very well.

But there are other questions I wish this man to answer. Justus, you admitted killing the children in Bethlehem."

"Yes," Justus said. "That was before I had learned the Way —before I'd come in contact with the Christ."

"Nevertheless, you admit that you are a murderer?"

"Yes. I killed those children. The Sanhedrin—as I told you —acquitted me on a technicality. My heart bears the scars of those acts. Still, Jesus told me that when I was baptized I became a new person in His eyes. He said that my sins were forgiven, and if He said they were, I'm sure they are."

"Yes, but don't you think a murderer should be disqualified from becoming an apostle?"

"Not necessarily, no," Justus replied. "If He forgave me, then I am no longer a murderer. I am a new man, ready and willing to serve Him. Jesus told me that I was to have a part in His kingdom—that I was to gather together His lost sheep. He said I would carry His Father's message to the ends of the earth. Perhaps He meant that I was to be chosen as an apostle. And if He thought I was qualified, then I am, in spite of the sins I committed in my other life."

Thomas considered. "There is another thing I want to ask. You have said you are only half Jewish—that your mother was Jewish and your father Greek?"

"That is true," Justus said, "but the Great Sanhedrin ruled at my trial that I was Jewish."

"Are you circumcised?"

"No."

"Do you follow our dietary laws? Do you . . . ?"

"No, I don't go to the Temple either," Justus said.

"What?" cried Peter. "You don't participate in the worship of our God?"

"Yes, but I believe with all my heart that Jesus' teachings differ from the Temple conception of worship. I find it hard to believe that He approved of the slaughter of animals and the

261

money changing transactions. And because I worship God through Jesus Christ, His Son, I believe that I can worship God anywhere—in the quiet of a room, in the beauty of a garden, or just in my mind and heart. I do not believe that Jesus told us we had to worship the Father only at the Great Temple."

"Nevertheless, Christ is the Savior of the Jewish people. So tell me, do you not believe He will destroy the Romans and rid our country of the infidels?"

Justus answered obliquely. "I believe that Jesus came to this earth, not just for the Jews, but for all the peoples of the earth — Jews, Romans, Greeks—all those who will listen, accept His salvation, and follow in His steps. He as much as said so on many occasions, and if it had been His plan to rid this country of the Romans, He could have done so with ease. So, because He did not destroy them, I feel that he considered even the Romans brothers to the Jews."

Peter interrupted, facing the room. "Yes, but each of us here has entered His church by complying with the Law. Each has followed the Code of Moses and the Torah, and each has been dedicated to God by circumcision. Each has paid homage to God through observing the prophets and the Scriptures, and therefore, I, for one, cannot agree that we should accept a Gentile into this brotherhood. Jesus was a Jew who came to save the Jews. Gentiles have been aligned against us for years and years, and they have sought to destroy us. Why else did Pilate order Jesus' death? No, it would be contrary to everything that we have been taught, to have a Gentile as one of Jesus' spokesmen. No one, except a man of our race and creed, should be a teacher of His Word. Justus is not only a Roman citizen, but a Gentile."

Justus was growing angry. Peter's fiery words were contrary to his understanding of what Jesus had preached about. Now for the first time he began to understand why Jesus had told him that a fight would develop within the church directly involving himself.

Suddenly his thoughts were interrupted by John who stood up and pointed at Peter, crying, "Peter, you know that Jesus told both of us that Justus was to be welcomed by you, me, and the other nine apostles. Even when we saw this man for the first time, on the day of the Last Supper, Jesus knew that the traitor would betray Him—that when Justus returned from being healed, Judas would have taken his own life, and that there would be only eleven apostles to greet Justus on his return. He also said that Justus was to find His Father's lost sheep and that Justus would travel to the ends of the earth for Him. Thus I interpret this to mean that Jesus was telling us Justus was to become an apostle."

Now, before Peter could answer, Matthew broke in. "Yes, and there is also this to consider: Jesus may have healed Justus so that he could walk, and, with his strong body show the true Way to others. Notice, if you will, how many times Justus' life has touched our Lord's. First, in the desert, whereby he became a living confirmation of the Christ's birth. Then, consider how his life was spared by the Great Sanhedrin and how he incredibly survived the stoning by Herod. And don't forget that Justus also confirmed the Magdalene's seeing Jesus after He'd risen and that the Lord spoke to Justus at the Mount. All events bear witness to the love that Jesus bore for Justus. Thus I believe these contacts Justus had with the Christ have made him the most qualified person in this room to give testimony of our Lord and His great love. Furthermore, Peter," Matthew held up his hand, "before you interrupt . . . did Jesus say to Justus, '*You are a Gentile*'? He did not. Did He tell Justus, '*You cannot be a part of My kingdom because you are a Gentile*'? He did not. He accepted Justus, and that acceptance commended him to us as the thirteenth apostle."

Again before Peter could answer, Thaddeus sprang to his

feet. "No, listen. If Jesus followed the Law, then we must, too. Had God intended for us to abandon the Temple worship, don't you know that He would have had Jesus avoid the Temple? Don't you know He'd have prevented Jesus' being circumcised? No! Every facet of Jesus' life bears out His belief in the Law. He objected to some of the practices at the Temple, yes, but He did not attempt to destroy it. Why, think of the ridicule that could be heaped on us as Jesus' leaders if the priests find that we have a Gentile apostle! No, I say. I feel that Justus is disqualified from that high position. I cannot stand by and see Christ's kingdom destroyed!"

Peter began, "The Lord didn't suffer for the Gentiles . . ."

John cut in, "I take issue with that! Regardless of how some of us feel toward Romans and Gentiles, Jesus said we were to forgive them. Did Jesus, in His ministry, first inquire about a man's national background before He taught or healed him? He did not. The central thread that ran through our Lord's teaching was a love intended for Jew or Gentile — rich or poor. Didn't He cure the Roman centurion's son? Didn't He heal Justus?"

Justus remained silent as the controversy continued. He wanted to speak out, but he felt that the argument in his behalf was being presented by men who had more influence and skill than he. Time was quickly slipping away; though it was already afternoon, no one in the room seemed tired or ready to leave because the arguments that were boiling around them were extremely thought-provoking.

John was speaking again. "There have been 'God-fearers' in the Jewish religion for years. All of you know Gentiles who love the Lord and participate in the worship of our God, even though most of them do not join the church because of the ritual of circumcision. Now, let me pose this question: Does the fact that they are not circumcised make Gentiles the less devout?"

264

"Yes," Thomas cried, "because Jesus is a Jew, and if those so-called 'God-fearers' really loved God, they would prove their love through circumcision."

"In other words, you would require them to demonstrate their faith to Jesus by becoming subservient to this Law?"

"Of course."

"Even though it was the 'masters of the Law' who sought to destroy Jesus?"

Thomas shouted, "I cannot account for *their doubts and fears;* I do not condone their actions, yet I think the priests *believed* they were following the Law — however misled they were by Caiaphas. And even if the priests acted to foster personal gains, I still believe Jesus meant for us to continue to follow the Law."

"Oh, come now," John said. "You know that many of Jesus' teachings were contrary to those of the priests. Didn't He threaten once to destroy the Temple?"

Justus could now see that the argument had almost eliminated him. What had started as a discussion of his qualifications had turned into a fight over Jesus' teachings versus the Jewish Law. The discussions were veering past his qualifications for the apostleship, centering upon the Gentiles' right to become followers of Jesus' teaching and their right to worship God. He wanted to cry out against the bitter words being flung from one side of the room to the other. The sentiments seemed to be shifting, with clear battle lines drawn between the apostles and some other members. It seemed that long pent-up fears and jealousies were coming out into the open here — that words were being uttered which would not be soon forgotten.

And, now more than ever, he felt that Jesus had foretold these arguments with him at their center. But surely, Jesus had not meant that Justus would become an instrument of destruction of His church. Sweat began to run down Justus' face; he felt he had to stop this fight at any cost, so he shouted, "Wait! This has gone far enough!"

The room became silent as a tomb as all the members turned to face him. Mary smiled at him, as if to approve of his halting this discussion that had gotten out of Peter's control, and he continued, "This all began as a discussion as to my qualifications for filling Judas' place among the apostles. Now, the tenor of discussion has changed from love to prejudice on both sides. What started out as a test of me, has degenerated into a test of Jesus Himself."

Peter started to speak, but Justus cried out, "No! Don't interrupt me. Let me have my say. We have been testing the will of God here, and I marvel at His patience. We, who were privileged to have known and loved Jesus, who have personally accepted His great love, during these past few hours have also attempted to destroy all that He gave us! I know that none of us would have done so by design, yet we have been doing just that. Perhaps it has done us good to express ourselves on these problems; that, only time will tell.

"As for me, I wanted to become an apostle — to be known as one of Jesus' teachers. I did not want to be merely a disciple — I wished to be an apostle. Was it false pride that led me to these desires? I say it was not, but an honorable pride based on my love of the Son. Still, from what has happened today, I see that I must, for the good of the church, withdraw my name from the nomination."

"No. We won't let you," John cried.

"But I must," Justus said. "The struggle prevailing here strikes at the base of our allegiance to Jesus. Were I to be chosen, there might be a split in the church. The way I see it, there are so few of us that we must band tightly together to gather forces for Jesus' victory on earth. If we had Him with us in body, He would show us the way, but now we must deal with His Spirit only. I would be proud to continue in this election, yet my heart and mind tell me I would be acting in Jesus' best interest if I withdrew my name."

"No," John shouted again, but once more Justus raised his hand.

"I claim to be Gentile, yet the Sanhedrin says I am an uncircumcised Jew. Thus I am neither fish nor fowl—and so, I rather think Jesus made me the cause of this conflict to demonstrate to all that His church stands at the crossroads, just as Jerusalem stands at the crossroads of the world. I believe that I could justify my membership in this church, yet I doubt that the church is ready to accept me as an apostle. And so, Peter, I ask that you withdraw my name."

"Then, so be it," Peter said with a hint of a smile. "Justus' name is withdrawn . . ."

"No, not yet!" Matthias cried. "I wish to speak. Throughout all these arguments and discussions I have sat silent; now I must speak from my heart. I do not want Justus to withdraw. I understand his reactions, for I too have deep feelings about this election. Some of you will vote for me to become this special apostle because Justus is not circumcised; some will vote against him because he was once the captain of Herod's bodyguards, and some, because he claims to be a Roman citizen. But those who vote against him for those reasons will not be voting for me because I am the more qualified man; and frankly, I want to be elected only because you feel me to be the one of us two who is best equipped to serve the cause of Christ."

Justus let his hand drift to the Magi's coin as Matthias' plea continued, and the man's slow, halting speech now assumed a commanding quality.

"Brothers and sisters, the sole question I want answered here today is: which of two men is the better qualified? And though I have been flattered by my nomination—I sincerely believe that Justus is the better qualified—therefore I ask those who believe in me to join me in voting for Justus."

"No," someone shouted, "we can't do that. He is a Gentile."

Now Peter stepped to the center of the room and held his

arms up for silence. "Justus' name has been withdrawn, at his own request. Therefore the election must go to Matthias by default."

"No!" Edith cried. "Justus was nominated by John, and John must agree that Justus' name be withdrawn!" She turned and looked at John whose eyes were lowered. "John, tell them you won't let Justus' name be withdrawn. If you had enough faith in this man to nominate him, then you must have enough to stand behind him."

John stood silent for a full moment; then he raised his head to face the others. "Brethren, I have been praying in silence, asking God to give me the answer to this problem, but I still do not know what to say. Any answer that might come could have far-reaching effects on the church. What we do here today could determine how others will view our trust and belief in Jesus. Now if God had sent an angel in answer to my prayers, our solution would be simple—if He had even given a sign, our task would be easy, but God has not, and so, my brothers and sisters, we must solve this problem in our own way."

Edith shifted her weight. "That's what we want to do—so, don't take Justus' name out of nomination."

John went on, ignoring her. "In summary, as I see our situation, if we turn Justus down, we are refusing all Gentiles the right to worship God and His Son. That decision will have the effect of telling everyone that Jesus' world is strictly a Jewish world, and I do not believe that Jesus's world is so confined. If God controls the stars and the birds in the heavens, the animals on land and the fish in the sea, why then, is His dominion and sovereignty confined to the Jews?"

John paused, and Peter shouted, "We have already heard all of this . . ."

John broke in, "No, wait, let me finish. What I'm trying to say is: only God Himself can set the limits of His Kingdom.

And He has already said through our Lord Jesus, the Christ, that His domain is boundless.

"Now, if I withdrew Justus' name, I believe that I would, in effect, be circumscribing God's kingdom, and this I cannot do. Therefore, I will not withdraw Justus' name, and I demand that we choose between these two worthy men."

"Then I won't let Matthias' name be withdrawn either!" James cried defiantly.

Peter shook his head in obvious disgust that the meeting had gotten so far out of hand, but Justus suddenly brightened. He stepped forward, speaking quickly. "Peter, I may have a solution. I know there is danger in splitting the church by allowing a vote between Matthias and myself. The arguments and discussion have created deeply searching questions which, perhaps, should not be answered by us now. Those who seek my election do so on a principle, just as those who desire Matthias' election do so on principle, and the division of those present seems almost equally divided.

"Now, each of us could vote, but since we are not sure which side is right, I propose that lots be cast."

Matthew jumped to his feet, shouting, "No. That would be gambling with God's church!"

But Peter said, "Even so, I see merit in Justus' suggestion. Look at it this way: suppose we should place two beads in a bottle and let one fall out . . ."

Matthew cut in, "It would still be gambling!"

"Now look, Matthew," Peter said, "if God has control of all the stars and each blade of grass, why should He not also have control over which bead falls from a bottle? Don't you see? He can solve this problem for us."

Matthew shook his head. "God gave men minds with which to make decisions. We must prove our faith by acting according to our own best judgment."

Peter spoke once more. "In small matters, yes—but with the

big ones we must ask God's help. Let me say a prayer, asking God to make the selection."

"I agree," John said. "Not that I think it will solve the Gentile problem—which I honestly believe we'll have to solve for ourselves—but I will agree to this to prevent a possible rift among our members."

Peter smiled. "Then, so be it. And no matter which bead God chooses, after His selection we must forget what has transpired here. I myself will pledge to do so, even though I have been strongly set against Justus."

"No, wait just a moment!" Matthew cried. "We have not voted to hold a lottery. If the group votes to make the selection in such a way, I too will agree, but the whole brotherhood must vote."

Justus could see Peter muttering in his beard as he extended his huge hands to silence the murmuring group; then the fisherman cried, "All those who want to cast lots will raise their hands."

A sea of hands shot out in front of him, and Peter beamed as he turned to ask Matthew, "Do you want me to call the 'no' vote? Or are you satisfied that most of us do not think this will be gambling?"

"I think most of you know it's gambling—and wrong," snapped Matthew, "but I will concede the method of selection if we all agree to give full support to the winner, no matter who he may be."

"Will everyone agree to that?" Peter asked. A chorus of "ayes" answered him, and he said, "Good. Now, who has a water jar?"

"Here's something," Edith said. "It's not a water jar—it's a wine bottle. Just a moment." She removed the wood stopper from the long-necked jug and took a gulp from the brown clay container, passed it along the line, then added, lifting a single strand of large beads over her head, "Here are the beads. Like everything else my late husband gave me, they are of little value, but I want them back."

"May I break the strand?" Peter asked.

"Yes, if you'll restring them," Edith told him.

"I'll try." Peter blushed.

"No, don't," Edith said. "With those big hands you'd never finish. Just break the strand, but let me have all the stones when you finish."

Now all the room watched as Peter's huge hands tugged at the thin leather thong that ran through the center of the irregular lusterless black and red beads, and the muscles of Peter's hands and wrists bulged as he held the string in front of his chest between his two hands and pulled. Finally, the leather thong broke, showering beads all over the room, and Peter glanced into his hands. Only two beads remained there — a red one in his right hand and a black one in his left.

"You big ox," Edith scolded. "I should have known you'd try to show us how strong you are. You're going to find every last one of my beads if it takes you all day!"

After the laughter had died and most of the beads had been passed back to Edith by searchers, Peter regained his composure. He held the wine bottle upside down and said, "See, it is empty." Then he turned it upright in his left hand, saying, "I now place one red bead in the bottle for Matthias. If the red one falls out first, Matthias shall be the apostle to take Judas' place."

The clink of the bead striking the clay bottle's bottom seemed to tense the backs of the members as their faces glowed with excitement, and Justus bowed his head to whisper a prayer.

Peter held up the black bead. "Now I will drop this black bead in. Should it fall from the bottle first, Justus will become our new apostle."

Again there was a hush over the room as the black bead fell,

271

and as Peter rolled the beads around inside the vessel, they gave off little dead thuds.

The bottle's neck was just large enough to allow one bead to fall, and Peter kept his huge thumb over the mouth to keep the tokens inside.

Justus noted that Mary had her head bowed as though in prayer, and others seemed also to be praying silently, so he quickly bowed his own head.

The beads seemed to bounce increasingly harder against the clay sides of the bottle; then Peter stopped shaking it, the two objects whirled to a stop, and Peter said, "We now come to the most important decision we have had to make since our Lord left us."

He bowed his head and his great body towered above the people who sat at his feet. The white robe draping his massive frame caught the sunlight that streamed through a high window, and as he moved his body, a beam of golden light fell on the wine bottle.

Peter closed his eyes and began, "We pray, oh God, to You who sent Your Son to us; You who have honored us with the privilege of knowing Jesus; You who allow us to serve You. We are here today for one purpose — to fulfill the Scriptures as You have directed and to choose a successor to Judas Iscariot. We are weak, and we know that You know what is best. Only You can fathom the future — You alone can command . . ."

Justus' head was still bowed as he listened intently to the big fisherman's words. *"There is truth in what he says,"* he thought, as he again asked God to help him to be selected.

"There are two stones in this bottle," Peter was saying, "the red for Matthias, the black for Justus . . . and only You, oh God, can decide which bead shall fall from the neck of the bottle. We confess that we are weak in asking You to help us, but the grave implications of our making the selection are more than we can endure. Therefore, oh God, let forth the bead, and we shall abide by its color."

Justus looked at Matthias, who looked back at him and smiled; then Justus raised his hand in salute to his adversary.

"Mary, will you please come here?" Peter asked. "It is only fitting that you, His mother, should first know of the choice."

There were smiles of approval as Mary arose and moved through the crowd to the center of the circle, where Peter stood alone.

"Now, I shall turn the mouth of the bottle into your closed hand," Peter said, "and when you feel the first stone escape, close your hand so that the other will remain in the bottle. The one in your hand will decide the apostle. Do you understand?"

Mary nodded.

"Oh God, please let it be me," Justus whispered. "Jesus told me I was to be His shepherd. Please Lord, let the black bead come first."

Mary placed her small hand over the mouth of the bottle, and Peter tilted the bottle. As its neck lowered, Justus could hear the two beads rolling toward its narrow mouth; then they came to rest, one behind the other, in the long neck of the bottle, and as Mary made a slight movement of her slim fingers, one stone dropped into her palm.

"I have one," she said, and Peter straightened the bottle and shook it so that the remaining pebble bounced in the clay container.

"Then will you show us the one that God has selected?" he said.

Mary held her hand close to her chest and slowly opened her fingers; then she quickly closed her hand, and Justus could feel his heart pounding so loud he was sure that everyone in the room could hear it.

"I have in my hand the token of the new apostle," Mary said, "but before I reveal the choice, I want to ask that the loser

273

pledge himself to work for God through my son. It would please me greatly—and I know that it would please Jesus."

Justus smiled weakly. "You have my promise," he said, and Matthias echoed, "You have mine, too."

"Thank you," Mary said. She held the bead aloft between her thumb and forefinger and spoke into the silence.

"It is the red, for Matthias."

XXXV

"The red bead was in Mary's hand," Justus told his friends, "and I didn't know what to do. I felt like running from the room, and perhaps I would have, if I'd been near the door."

"So, what did you do?" Judith asked, pouring two cups of wine.

"Well . . . I think I tried to smile at Matthias, but I was so stunned, I can't remember. Have you ever wanted something so much you just *knew* you were going to get it? And have you ever felt the terrible disappointment when you didn't?"

Silas nodded, and Justus continued, "I was sure Jesus had told me I'd be the one selected. I know now that He hadn't, but it hurt me to lose just the same."

"Did they laugh at you?" Judith asked.

"No." Justus chewed a piece of hard bread. "They were all very considerate, and I think they sensed how disappointed I was."

Silas cut a piece of soft cheese with a dull knife. "Well, are they going to throw you out of the group?"

"No. Even Peter who'd been so much against me, asked that I not desert them."

"But . . . I thought you said he believed that only Jews could belong," Judith said.

"I know. Maybe the fisherman wanted to make me feel good

274

—or maybe he saw that he was wrong. Only time will tell. Anyway, he did invite me to stay."

"Do you think he meant it?" Silas asked.

"Yes. He's not the type to lie. I think he is very sincere."

"What about the others?" asked Judith.

"Well . . . although everyone pledged his support for both Matthias and me, I'm positive some of the members will never forget their prejudices. I'm afraid if I remain in Jerusalem it might do more harm than good. You know how things like this grow on people. Little things seem to magnify in importance, and honest differences of opinion often grow into hate and distrust. Therefore, since I believe so strongly in Jesus, I cannot take the chance of such a situation arising in His church in Judea."

"Then you're going to quit?" Judith questioned, offering more wine.

"No. I'll just move. You see, Jesus told me, 'In the end you will have to fight alone. Your loss will be the foundation of victory for Me. Time will justify you.' And what He said has come to pass. I will have to fight alone. His words to Matthias also came true, for Jesus said that he would be the mortar that would bind the stones of the church. So, since everything has happened as Jesus said it would, I know I must leave Jerusalem for good."

"Oh, no," Judith cried.

"Yes, I must. Jesus told me that I would be His shepherd, and there are flocks in other lands. If I can't work effectively for Jesus here in Jerusalem, then I shall go where my presence will be welcomed."

"But where will you go?" Silas asked.

Justus hesitated. "I thought about that all night. I couldn't sleep, so I walked through the still city. I walked to the Temple, to Antonia, to the Garden where He was placed in a borrowed tomb, and even to the Place of the Skull. I walked all night, and everywhere I walked, I relived old memories. I thought of my 33 years of pain—of my trials before the Sanhedrin and Herod. My life was spared for a purpose because that stoning would have killed any normal man. And how can I forget His healing? He gave me back this body, so I must work for Him."

"Did you talk to Jesus last night?" asked Silas.

"Yes. I think so. He did not appear before me, if that's what you mean, but He was in my mind and my heart. I know He was with me as I walked through my past, and I realize now it was He who told me to take that walk. Through having my past life pass through my mind, He has shown me the way into the future—and so I have decided to leave this country."

"Oh no, Justus, please," Judith's eyes gleamed wetly.

"Yes, Judith, I *must*. Can't you see? If I stay, I could harm Jesus' church. If I leave, I can establish other churches—assemble groups that will one day join those here in Judea. They will all be united some day."

"Then, you will try to get Gentiles to believe in Jesus and God the Father?" Silas asked, great-eyed.

"Yes, look at it this way. You know that Jesus is the Son. You know of His power . . . power that only God has. Look at me. If I wanted to tell of His miracle in healing me, I could surely attract thousands. But I want to tell people only of Jesus' love, by which He became victorious over death . . . and Herod . . . and the Romans. I want to tell the world of His prime purpose in coming to earth. I must tell everyone of His blameless life for mankind and His fight against evil. I want to tell of His promise to each of us who believes in Him. Since Jesus did not limit His promises to Jews alone, I will not limit myself in my teaching. I will say that all men—everywhere—can partake of His love."

"But you could teach in Jerusalem," Judith pleaded.

"Yes. I suppose I could convert some people here. But

276

He has told me that I must be the shepherd of His lost sheep, and I know I can do more good elsewhere."

"Why don't you tell them you are a Jew? Then you can stay," Judith said. "Renounce your Roman citizenship; that would solve everything."

"No, please," Justus said. "You must understand I am not merely concerned with the people of Judea. Peter and the others will some day come to the obvious conclusion that Jesus came into this world to help everyone—not the Jews alone. But when they do, I shall already have expanded His Kingdom on earth."

"But how can you be sure?" Judith cried. "Surely Jesus talked to Peter and the other apostles more than to you. Maybe Peter is right and you are wrong."

Justus shook his head. "I can't believe it. I don't know just how, but I feel very sure I am right. I believe Jesus meant for me to lead interference for Him, and I am a soldier, ready to go into battle. I have learned, from the apostles, of Jesus' promise to those who believe, and armed with this knowledge, I can become the Christ's personal missionary throughout the world."

"Oh," Judith said. "I still don't understand. Why must you go alone?"

Justus smiled. "Because I was chosen—for many reasons. First, because of my background. I speak many languages, which I learned as a soldier; next, I am familiar with the geography and customs of other lands. Both Rome and Athens are known to me."

"Yes, but . . ."

"Be quiet, old woman," Silas snapped. "Let the man finish."

Justus patted Judith's hand to comfort her. "You see, His acceptance of me—after the life I had led—will give hope to everyone. It will prove that the only way to God is through an acceptance of Jesus Christ. He has already accepted us—we need only to accept Him as our Savior — even though we are not worthy."

"What do you mean?" Silas asked.

"Well . . . I believe that God chose me for a purpose, even before I became a soldier, but it was not till years later that I was led to accept Him. So I think, if a man needs Jesus, then Jesus will find him, just as He found me — for what I was really seeking, all my days as a crippled beggar, was Jesus, though I certainly didn't know it at the time."

"Justus . . . where will you go now?" asked Judith.

Justus squeezed her hand. "Be patient, and I will tell you. You see, I claim my Roman citizenship for only one reason. I believe that the Roman political empire is the greatest on earth. At the same time, I believe in Jesus, the Christ, with all my mind and soul — and I feel sure I am supposed to work for Him and His Father throughout the Roman Empire."

Silas drew a circle on the rough tabletop with his finger. "Then, your mind is made up?"

"Yes. I will leave tomorrow for Athens. I have no money, so I'll have to work my way across the face of the Empire, and as I do I shall tell everyone I meet of Jesus and His love. I am happy for the first time in my life, for I am confident that I have at last found what I was destined to do. I know that there will be hardships. There will be those who will reject me and my message, but if I succeed in helping even a few, my mission will have been fulfilled." Justus fingered the Magi's coin. "I know, too, that I shall be protected, and I shall walk without fear, knowing that He is beside me."

"But what will you get out of this?" Judith questioned.

Justus smiled. "Dear Judith, I have possessed gold and jewels, and I have had high position; but those things availed me nothing. Now, all I want is one day to look again into the face of my Master and say: 'I gave You the best I had. I tried to live the kind of life You wanted me to live.' If I can say to Him that I gave my best—if He says to me at the end, 'Justus, you have done well,' my life shall have been successful. So, tomorrow I leave for Caesarea."

"Justus," Judith blinked at him. "Will you remember me?"

"Yes, Judith. And I will baptize you and Silas before I leave."

Awed that Justus had read his innermost thoughts, Silas whispered, "Thank you."

"No, thank God that you wish to accept the Christ." Justus smiled. "Your acceptance of Him will open a new way of life for you—you will see. Meanwhile, I am happy that you have chosen to join me in this new life—happy that my two most loved friends have been the first to accept Jesus, the Christ, through me."

Justus sat smiling at them, and a surge of joy swept through him—now that he was sure his future would be fruitful. He looked forward to his travels with exhilaration, confident that he would serve Jesus of Nazareth with honor and dignity—that he would travel far, but always with the Master at his side.

"Justus, if people should question," Judith asked timidly, "I mean . . . if we, who have accepted Jesus, can no longer follow the orthodox Jewish religion . . . what shall we call ourselves?"

Justus sat silent. This was a question he had never considered, and he doubted the apostles had either. But, of course, Judith had a point: this meant breaking away from the old religion and worship of the Jewish people.

He hesitated and for a moment his hand unconsciously moved to the Magi's coin. Then his chest swelled with pride as he smiled and said: *"Call me a Christian!"*

THE END

Composition — 12/15 Baskerville slightly reduced for printing.
Display type — hand-lettered adaptation from original Roman
 alphabet on base of Trajan's Column, Rome.
Paper — 70# Warren's Antique.
Binding — Whitman's Buksyn.
Design — Edward Q. Luhmann

First to see merit in the manuscript was A. J. Buehner,
who researched and edited the copy and prepared the sketch
of the Jerusalem Fortress area.